MOTHER ISLAND

MOTHER ISLAND

Bethan Roberts

Chatto & Windus

LONDON

Published by Chatto & Windus 2014

2 4 6 8 10 9 7 5 3 1

Copyright © Bethan Roberts 2014

Bethan Roberts has asserted her right under the Copyright, Designs
and Patents Act 1988 to be identified as the author of this work

First published in Great Britain in 2014 by
Chatto & Windus
Random House, 20 Vauxhall Bridge Road,
London SW1V 2SA

www.randomhouse.co.uk

Addresses for companies within The Random House Group Limited can be found at:
www.randomhouse.co.uk/offices.htm

The Random House Group Limited Reg. No. 954009

A CIP catalogue record for this book
is available from the British Library

ISBN 9780701185855

The Random House Group Limited supports the Forest Stewardship Council® (FSC®),
the leading international forest-certification organisation. Our books carrying the FSC
label are printed on FSC®-certified paper. FSC is the only forest-certification scheme
supported by the leading environmental organisations, including Greenpeace. Our paper
procurement policy can be found at www.randomhouse.co.uk/environment

Typeset in Adobe Garamond by Palimpsest Book Production Limited,
Falkirk, Stirlingshire
Printed and bound in Great Britain by
Clays Ltd., St Ives plc

For my father

This thing of darkness I acknowledge mine.

The Tempest, Act V, scene i

Prologue

The night before she takes the child, she hears her brother's voice.

'Maggie,' he says. '*Maggie.*'

It is night-time and the room is warm with his urgent breath.

'Wake up. It's me.'

Is he really talking to her again? Can he really be here, in the brown dark?

'Joe?'

But even as she asks, she knows the answer. She can smell him. She sits up in bed, rubs her eyes. 'What is it?' she asks. 'What do you want?'

'Nothing,' he says. She cannot see him, but his voice is close, just as it used to be when they played together behind the curtains at the old house.

'I was just checking,' he says.

'Checking what?'

'Checking on you.'

And she lies down and closes her eyes, because it seems that he will be there in the morning, that he is actually back. And soon she is asleep again. But in the morning, when she wakes to her bare Oxford flat, her brother is nowhere to be seen. How could he be? Still, for some minutes after she wakes, she's unsure whether this actually happened, or whether it was a fantasy. As she dresses for work, pulling on her usual black jeans and T-shirt, she can hear her brother's voice. It's there as she selects the old, slightly rusty key from the kitchen drawer and slips it in her pocket. And it remains with her as she skips breakfast and hurries from the flat, thinking only of the island, and how she will get there.

A hot morning in late June. The rush-hour traffic pulses in the road outside the Shaws' large Victorian house. Maggie's hire car, a blue Fiat Punto, is parked on the corner, just out of sight. Samuel is in his mother's arms, watching Maggie from the window. Maggie waves to them both and his face brightens. Nula opens the door, her body tight with tiredness. They have been awake, she tells Maggie before saying hello, since 4 a.m. Maggie pulls a sympathetic face, touching Nula on the shoulder as she steps into the shade of the house with its familiar smells of beeswax, baby-wipes and last night's salmon.

'Why don't you go back to bed? We'll be fine now, won't we, Samuel?'

Samuel laughs.

Nula's shoulder sags under Maggie's touch. 'Are you sure?' she asks, her foot already on the first polished step of the stairs.

'Of course,' Maggie says, reaching for the child. 'You need sleep.'

Nula nods, wearily. Maggie has said it so many times since she arrived at Nula's house a year and a half ago, and it is still true. Nula looks back and touches Samuel's cheek, but he is with Maggie now, gazing at her face, saying, 'Gee-Gee.'

'What would I do without you?' Nula asks. It is her usual response. But it is always, Maggie knows, heartfelt.

4

'Go on,' Maggie says.

A line of spit, clear and heavy, runs out and over Maggie's hand as Samuel watches his mother disappear, one step at a time. After she's reached the landing he waves frantically and grins at Maggie.

Once Nula has gone, Maggie does not rush. Her heart does not speed up and her breathing remains steady. She knows that this is the right thing to do. She takes the boy upstairs so she can pack a few things in a cloth bag. A pair of pyjamas. A couple of long-sleeved T-shirts and trousers. Nappies. Wipes. His favourite toy – Leggy Monkey. For a while they play together on the floor; she allows him to crash his plastic digger into the wooden legs of the cot. 'Cr-uuck!' he repeats, as he does it again and again, especially delighted when the toy man in the driver's cab falls from his seat onto the rug. 'Not too loud,' says Maggie, afraid that Nula will wake. Samuel laughs and makes the sound again, louder. She puts her finger to her lips and he tries to copy her, blowing through his splayed hand and making a wet raspberry sound. 'Don't get me in trouble, now,' says Maggie, smiling. And she closes the bedroom door, just in case.

It is important, Maggie thinks, to maintain their routine as much as possible, for as long as she can. And so the two of them attend their usual toddler group at the local church hall. Whilst there, she tries not to check her watch and avoids talking to the other women. Samuel cries when another boy pushes him away from his favourite toy toaster. Usually Maggie would smile resignedly at the boy's mother, say something about them being 'all the same' and try to distract Samuel. But this morning she snatches the toaster from the other boy's sweaty grip, hands it to Samuel, then sits protectively between the two of them. The mother tuts loudly and takes her son to play elsewhere. Maggie remains where she is, unrepentant, slightly breathless.

On the way back, Samuel's head begins to nod in his buggy. A nap would interrupt their schedule; she needs him to sleep in the car, later. She manages to keep him awake with a pouch of peach smoothie and a loud rendition of a song.

'Three little ducks went swimming one day, over the hills and far away. Mummy duck said *quack-quack-quack-quack*, and only two little ducks came back . . .'

Suddenly realising what she is singing, she switches abruptly to 'The Grand Old Duke of York'.

Coming into the house, Maggie calls up the stairs for Nula, just in case she hasn't made it to work yet.

Silence.

It's twelve-fifteen.

There's the usual note on the kitchen table. 'M – Thanks for this morning. You're a life-saver. Have fun today! N xx P.S. Frittata in the fridge – help yourself. Maybe S will eat for lunch, too?!' Ignoring this, Maggie makes cheese sandwiches. While Samuel eats, she takes a couple of bananas, two toddler muesli bars, a six-pack of yoghurt, two jars of Peter Rabbit tomato sauce and a packet of pasta shells and stuffs them all into his changing bag. Maggie has often wished that Nula would empty out and wash this bag; it's full of chewed straws, stray raisins and chunks of stale rice-cake and is beginning to smell. No matter, though. Soon she will be able to clean and organise the bag herself.

She allows herself a glance at the clock. Twelve-thirty. She sits and watches Samuel chew, leaving her own sandwich untouched.

When he has finished, she is careful to wipe the table and stack the dishwasher, as normal.

Another glance. A quarter to one.

She wipes his hands and face, and takes him in her arms. 'Shall we go out again?' she asks.

He looks confused for a moment. This is usually when she insists that he have a nap.

'Samuel? Shall we go out in the car?'

'Car! Car!' he shouts. She puts him down and he barrels towards the front door and hurls himself at its glass panel, beating with his fists to be let out.

Reaching for her bags, she glimpses her own wrist and realises she has forgotten to put on her bracelet. Clasping the naked arc of bone, she briefly considers a quick detour to her flat to collect it. She pictures herself scooping it up, slipping it back where it should be. Then she decides it's not worth it; she can leave the bracelet on the table, by her bed. Now that she is returning to the island, there's no need to wear it.

Maggie chucks the bags into the buggy. She balances Samuel on her hip and, steering the buggy with one hand, leaves the house behind.

His precious legs. So round and cushioned. His knees dimpled like a doll's face. They hang without a care over the lip of Maggie's car seat, which she transferred to the hire car earlier this morning. He is a good boy on the journey, remaining quietly awake for a while before sleeping with his head on one side, his mouth open. Every few minutes Maggie checks the rear-view mirror for him, and he is still there, still perfect, still asleep. Each inch of his flesh is perfect, thanks to the oil she massages into his skin at nappy changes. His mother sometimes says it is a miracle, the way Maggie has transformed her child. Maggie wants to tell her: he is the miracle. Samuel.

They drive for over an hour and he doesn't make a sound. Maggie stops for petrol, looks no one in the eye. The man behind the cash desk says, 'Hope you've locked your doors. Got to keep the little ones safe, eh?' And she smiles and thanks him.

As she drives, she thinks about their destination. The place they are heading for is across the water, which runs fast in all directions. This makes it difficult to swim, unless you know the times and the tides and where the sandbanks are. You have to be sure of all this in order to get in the water. If you're not, God help you. Soon they will play together on the pebble beach and Samuel will know the place, too.

Joe used to tell her, when they were younger: 'This island is the Mother of Wales.' 'How can an island be a mother?' she asked. 'Because she is fertile and giving,' he said, importantly. He'd read that in a book. Maggie must have looked confused because he added, 'You know. Good for growing crops, feeding people.' She nodded, as if she understood. 'But also,' he said, 'I think it's because people come here for holidays, like we used to. They come here when they need a rest.'

The pylons flash past in their pointy beauty. Where they are going, Maggie thinks, there will be few luxuries. But there will be safety. That is the trouble with luxury, such as Samuel's mother has. It can make you feel safe when really you are not.

It's 7.30 p.m. in the Shaw house, and Nula is alone, trying to get through to Maggie's mobile. She has fetched herself a large glass of Cabernet Sauvignon and is sitting on the sofa, going through the possibilities, trying to remain calm. Over an hour has gone by since her return and her two-year-old boy and his nanny are still not home and she has no idea where they are. Her feet, still in her work shoes – zebra-striped pumps – are sweating, but her hands are chilled. Sometimes they are late back in the evening, delayed by the traffic, but never this late. Six-thirty has been the latest. Maggie knows that Samuel needs to eat no later than six, ideally an hour before that. Nula tries not to imagine car accidents. Lorries veering into the hard shoulder. Bodies crumpled by warped metal. She checks the local news for traffic reports around Oxford. Nothing. She reaches Maggie's answerphone again and her stomach hardens with anxiety. She picks at a hangnail on her thumb until a bead of blood rolls down her wrist.

She remembers the time Samuel cut his head open on the corner of the garden steps and she'd been so shocked that she'd laughed. She'd heard the bright, brittle note in her own laughter and had been glad of it – glad she was still capable of laughing instead of shouting or crying as she lunged forward to grab his little arm, feeling his usual resistance to being picked up, and foresaw the approaching long half-hour of screaming, of wrestling with blood and plasters, tissues and wipes, before his skin healed enough to stem the worst of it. He'd kept writhing in her arms, rubbing at the wound with his fist, smearing blood over his cheek and her blouse.

Blood and sweat. So much of child-rearing is blood and sweat, she thinks, and she can clearly imagine the way Samuel's back will be sodden with sweat from Maggie's car seat, wherever they are, because Maggie has not taken his sheepskin with her. It is this, more than anything, that makes Nula worry for her son's safety. Because Maggie isn't the kind of person who would be thoughtless enough just to forget to call. Nula knows her cousin can be a little – strange is too strong a word. Odd. Eccentric, perhaps. Isolated, maybe. Yet with Samuel she has been such a careful, caring person.

But this oversight – the sheepskin left in his spare buggy – makes Nula very afraid. If Maggie has forgotten this, what else will she overlook? What detail will go unattended?

She's called Greg several times, but can get no answer from him, either. Probably he's driving home, she tells herself. Then again . . . Perhaps, she thinks, perhaps they are together. Perhaps they have planned this. Perhaps this is her punishment for her various and unforgivable sins. Perhaps Greg has arranged for Maggie to get Samuel out of the way so he can do his breaking-up speech. She hopes this is the case. She hopes that Maggie is with Samuel somewhere safe – perhaps a Cotswolds hotel – waiting for Greg to arrive with the jubilant news of his forthcoming divorce. She hopes the two of them will be happy together, so she can get her boy back. Once Greg has done his 'We-both-know-we-should-go-our-separate-ways' speech, she can retrieve Samuel and everything will be all right. If Greg thinks he's keeping him, he's more deluded than she'd thought. But none of it will matter because she will have her son.

She rehearses the speech in her head. She won't deny anything. Calmly, she'll admit she was wrong. It would be rash to aggravate him. She won't point out the years of suspicion she has endured. The text flirtations with various women. She won't mention what she saw last week, when she came home from work to the two of them in the sitting room. Perhaps they weren't holding hands, but they were close enough. And she saw the look in her husband's eyes as he listened to whatever Maggie was telling him. Knew what that look meant. She couldn't see Maggie's face, but her cousin's head was bent towards Greg's and her hair looked thicker, more alive, than before. She must have used some sort of glossing treatment, which was unlike her. It had slipped over her shoulder as she turned. Samuel had been sitting by the fireplace, banging his plastic fire truck into the skirting board. Nula marched in, swept her boy into her arms and kissed him. He'd held onto her neck and said 'Mummy, Mummy, Mummy', and she hadn't looked at either of them as she carried him away.

She would not mention that she'd known, then, that she was off the hook. That Greg, too, could take his share of the blame.

I

Nula had met Greg at work. He'd come to the office to discuss building a website for her company and she'd spied him bounding up to her boss's room. When she'd heard Greg coming back down, two stairs at a time, she'd deliberately stepped out of her own office to the photocopier on the landing and had caught a flash of his broad shoulders in their lime-green shirt and his delicately sculpted head – his hair was shaved very short but, unlike most men who attempted this style, Greg could carry it off as his features were absolutely even. Sometimes, she thought now, a little too even. But then he'd flashed by like a Hockney drawing, languid and yet masculine, and she had decided to take an early lunch. Without quite knowing what she was doing, she'd grabbed her coat and bag and followed him out into the street. He walked with flat feet and an incredibly straight back, flicking the occasional glance at the shimmering shop windows along the Turl. Nula held her bag close to her body; it was a cool May morning and had been raining heavily when she'd left for work. She was careful to keep some distance behind Greg and to tell herself that she was not following him, that what she was doing was heading for the covered market to buy a sandwich and it just so happened that this web designer, Greg Shaw, was walking quickly ahead of her. The clock of Exeter College chapel struck twelve. Her stomach turned over, but that, she reassured herself, was just hunger. She felt herself becoming warmer with the effort of keeping up with him. Already people were dressing for summer – the students in their short flowered dresses, pumps and cardigans or scarves – but Nula was wearing her heavy grey coat and black boots. She often feels cold in this city. Her father calls it a damp pit; 'It's not a seat of learning,' he'll say, 'it's a damp pit, where a man can't breathe the air for all the bloody spires.' Despite this she's always loved the mists that hang around the parks and the quad lawns; and she likes that she is surrounded by towers and bells, it gives her a feeling of protection. Once her family went on holiday to Norfolk and she'd hated the flat openness of the landscape, the way the sky went on for ever, the fields an endless earthy monotone. She likes to feel there's a boundary somewhere, as, she thinks, on the south shore of Anglesey, where the peaks of Snowdonia provide an edge to the view, like the hem of a skirt. This is where one thing ends and another begins, they say. Come over here, if you dare. Greg turned into the market and she knew that he was going to eat, too, and that from this point on it would be easy. All she had to do was stand near him in the queue and say, 'Aren't you the guy who was just in my office?'

Just as she had hoped, he'd smiled and asked her to join him.

Nula was twenty-nine when she married Greg. The act of marriage seemed to untether her desire for a child. Even on their honeymoon she was thinking about the mysteries of her menstrual cycle, wondering if last night's activities had hit the right moment. Because, Nula knew, the moment had to be exactly right. In their slightly disappointing Roman hotel, Greg had made something of a project of their lovemaking. Greg's goal was to get it absolutely right, every time. 'Come to bed,' he would say each night, as if there were any possibility of her doing otherwise, and would grab her, still fully clothed, pull her towards him and kiss her neck with self-consciously dramatic abandon. She sometimes thought, in that hotel room, of the place on the shore by Plas Coch where the Menai Strait glittered blue and green and ran faster than any water she had ever seen, where she'd been with Joe that summer all those years ago and had felt herself revealed; and she sometimes longed not for love, but for this revealing of herself to a man, for a moment when she could slip off not only her clothes but also her nails, her make-up, her hairstyle and her past – all of it – so he would see her in the reflected light of the water, fully herself for the first time.

As the months after marriage went by, Nula felt her family's glances travelling to her stomach, and was aware of the gaps in her conversations with friends who were already mothers. They said nothing, but in their silences Nula read their desire to ask the question: when? When are you going to be like us? When are you going to know what it is to bear a child? And where is your place among us? Their children seemed frightening to Nula – so needy, so uninhibited, so alien, with their massive faces and small hands. And yet she was surprised to find herself feeling it keenly, the famous hunger. She had thought all that would be of no interest to her. She'd thought she had left all that behind in the discreet Summertown clinic. She'd been determinedly uninterested in Mothercare or nuchal folds or breastfeeding, but now she felt a longing to become like her friends, to become one of those women.

What she had been really angry about was how disappointing the whole experience of actually being pregnant turned out to be. *Euphoric* and *glowing* were words she'd expected to use about her pregnant state. She was, after all, *expecting*. That meant everything was to come, didn't it? It suggested a state of constant bright-eyed excitement, such as in a child waiting for Christmas. And wasn't the pregnancy actual, physical evidence of the usefulness of Nula, of her ability to be a woman? And wasn't she the same as her friends now? Before her pregnancy, she had surprised herself by looking forward to growing in size, to buying maternity clothes and having breasts so full – having such an abundance of herself – that she leaked milk, or something like milk. But the reality was very disappointing indeed. For weeks after she found out she was pregnant she felt as though she were on some terrible sea voyage, constantly negotiating the swells of sickness and tiredness. It was good, one stormy day, to take a trip to the seaside and actually smell the sea, to feel the damp spray of salt water on her skin. For a few hours, how she felt had at least made sense. And then her body had grown out of control. She stopped looking at herself in mirrors, hardly recognising the inflated woman whose ruddy features were softened and obscured by extra flesh bouncing rudely back at her.

After months of waiting, things happened alarmingly fast. One day near her due date, Nula felt unwell and went to see their GP, the understated Dr Grigson. In a quiet voice, he told her to go straight to the hospital, and to take an overnight bag. Probably nothing to worry about, but they should keep an eye on things. Once there, she was told the baby's heartbeat had become a little irregular. She was hooked up to an ultrasound monitor, pages of paper streaming out beside her bed, a needle etching the baby's heartbeat. She watched those lines go up and down like some sort of religious sign; she was unable to understand what they said, but knew they were the only important thing in her white hospital room. The movement of lines was all. And when, less than an hour after being admitted, the movement grew erratic, she pressed the buzzer for the nurse. Within minutes she was being wheeled into an operating theatre.

It was noisy in the hospital. And the operating theatre was the noisiest of all. There were seven people in that room, not counting Nula. All of them talking over her tented lower half. They tilted the bed so the umbilical cord wouldn't be compressed. Everything, then, was at an angle. The anaesthetist had a soft, sympathetic face with a comically large black moustache; he kept giving her the thumbs up and she found herself focusing on him, chatting to him even, about where he was from (Cairo), and where she was from, and what had brought him here. It was a relief to focus on something else. Behind the curtain, several men tugged at her abdomen. She felt their hands rummage inside her, heard one say to another, 'God, well done' when they finally pulled the baby free.

She would realise only later that the red she'd seen in the huge ceiling lamp was a reflection of her own insides. Greg sat at her side and held her hand. His face, beneath his green surgical mask, was absolutely grey, like overworked dough. She kept her eyes on his, knowing they would immediately signal anything wrong. Greg tried to keep a calm exterior at all times and many people were fooled by his apparent coolness, but the reality was that, under emotional pressure, he was much worse than Nula at hiding how he felt. If he told a lie he began to sweat almost immediately, and his veins would stand proud of his forehead. She had first seen this when he'd told her his company had five employees, early in their relationship. She'd felt sorry for him because she could tell he was trying to impress her with a lie. It was this, partly, that had endeared him to her: the way he was vulnerable and could barely cover for himself.

There was a cry, wonderfully loud and alive, so animal-like and wholly inappropriate in the antiseptic whiteness of the operating theatre that Nula, her abdomen cut open and bleeding, pinned to the operating table by the epidural, let out a loud laugh.

'You have a baby boy, Mrs Shaw,' said the surgeon. 'Congratulations!'

She'd imagined a girl, someone with whom to share secrets and dresses and the intimate knowledge of *what men really are*. But that hardly mattered now.

The euphoria of knowing he was alive was quickly followed by panic. She didn't know where he was in the room. She only knew he wasn't part of her any more. 'Where is he? Where is he?' she asked Greg, but Greg was standing up now, straining to see his son being cleaned and weighed in the corner of the room. 'It's all right,' he said, 'he's there. Over there.' Over there was much too far away for Nula, and she began to cry. 'Where is he?' she begged. When the baby was finally displayed to her, he was wrapped in a green blanket and held by the beaming nurse, as though he were a package Nula was considering buying. His face was so red, so pained, that Nula knew her son didn't want to be here, either.

'He's on the small side, so we need to get him properly warmed, all right?' said the nurse. 'You can hold him later.'

Nula wanted, more than anything, to touch his skin. But he seemed such a delicate, precious, alien thing. Too impossible to touch.

'He looks like you,' said the nurse. 'The same eyes.'

To Nula, he looked like nothing on earth.

Greg said: 'You've got to do something, Nula. You've got to help yourself, darling' and touched his wife on the hand. They were sitting in the garden, faces turned to the warm sunlight. It was three weeks since they'd brought Samuel home from the hospital.

That *darling* took her by surprise. It was unusual, yes, but it was also accusatory. *You are my darling, still* was what he meant. *Therefore you owe me this. You owe me your sanity. You will remain my darling on this condition.*

But then, Greg had never got these terms of endearment quite right. *Little cat*, he sometimes called her, even though she was neither small, nor, she thought, particularly feline. He didn't pay enough attention; that was the trouble. He was too busy, always, with work. Recently his business had become quite immodestly successful; he would regularly come home somewhere near midnight and expect her to be pleased to hear his tales of client dinners and drinks and the promise of huge contracts. She wanted to tell him: look at me. I'm almost as tall as you. Yes, my hair is glossy and my nose is stubbier than it should be, but do I wash myself behind my ears or curl up on your lap purring? I don't recognise myself in your phrasing.

Since the baby, Greg hadn't used any term at all, as if he were unsure of what his wife had become. Mothers, Nula reflected, couldn't be little cats. Mothers were more like big, screeching moggies. Or ferocious dogs. Perhaps that was it. She'd become a bitch, ready to bite anything that threatened her pup, but also desperate to push that greedy little mouth away from her aching teats.

Darling was a new one, then. Greg was not, he had always been proud to say, from the sort of family who would use the term lightly. It was too large, too gushing a word. Oddly, *love* and *my love* seemed much safer options for Greg: less romantic, less puffed up. More domesticated and contained, like his mother Lilly, whose kitchen was, as Greg always said, 'the heart of the house'. Even now her son has left home you need never ask whether anything at Lilly's is home-made. It is an unquestionable fact.

Greg shuffled in his seat, uncomfortable on the steel garden chairs Lilly had given them as a wedding gift. 'Darling?'

The patio was gritty beneath Nula's foot as she swept her lower leg back and forth, trying to gather a thought.

'How are you feeling?' Greg asked.

'Shaky,' she said.

'Bound to be, at first.'

But she meant it literally. Her hands were shaking. Her eyelids seemed to flutter. Her stomach jerked and rolled. Her legs no longer felt solid. Her whole body appeared to be untrustworthy. The garden itself looked shaky, the wind blowing twigs and grit in uneven pulses, making the rose petals tremble. Seeing her own reflection in Greg's goggle-like sunglasses, she had to turn away. She looked instead towards the back of the house, through the kitchen window. After several turns around the block she had managed to park the pram in there without waking Samuel. She commanded herself to relax. It was a warm day; the baby was asleep; she had a few moments to herself and her husband was here by her side. Relax. Just relax.

She tried to remember how to do this. Something to do with letting the muscles go slack. But Greg was talking about doctors and periods of adjustment, and how long had Samuel been asleep now? It must be twenty minutes, she thought, which gave her perhaps twenty more before it would be time for another feed (how many today? three or four? she'd lost count). So when she heard Greg say, 'You don't seem to be coping very well', every muscle in her body was in fact straining towards the house, on alert for Samuel's cry.

Focusing on Greg's mouth, so as not to have to look at herself in his sunglasses, she noticed a speck of bread on his bottom lip and reached to swab it away with her thumb. He caught her hand deftly and held it in mid-air. 'Nula. Darling.'

'You have something stuck—'

'I'm trying to talk to you.' He pushed his sunglasses to the top of his head. 'You always say this is what you want. To talk more.'

She couldn't remember making this specific request. It could be something Madeleine had said. Greg and Madeleine's five-year marriage had ended not long before he met Nula, and occasionally Nula felt sorry for her husband's plight, the way he had to sift through so many memories and preferences to make sure he had selected the correct woman before opening his mouth. But today she did not feel sorry for Greg. Today she said, with almost gleeful spikiness, 'Are you sure you're not mixing me up with Madeleine?'

He did not rise to her challenge. 'I'm just trying to talk—'

'It wouldn't be the first time.'

Greg sighed.

Nula pressed on. 'It just doesn't sound like something I'd say. I don't say that sort of thing.'

Greg slapped his sunglasses on the table. 'It's the sort of thing women say, though, isn't it?'

'So it's generic. *I'm* generic.'

A wail from the kitchen. Low at first, but quickly accelerating into a wild scream. Nula jolted from her seat, the initial shock of the cry immediately followed by a feeling of resigned relief. This was what she'd been waiting for, and now it had happened. Now that she could go to her baby she actually felt herself relax, just a little. Pausing at the edge of the lawn, she half-turned to her husband, mumbled, 'Sorry', then hurried into the house.

When Nula and Samuel were alone together during those first few weeks, this is what she saw: fists and feet, curled, cringing in the open coldness of the air. Startled eyes, looking towards any chink of light, any moving thing. Open mouth, pink and angry, always searching for her breast. When she held him he would swim towards it, rubbing his face into her shoulder, armpit, smelling his way to her milk. And she experienced something disturbing. Her mind became locked – almost paralysed – in such a way that she thought she now understood what women meant when they said their brains had 'gone to mush' following childbirth. Prior to having Samuel she'd thought this 'mush' must mean a kind of bliss, a swapping of feverish anxieties for the cuddly mess of the mother's brain. But this was not what happened. She went through the routines she had learned to perform for the sake of her child's welfare – nappy change, feed, rock to sleep; nappy change, feed, rock to sleep – without thinking of other things, but this was not because her mind was now free of other things. It was because her mind had locked exclusively on Samuel and had no air to breathe or room to stretch. There was only this: nappy change, feed, rock to sleep. It was a deadening stranglehold, and it made her cry. She had never cried so many tears in her life. They came to her eyes without warning, flowing down her cheeks with indecent ease and without any apparent provocation. As she changed Samuel's nappy, she cried. She tried to keep singing as she did so. 'Baa, baa, black sheep, have you any wool?' she sang, thinking that it must be impossible to sing nursery rhymes and cry at the same time. When she could no longer sing she apologised to Samuel and there was a part of her that could see herself in this state, changing nappies and weeping, a part of her that thought: I am like someone in a kitchen-sink drama, but still she was powerless to stop it. Sometimes Nula and Samuel cried together, and she picked him up and held him close to her face, their tears mingling on her cheek, and she was grateful for the terrible noise he made, for the way it covered her own.

Sometimes she looked at him and thought: do I love you enough yet? Or: why don't I love you enough to enjoy this?

The health visitor, a thin woman in her mid-forties with dyed blonde hair, recommended that Nula 'come to group'. It sounded to her like an invitation to join a cult. 'Come to our post-natal group and share your experiences,' the health visitor said. 'Most people find it helpful to know they're not alone.'

But I am alone, Nula thought. One afternoon during Samuel's first week at home she had heard visitors laughing with Greg in the kitchen and she'd suddenly shouted, 'I'm on my own in here!' because she was, as usual, feeding Samuel on the sofa. 'You're not alone,' said Greg, popping his head around the door. 'You've got Samuel.'

*

Before Samuel, she had estimated breastfeeding to be a lifestyle choice, which she could either accept or reject. But Nula found herself in its thrall. If I can do nothing else for him, she thought, at least I can do this. In some respects it came easily to her: she found she had enough milk, and she avoided the horrors of cracked nipples or mastitis. If I have the milk, she told herself, then I must get it to him. That is what a mother's love is. Sustenance. What would the point of it all have been, otherwise?

She had arranged a comfortable chair, a low light and a radio by the bedroom window. Her feeding station, Greg had joked. Maternity pillow propped in readiness, tissues and a glass of water to hand. The radio tuned to the BBC World Service. She'd imagined, when she first prepared this scene, before the baby came, that hearing another voice in the early hours of the morning would make the whole process less lonely. It did not. She was too afraid to leave the volume turned up, lest she disturb Samuel, and so she found herself straining to hear every other word, even though the programme held not the slightest interest for her. Later, after about five minutes of *The Strand* or *Hardtalk*, Nula wished she could kick the Off switch without disturbing the baby at her breast. She hated the announcers' confident voices, hated that they were in lit studios, talking, when she was in a darkened room, feeding. She imagined the paper coffee cups, Post-it notes and lip balms littering the desks, their mobiles lighting with texts from lovers and friends.

And this is how it went at the feeding station: Samuel fed for twenty minutes, then slept. By gently inserting her little finger into the corner of his mouth, as the health visitor had advised, Nula was able to remove him from her nipple. Ten minutes of rocking whilst in the chair, another ten minutes of rocking whilst pacing the room. Then began the process of lowering him into the cot through the cold, motherless air. Sometimes he didn't wake on hitting the mattress, but waited until she'd removed her hand from beneath his back before letting out a horrified scream. But usually he woke as soon as she peeled his hot face from her shoulder. And the whole process would be repeated: feed, rock, rock, peel, lower, wail. And again. And again. And again. Often this routine lasted for an hour, sometimes two. Having finally reached her cold bed, she explored the possibilities of how much time she might have until the next feed, calculating how long ago Samuel took some milk, how long he'd already slept and what the average time had been, during the last three days, between feeds. Sometimes she thought about rising from her bed and preparing a spreadsheet to properly evaluate this data. Rarely, she fell asleep and was not woken for an hour or so. Several times Nula made it back between the sheets and lay in this hyper-alert state for less than ten minutes before Samuel woke again.

Christ, it was torture.

One night during the sixth or seventh week of these labours Nula had peeled her son from her shoulder and managed to lower him halfway into the cot when he opened his eyes and looked directly at her. It was three o'clock in the morning, and she had yet to manage any sleep at all. His eyes were bright and, she thought, rather triumphant. And so she dropped him. As she did so, the image in her mind was not one of dropping, but of throwing, first gathering the baby to her chest like a netball she was about to shoot at the goal. She wanted to hurl him out of the window and into the street for the wandering foxes to nurture or tear to pieces, as they liked. She imagined all this, and she opened her hands. It was quite a long drop – about a foot, she guessed. 'Just. Go. To. FUCKING. Sleep!'

If her shouting wasn't enough to wake Greg, who was in the spare room, Nula stumbling down the landing shouting, 'For fuck's sake for fuck's sake for fucking fuck's sake', then kicking the bannister and slamming the bathroom door certainly was. She slammed it twice because the vintage glass knob that Greg had chosen for a handle was difficult to pull towards you at great speed without losing your grip. As she slammed it she asked herself why she hadn't gone against Greg's wishes and bought the ugly brass lever-handle instead. Then she could have given the thing a really good whacking.

The baby was, of course, screaming. As Nula slid to the floor, still shouting, she could picture her son's face, red as a blister; she could picture his raised fists, his stretched mouth, his tongue firing out like a furious lizard's.

Greg passed the crumpled shape of his wife in the bathroom without a word and picked up the child. Samuel quietened a little, exhausted by his trauma. Nula waited, gripping handfuls of her own hair and pulling until it hurt, wondering if physical pain would give her the right to sleep. Perhaps, she thought, now Greg had the baby, she could just lie down on the bathmat and close her eyes. Perhaps she could tell him that she had wanted to throw the child from the window, and he would have to hospitalise her. She'd heard of such things, of mothers being taken away from their own infants for everyone's safety. It didn't sound dreadful to Nula, the idea of a few weeks on a ward in Littlemore or some such institution for psychotic women. A few weeks alone.

She felt Greg staring down at her, holding the baby above her head like a threat. 'What happened?'

She grabbed at another handful of hair.

'Nula? Why was Sammy so scared? Why were you shouting?'

There was to be no talk, then, of her own fear.

'I lost it,' she mumbled.

Greg shifted Samuel to his other shoulder. The boy was drowsy now, his mouth and body slack.

'Go back to bed. You need to sleep.'

'I've got to feed him.'

'I'll do it. Let me do it.'

'You can't. I haven't expressed.'

'We've got that formula. Go on. Get some sleep. You go in the spare room.'

It was a demand, not a suggestion, but she could not move.

'I lost it,' she said again. 'Sorry. I lost it.'

For this was about loss, she saw that clearly as she spoke the word. She'd never imagined that having a child would involve such loss. It had seemed to be about *becoming*. Becoming pregnant. Becoming a mother. Becoming a family.

'Christ,' Greg said under his breath. He looked pink-cheeked, bleary eyed, but healthy. He looked like a father who had rescued his child. Nula felt a pang of jealousy. She had just handed Greg a bonding moment with his son, and she was reduced to crouching on the floor, yanking at her own hair, like a woman on the street who'd lost her child long ago.

Scrambling to her feet, she followed Greg into the bedroom and watched him place the snoring Samuel in his cot. The child remained quietly asleep. She looked down at his beautiful face, the creases now all undone, and began to cry. Greg put a hand on her shoulder. 'Sleep,' he commanded.

A few weeks later, Nula and Samuel slept for a five-hour stretch. Between the hours of 1 a.m. and 6 a.m. they both remained asleep, and Nula woke with a strangely light feeling in her limbs. She scooped Samuel, who was just beginning to mew, out of his cot and sat in the chair by the window to feed him. She stroked his forehead and he looked up at her, his eyes bright and clear. After a few minutes of greedy gulping, he stopped sucking and let her nipple fall from his mouth. A yellowish line of milk ran from his lip and down her wrist and she panicked: he hadn't had nearly enough, he'd been asleep for hours; if he didn't have a good feed now he would be grumpy, and she wouldn't get her usual hour between nine and ten to clear up the kitchen and check her emails. But she managed not to frown, because he was holding her eyes with his so intensely, and suddenly it was there, his mouth turning upwards. A smile. Samuel smiled at his mother, and she said, 'You're smiling at me' and he smiled some more. She could not take her eyes from the sight of his smile, and it was Samuel who looked away, found her nipple once more and began to suck. As he fed, concentrating now on his task, Nula watched his face for signs of another transformation. It was only a moment of reward, but it kept her sitting in that chair even whilst Samuel slept, even though all the things she could have been doing instead came rushing into her mind; she chose not to move but to stay where she was, stroking the face of her boy who had just smiled at her, holding him whilst he slept heavily in her aching arms, and for a few minutes it was enough to think: perhaps later we will take a walk into the gentle August afternoon and he will smile at me again.

On a bright December morning Maggie arrived at Nula's home, saw the Shaws' shining black four-wheel drive squatting outside the house like a huge cockroach and thought: this is the right place. I can do good here. This place has room for me.

The glazed red bricks of the drive clacked beneath her feet. The front door, painted sea-green, was wide, its long glass panel gleaming. She had to knock twice. On the phone, Nula had sounded surprised when Maggie said yes, she would be interested in working for Nula; and, no, of course there was no reason why they shouldn't see one another. It would be lovely to get reacquainted. Nula had breathed out audibly and said, 'I'm *so* glad' and, just as Maggie was hanging up, added, 'I can't wait for you to meet Samuel.'

A man with a baby of about six months in his arms opened the door. The baby looked at Maggie with his face half-turned into the man's pink neck. He had blond curls and his eyes were light green with grey flecks. Their clarity was alarming. There was something adult about such clarity. Maggie remembered seeing something similar in his mother's eyes, years ago.

'You must be Maggie,' the man said, holding out a hand. His fingers were long and slightly damp to touch. 'I'm Greg. Come in.' He paused and looked at her quizzically. 'Sorry,' he said. 'It's just I sort of assumed you'd be younger.'

Not knowing how to respond, Maggie laughed. 'Thirty-two is young,' she said. 'Isn't it?'

He didn't seem to have heard. 'Nula!' he shouted, ushering Maggie inside. 'Nula! Your cousin's here.'

Maggie looked up and there she was, coming down the stairs. It had been sixteen years – Maggie had counted every one – since they were last together, but Maggie was not surprised to see that her cousin still had the same polished appearance. Tall and thin with artfully dishevelled shoulder-length hair and eyes like the child's. Too bright. The darkness around them made them brighter.

'Here she is,' said Greg.

Nula smiled. The baby held out his arms, and she lifted him in the air and kissed him lavishly. 'And this is Samuel,' she said. 'Say hello, Samuel.'

Samuel hid his face in Nula's hair.

'I'll let you two catch up,' said Greg, disappearing.

Nula led Maggie to the sitting room, in which everything was cream, apart from the boy's toys, which were kept in a wooden crate painted with hot-air balloons. The floor was polished parquet like, Maggie thought, an old school hall, and the television was flat, large and turned off. Samuel looked at it and made a loud 'ah!' sound.

'It's not time for television,' said Nula, placing him on a bright-green mat with toys hanging from its padded arches. 'It's time for Jungle Gym!' She rolled her eyes at Maggie and sat on the sofa. 'Have a seat. It's totally – lovely to see you.' She touched Maggie lightly on the forearm. 'It's been too long, hasn't it?'

'Yes,' said Maggie, moving her arm away.

Maggie sat on the floor next to Samuel and flicked at a hanging giraffe. 'He's already sitting up by himself,' she observed. 'That's good.'

Nula smiled proudly. 'Quite the little genius, eh?' She passed Maggie a couple of cushions. 'Best to prop him up, though. Just in case.'

As Maggie arranged the cushions around Samuel, Nula said, 'You look just the same, you know.'

'So do you.'

Nula sighed. 'Don't think so. Not after having him.'

'You look great,' said Maggie. 'Like you always did.'

Nula cleared her throat. 'So. I was amazed when Mum told me you'd come back to Oxford.'

By chance, Maggie had met her Aunt Eleanor at a toddler group where Eleanor volunteered. Eleanor had mentioned that Nula was looking for childcare. 'It would be perfect, wouldn't it?' she'd said. 'A professional relationship, but also a personal one.' Maggie had been shocked, and then intrigued. Getting back in contact with Nula had suddenly seemed like a good idea, perhaps even the first step towards some sort of family reconciliation.

'I've actually been here for ages.'

Nula nodded. 'Mum said.' She paused. 'So. How's everything – back at home?'

Maggie said, very slowly and carefully, 'Fine, I think. I don't hear much. You know what it's like, once you've left . . .'

Nula brushed a hand up the back of her neck and seemed to be about to say something. To stop her Maggie added, quickly, 'I came here to study.'

Nula raised her eyebrows. Although they'd been plucked into neat wedges, they were still thick and expressive.

'English Literature,' said Maggie. 'Jesus College.'

'Blimey,' said Nula, with a bark of laughter. 'That's better than I managed . . . I did bloody Media Studies at Kent.'

Maggie shrugged. 'Looks like you've done all right, though.'

She was still taking in the plump sofa, the springy rugs, the tiny hi-fi system, and was that a DVD projector hanging from the ceiling? And the quietness of the place: Maggie could hear no evidence of neighbours, apart from the occasional confident roar of an engine as another car negotiated the speed-humps in the road outside.

'Well,' said Nula, 'I suppose I have.' She gazed at Samuel, who was now batting madly at a jingly lion. 'Maggie, I hope you don't mind me asking, but how come you're – you know . . .'

Maggie looked at Nula blankly, waiting for her to say it.

'If you have a degree from Oxford, how come you're working as a nanny?'

'I don't have a degree from Oxford. I didn't finish it. It wasn't really for me.'

Nula smiled and seemed relieved. 'Well. It's the experience that counts, isn't it? Degrees are two-a-penny these days.'

'So they say.'

Maggie handed Samuel a red cloth elephant with pink ears. He stuffed one of the ears in his mouth and looked longingly at his mother.

'But I love working with children,' Maggie said.

'What do you love about it?'

Maggie stiffened; this encounter was turning into more of an interview than she had envisaged. 'Well. They're different every day. Always changing. That's exciting, isn't it? It's challenging, but you get so much back. And they're funny. Samuel's funny, aren't you, Samuel?'

The child blinked at her.

'Oh,' said Nula. 'Samuel's hilarious.'

'And, you know, it's great to work with people. I couldn't be stuck in an office. Looking at a screen.'

'That's what I do,' said Nula, with an apparently rueful shake of her head. 'Or what I used to do – what I will be doing again if I – if you – if we decide . . .'

'What is it you do?'

Nula stared deliberately out of the window and said mildly, 'Oh, a bit of TV work . . . nothing major. For an independent company. We make programmes about all sorts of things, but always on a low budget and usually on a minor channel.'

Samuel made a sudden grab for Maggie's bracelet.

'Samuel, no—'

'It's all right,' Maggie said, slipping it off and giving it to the boy. 'He can look at it.'

'But isn't it too little?'

Maggie had made the bracelet herself from chunky plastic beads and one small pebble, collected from the beach at Llanidan. It was the kind of jewellery she didn't usually like. But the pebble had once been Joe's, and so she wore it. Every day she thought: I must take this thing off. And every day she left it on.

'It's OK,' she said, 'it's pretty sturdy. They won't come off. I'll watch him.'

Drool fell from Samuel's mouth as he munched on the bracelet. Maggie wished she had that pebble in her mouth, too. Wished she could roll its hard saltiness around on her tongue.

But Nula leaned forward and tried to wrench the bracelet from the boy. He resisted. She tugged at the thing, and he clenched his jaw down hard and stared at her. 'Samuel, darling,' she said. 'Give Mummy the bracelet.'

He let out a cry of dissent, flapped his arms in fury.

Nula looked helplessly at Maggie. 'Come on, sweetie,' she said and, clasping his shoulder, she wrenched the jewellery from his mouth. He let out a long, loud wail.

'Sorry,' she said, handing the soggy bracelet back to Maggie. 'Sorry. I was worried. There's so many things to worry about, aren't there?'

Samuel's wail became louder and his face was puce. His mother picked him up and cradled him, but he pushed at her shoulders and cried louder.

'Shall I try . . . ?' asked Maggie.

'It's OK,' said Nula.

Samuel began to arch backwards in Nula's arms. He was screaming now.

'Oh, Sammy, Sammy . . . come on, darling . . .' Nula's eyes filled with tears as she paced up and down with her son, attempting to console him.

Eventually she held the boy out to Maggie, saying, 'Maybe you'd better have a go.'

The shock of being with someone new broke the rhythm of Samuel's screams. Maggie bounded towards the window with him. 'Look!' she cried. 'Look at that bird, Samuel! Wow! He's flying!'

And, thank God, a pigeon flew right past. Samuel took a big breath.

'Look!' Maggie said again. 'Where's he going now?' She jiggled the boy up and down on her hip. 'Whoosh! The birdie's flying!'

He stopped crying and stared out of the window in silence.

Behind Maggie, Nula sighed. 'Well done,' she said, patting her on the shoulder. 'Well done.'

It was agreed that Maggie should start right away. There would be a trial period of two weeks, during which Nula would be around for most of the day. Her office was very flexible, she told Maggie, and they would let her work from home whilst Maggie settled in. After the trial period, though, Maggie would be alone with Samuel, working Monday to Friday, eight-thirty to six-thirty. Nula said, 'I'm so glad Sammy will be looked after by family' and she gave Maggie a printed contract, which they both signed. It stipulated that the employee should *Arrange and supervise a stimulating and child-centred day with age-appropriate activities* and *Provide a safe environment and highlight the potential dangers in and around the home.* Nula explained that she'd downloaded the contract from the Internet; it was a standard thing, which Maggie should feel free to amend if she wished. They didn't have to have a contract at all, she said, if it made Maggie uncomfortable. 'I just want you to look after him,' she explained, with a smile. Then she added, 'Keep him happy.' But Maggie was glad of such formalities, because when you worked in someone's home it was important to keep things professional.

Soon Maggie began to ask Nula questions. Not questions about the past, but questions about becoming a mother. This, she had found, was what new mothers wanted: to tell you how difficult it had been, to share their burden. It started during the second week, when Nula was still working from home. Samuel was napping, and Nula made Maggie tea and told her about his birth, about her sudden hospitalisation and emergency Caesarean section. All the mothers Maggie had worked with had been disappointed by what they called their *birth experience.* They had been prepared for a natural birth, at home, without drugs. But this was not what any of them got. What they got was pain, a hospital bed, stitches and as many drugs as they could take. Every mother she'd worked for had been the same:

disappointed by the disruption to her plans, the bombsite of her days.

The two women sat in the kitchen and Maggie took three digestive biscuits from the tin because she knew she would be spared no detail. They had reached day two of Nula's hospital stay, and she was in full flow, eyes wide, bangles jangling on the table as she jabbed her arms around, making her points. 'God!' she said. 'Nothing can prepare you for it. Not that I want to put you off, Maggie. But, Jesus. *Jesus!*' She stared at the table, speechless.

A wail from Samuel saved Maggie from the rest of the horror.

Towards the end of her second week at the Shaws', Greg took Maggie aside and said, 'Look, Maggie. Nula's not been herself for a while. Baby-blues. So if you see her crying, don't worry, OK? I'm sure she's going to get better, now you're here.'

Maggie knew that the 'baby-blues' were not supposed to last more than a week or so after giving birth, and she had never thought of Nula as someone who cried easily. She couldn't remember her cousin crying during that summer on Anglesey. This chip in Nula's polish intrigued her, and she began to look for evidence of the malaise.

On arriving at the Shaws' the next morning, when Maggie had expected Nula to be working from home, no one answered the front door. She looked through the bay window into the sitting room. Samuel was propped up by cushions into a sitting position on the rug, his favourite monkey stuffed into his mouth, drooling at the television. She knocked on the door again and Samuel swivelled his big head round. She waved at him and he sucked harder on his monkey. But still no one answered the door. So Maggie let herself into the house with her key. The television was very loud. Justin Fletcher was shouting, 'YOU SIGN! DOG BASKET. DOG BASKET.' She called up the stairs, but there was no reply. She picked up the child, said hello. He pulled her lip and smiled. 'Shall we turn this off?' she asked, hitting the remote. Then she heard the sobbing clearly: great shaky cries followed by wheezy intakes of breath. Maggie sat on the sofa with Samuel on her lap. The boy looked upwards, towards the noise, a frown gathering on his smooth brow. Switching the TV back on, Maggie placed Samuel on the rug, propped him up with the cushions again and promised to be back soon.

The noise was coming from the bathroom. Outside the door Maggie hesitated, then knocked.

'Nula?' she asked, gently. 'Are you OK?'

The crying had lessened; she could hear her cousin gulping for air, tearing sheets off the toilet roll, blowing her nose.

'Nula?' Maggie asked again. 'Can I come in?'

No reply. She edged the door open. It was a beautiful bathroom, with tiles hand-painted with species of exotic birds that Maggie couldn't name, and a shower that looked like a medical implement. Nula's face was puffed and shiny, her eyes pink and pickled-looking. But she faced Maggie and managed to say, 'Is Sammy OK?'

Maggie nodded. 'He's watching *Something Special*.'

There was a pause.

'Are you OK?' Maggie asked again.

Nula blew her nose. 'Sorry,' she said, 'sorry.'

'Can I get you anything?' asked Maggie. 'A cup of tea?'

Nula shook her head and wiped beneath her eyes with one finger, as if trying to save her already-destroyed make-up.

'Thanks,' she whispered, then cleared her throat. 'I'd better get myself together. Get on with some work.'

'Maybe you shouldn't work today . . .' Maggie began.

'I'm fine,' said Nula. 'Time of the month, that's all.' She tried to smile. 'That's the downside to giving up breastfeeding.'

The two women looked at one another for a moment. Then Nula started off down the hall.

As Maggie turned to go back to Samuel, Nula called to her, 'Maggie? Don't say anything to Greg about this. OK?'

It wasn't long before Nula was spending most of her days at the office, which Maggie much preferred.

Still, she was sometimes surprised by Greg. One lunchtime, not knowing he was in the house, Maggie gave a little jump when he appeared in the kitchen. His hair was shaved close enough to make him look, she thought, like a prisoner. Which was a shame, because he had a soft face. He wore collars so high and stiff she was always surprised he could move his head freely. But they were bright, these shirts: orange, fuchsia, turquoise. As if Greg hoped his shirt would speak for him.

'Samuel still asleep?' he asked. Today's shirt was mauve.

Maggie nodded. 'He's a good sleeper.'

'For you, maybe. You're so great with him.' Greg leaned over her and helped himself to a biscuit from the tin.

Already Greg often told Maggie she was doing a good job. 'Thank you, Maggie, for your work,' he would say, as she left the house. 'Thank you for looking after our boy.' He thanked her over and over, as if, she thought, she were some kind of god. But even as he thanked her, he watched her. Maggie could sense him looking for a clue, hoping she would respond in a way that would reveal something of herself to him. But Maggie had no wish to reveal herself to Greg.

Now he said, 'Coffee?' and walked to the glinting machine. Greg wasn't particularly tall, but he walked as though he was.

Maggie refused; she already had tea. He shrugged and fiddled with the knobs and levers of the machine. She sensed that he hoped to impress her by making cappuccino without help from his wife.

He sat next to Maggie with a matt black cup full of white foam. 'Got to have chocolate,' he stated, poised with the sprinkler, 'although I shouldn't.' When the Shaws were not in the house, Maggie had taken to sprinkling the tray on Samuel's highchair with chocolate until it was covered with brown dust. Strapping him in, she would encourage Samuel to slap his hands in it whilst she drew lines through the chocolate with her fingers, licking as she went. Together they made railways, trees, people, pylons, shops. They drew until they had a whole city on the tray. She was always careful to clean away every scrap of evidence afterwards, knowing the Shaws were not in favour of chocolate for the under-ones.

Greg looked at Maggie and said, 'I've been meaning to have a word.'

Maggie sipped her tea. Greg stirred his coffee until it spilled from the cup. 'How are you getting on?'

'Good,' she said. 'Thank you.'

He nodded. 'Nula thinks so. That's what she tells me. Maggie's an angel – that's what she says.'

'Nula's very generous.'

'It's been – how long now?'

'Six weeks.'

He raised his eyebrows. 'God! Already?' There was a little pause, then he added, 'And how do you think she is, lately?'

Maggie put her cup down. She had been expecting a question about Samuel, or perhaps even about herself. Not a question about his wife.

'Nula?' she asked, buying a little time.

She knew how it went, from other houses she'd worked in. The husband started asking the nanny about his wife. The wife started asking the nanny about her husband. And no one could tell anyone anything, except perhaps something about themselves. And then everything got lost. Maggie did not want that to happen again. Having to consider the parents' lives and emotions was very distracting when you were trying to care for a child. In all her nannying jobs – and there had been many since she'd dropped out of university – Maggie had tried to put the children first, always. But sometimes the parents made this difficult.

Maggie knew she should not get involved. But, she reasoned, it couldn't be helped. After all, she was already involved with Nula. And so she said, 'If you really want my opinion, she seems . . . agitated.'

She also knew that Greg did not want her opinion. He wanted a mirror. A friendly, warped mirror that would reassure him he was right about everything, and everything was all right.

'Agitated? What do you mean?'

'Unsettled.'

'Like the baby.'

Maggie smiled. 'Samuel's almost eight months. He won't be a baby much longer.'

'I suppose not.' Greg tweaked at his ear. 'Can you give me an example? Of what you mean?'

Maggie took a long drink of her tea and decided he could take it. 'I've heard her crying. She goes into the bathroom and she cries. A lot.'

Greg let go of his ear and looked at Maggie. 'I was afraid of that. Thank you for telling me.' And he looked very, very tired.

II

Anglesey was all this. The trembling trees. The stars of garlic flowers in spring. The glimpse of the Menai Strait through the leaves as she walked down the lane at Llanidan. The tide right up to the boathouse, the water full and blue. Mudflats appearing and disappearing. The sounds of sheep and birds and boats and the scream of the white peacock in the old chapel-house garden.

At school Miss Bagshawe would say: 'Get your education, Maggie, and don't look back. You can do whatever you want.' Which meant: leave this place.

At home her brother would say: 'You're lucky. I've got nowhere else to go.' Which meant: leave this place.

In the back yard Maggie's father said: 'Don't be like me. Never doing what you really wanted.' Which meant: leave this place.

In the kitchen her mother said: 'What will I do when you go? Whatever will I do?' Which meant: leave this place, but I will never forgive you. But leave. Leave, because if you don't, I will never forgive myself.

Until she had caused their family to unravel, Maggie hadn't given a great deal of thought to her mother. Fiona was a small, delicate woman with lots of hair the colour of treacle sponge. She favoured jeans and sandals, silk shirts. As she worked only a few hours a week at the local council offices, she was usually at home in their terraced house in the shabbier part of Summertown. She was a constant presence, so close to Maggie that she never quite came into focus.

Fiona talked a lot about her childhood days on Anglesey. She talked about her pet pig, and how she cried when her taid had to take it to market. How she refused to eat pork for a week, but learned not to be sentimental about animals when there was nothing else to eat on the table. And how that lesson was reinforced by the back of her father's hand. Maggie imagined her ear burning all night from the blow, her head ringing even in her dreams. 'Be thankful,' Fiona would tell her daughter, 'that your father is different. He may be difficult, but at least he's not like some men.'

But Maggie always wanted a pet pig, and the stories such a pig would give her. She had always wanted her own stories, because at home she was surrounded by ones that did not belong to her. Every Friday afternoon in Oxford she would sit in the kitchen with her mother, her mother's friend Jess and the neighbour, Rita. Jess was sophisticated; she smoked longer cigarettes than the rest and wore polo necks made of shiny fabric. Rita was the fat one – her jumpers rode up at the back and exposed flesh the texture of lumpy mashed potato – but she had the most stories, and could imitate voices with great accuracy. 'She should have been on the stage' was always the comment Jess made after Rita had left to cook tea for her two good-for-nothing sons. All Friday afternoon the women smoked and talked. Maggie and her brother Joe listened whilst running their Matchbox cars over the floorboards. There was a large gap in the boards near where her mother sat, and if Maggie got close enough she could see the darkness beneath, speckled with stray Rice Krispies and biscuit crumbs. She stared through the gap, pretending to play, but really she was inhaling words and smoke, and she knew Joe was, too. She loved the smell of their struck matches, that flinty spark, which so often began a new tale. There were stories of their own childhoods, of their mothers, of their babies, of their men. But there were most often stories of other women in the street. Martha, whose husband was following her every Saturday to Witney, because he'd figured out that's where her lover lived. Dolly, whose mother had moved back in and would bang on the bedroom floor with her walking stick for attention. Cathy, whose son Darren was picked up by the police for shoplifting. He'd hidden behind her sofa when he saw the lights flashing through the window. As if his mum could protect him. Stupid sod.

Once she'd inhaled so much smoke and stories that she'd yelled, 'Shut up! Can't you stop talking for one second?' There was a shocked silence. But instead of sending the girl to bed, the women had laughed. They'd all laughed, and Joe had laughed the most.

But, for Maggie, not being taken seriously was much worse than being punished. She was jealous. When would she have stories to tell? She was too young, she knew, to join in. Perhaps this was why, afterwards, she insisted to Joe that there had been a time when she was older than him. She would start a story with, 'When I was older than you . . .' and tell him what had happened during that time when she had greater knowledge, experience and memories than her elder brother. She insisted that she remembered things Joe would never know. And in her imagination these were secret, women things.

*

Her brother had beautiful hair. It was almost black, it shone like oil, and it hung in curls around his ears. Her mother and her mother's friends all agreed that such hair was wasted on a boy. Joe's hair seemed to make him cross, though; he would gaze up at his fringe, a dark frown scribbled across his brow. Once he stole his mother's sharp scissors and cut it himself, making her weep.

Although Joe was older by two years, there had been a time when he'd seemed to need Maggie more than anyone else. When he was eight and Maggie six, Joe started to trip on words beginning with a hard sound. His mother consulted his teachers and their GP, to no effect, but Maggie simply waited. She knew not to provide the sound, but to wait for Joe to be ready to speak. Even before he stammered, she heard the click of his tongue in his dry mouth, as if his words were stuck, reluctant to be born. At last they would come forth: 'c-curtain,' he'd say. 'Hide behind the c-curtain.' This was something they performed often: a sort of short play, directed by Joe, in which he was the teacher and she was his pupil. It usually took place in their father's small study. Maggie felt, even then, that it was important to listen, to let Joe express himself. She had to be prepared merely to watch as he pointed his long wooden ruler at her, telling her to stop hiding and come into the classroom. When she stepped from behind the curtain, the game would become confused and they would both turn into naughty schoolchildren, throwing their father's papers around the room. After Joe had given her a thorough ticking off for her bad behaviour (she sometimes feared he would bring the ruler down on the back of her hand, but he never did), Maggie would be the one to tidy up the paperwork.

Together the two of them watched and wondered about their father. Every day Alan put on what he referred to as his 'work-stripes': a grey pin-striped three-piece suit and a rather flashy tie (he often wore purple, or pink), picked up his battered leather briefcase and left the house in his rickety French family car for his job as an accountant for St Hugh's College. One morning Maggie took his box of Clairol hair dye from the top of the bathroom cabinet and trotted into the kitchen, where her father was eating a slice of wholemeal toast and listening to Classic FM.

'Can I try this, Dad?' she asked.

Alan put down his toast and reduced the radio's volume. 'You'll have to ask your mother. But I think she'll say no. You're far too young for such things.'

'But it's yours, isn't it?'

A smile flickered across his lips. 'Whatever gave you that idea, Maggie-May?'

Something stopped Maggie from saying: the fact that it's the colour on your head.

'Must be your mother's,' he said, returning to his toast.

Joe, who was sitting across the table, said, 'But I've seen you, D-Dad. I've seen you putting on that d-d-d. . .'

Maggie waited for him to say it.

'. . . that hair dye.'

Their father closed his eyes for a brief moment. He took a deep breath. Then his lips twisted horribly as he mimicked his son. 'I d-don't use hair d-dye, J-Joe!'

As soon as Joe pushed his chair back, Alan started to apologise. But Joe raced from the room before his father could rise from his seat.

When Maggie made to go after her brother, her father caught her arm and held it tightly.

'He'll be OK,' he said. 'He just has to toughen up a bit, that's all.'

The following day the box of dye was no longer on top of the bathroom cabinet, where Maggie had carefully replaced it. And, after that, Joe avoided speaking to his father as much as possible. Rather than be humiliated again, he seemed to absent himself from the family, adopting a policy of almost total silence at mealtimes. In the end, he even avoided speaking to his sister any more than was necessary. For a while, he passed notes to her. *Can you ask Dad for some money?* Or *Remember to give your KitKat to me on Friday.* He slid them into her lap under the table or pushed them beneath her bedroom door. As Maggie opened the notes, she imagined Joe might have written: *Want to come for a bike ride?* Or even: *I miss talking to you.* He never did, but Maggie still treasured these notes from her brother, and kept them all in her blue box beneath her bed, and tried to believe that the day would come when Joe would need her again.

One Saturday morning, her mother took Joe to a private speech therapist. Maggie went too.

It rained and Maggie was pleased to be able to unfurl her new tartan umbrella on the way to the bus stop. Its colourful canopy seemed to brighten everything beneath it, even the grey paving slabs. Joe wore his wellies and a zipped-up parka and refused to share her shelter. He kept his head down and said nothing as Maggie trotted behind him, trying to keep up without poking him with the umbrella's spokes. On the bus she wedged herself into the seat next to him and deliberately let her umbrella drip onto his jeans, hoping to provoke some response, but he stared out of the window, unmoved.

The therapist's office was on the top floor of an old building made of the same yellow stone as the colleges. Their mother was buzzed in and they clanked and dripped their way up the iron spiral staircase. In reception they were told to wait by a woman with a tight bun and discoloured teeth. Fiona flicked through the *Oxford Times*. Joe paced the room in his wellies, leaving dirty wet streaks on the linoleum. Through the long window Maggie could see the dome of the Radcliffe Camera. Joe pointed at the view. 'The d-dreaming spires,' he said. 'How totally d-dumb.' It was the first thing he had said all day, and the first time he'd directed a comment to her for many weeks.

'Why are they dreaming?' Maggie asked.

Before Joe could answer, their mother said, 'Maybe they're dreaming of escape. That wouldn't be so dumb, would it?'

Joe and Maggie looked at one another. In that moment she wanted to catch his arm and say something that would let him know that she was on his side, that she was ready to help him, but a clipped voice called for 'Joseph Wichelo', and Joe had to follow a man with a pink bow tie through a large door.

Whilst they waited, the woman with the bun offered Maggie a beaker of orange squash, which she refused. She tried to hear what was going on behind the door, but could catch only the occasional deep laugh, which must have come from the bow-tied man. Her mother told her to sit down, but Maggie stayed at the window, watching the rain grow heavier. It clapped against the pane as the wind blew it first one way, then the other. It was so absorbing that it was a while before Maggie noticed that her mother was doing something strange. Fiona was leaning forward in her chair, her elbows on her knees and her head buried deep in her hands.

Without saying anything, Maggie sat on the plastic chair next to her. Then, at a loss for what else to do, she leaned her head against her mother's wet sleeve. Her mother tried a little laugh. 'Don't mind me,' she said, straightening up and letting out a long sigh. 'I'm just a bit worried about poor old Joe. We've got to look after him, haven't we?'

Maggie nodded.

'Good girl. We can do it together, can't we?'

Maggie nodded again and was rewarded with a long squeeze. For the next ten minutes she remained safely cradled against her mother's warm, damp body.

When Joe emerged from the office, moments later, his cheeks were flaming red, and he was carrying his parka over his shoulder. His T-shirt looked comical; it was faded and too small, and flapped above his belt.

Their mother stood abruptly, causing Maggie to almost topple from her chair, and asked him how it went.

Without looking at her, he said, flatly, 'Brilliant.'

The therapist recommended that Joe come to twelve more sessions. Maggie's mother warned her father not to complain about the expense, and said it would be better for Joe if Maggie stayed at home. As the weeks went by, Joe's stammer lessened. But to Maggie's disappointment he didn't speak much more to her. If anything, getting better seemed to render Joe more distant, more unreachable, and Maggie more alone, than before.

When Maggie was fifteen, her mother bought a pair of high-heeled yellow shoes and began going out on her own.

One evening, Maggie had stayed up late reading *Gone With the Wind*, when she heard a door slam. Sitting up in bed to listen, she glanced at her plastic clock. Twelve-thirty. Later than she'd thought. She had been using the gripping narrative of her novel as an excuse to stay awake until she was sure her mother was back.

Now there was shouting. Maggie couldn't make out the words, but she could hear the breathless anger in her mother's voice, suddenly drowned out by her father bellowing the word 'ENOUGH'.

Maggie leapt from her bed and crept downstairs. She pressed an ear to the sitting-room door.

'TELL ME,' her father shouted.

Her mother gave a little cry of outrage and Maggie's hand flew to the door handle, ready to turn it should her father shout again.

'TELL ME!'

Maggie made her entrance, calculating that the sight of their daughter in her pink pyjamas (two sizes too small) would stop her parents arguing.

Her father had his tie – turquoise, paisley-patterned, the one he wore on Thursdays – rolled tightly round his fist. He wasn't a large man, but standing over her mother, who was sitting on their old Laura Ashley sofa with her head in her hands, he suddenly appeared gigantic. If either of them noticed Maggie, they gave her no acknowledgement, and her presence was not enough to stop Alan bringing the end of his tie down on her mother's shoulders, nor was it enough to stop her mother letting out a ferocious laugh, followed by the words, 'If you think you can hurt me with that thing, you're wrong.'

Maggie's father let the tie drop to the floor and looked at his daughter. 'Go back to bed,' he said. 'Everything is fine. Go back to bed.'

Maggie looked at her mother's back, but she did not move. Eventually, without turning round, Fiona said, 'Do as he says, love.'

From then on, Maggie was alert to her mother's secrets. She wanted to know whatever it was that her father had wanted to know, whatever it was that her mother's unmoving back had refused to offer up. TELL ME, she thought to herself. TELL ME. When she came home from school she had half an hour alone in the house before Fiona came back at four (Joe never arrived home before six; what he did in the hours after school was a mystery to her, and, as far as Maggie knew, to everyone else). During this time she went into her parents' bedroom and looked for clues. In her mother's underwear drawer she found nothing but the usual knickers and bras, labels washed until limp, lace trims grey and often fraying. In the bottom of the wardrobe she found the normal collection of old shoes and bags. She let herself examine the one covered in tiny gold beads, now losing their lustre. She'd often played with this as a younger girl, filling it with her lip balms and the tortoiseshell comb that was a present from her Aunt Sandra, her mother's sister who'd never married, but had instead moved to Canada. Aunt Sandra had visited Oxford once, and the whole week had been filled with anxiety and excitement for Maggie. Sandra smoked roll-up cigarettes and complained about the lack of a shower cubicle in the bathroom. She'd sat on Maggie's bed and combed her hair into French plaits for hours, talking all the time of the pros and cons of dating Canadian men – real men who wore plaid shirts and did things with axes. When she had left, she'd held Maggie's chin and said, 'Come visit me when you're older and you've had enough of these guys.' Fiona had held on to her daughter's shoulder and Maggie had swallowed her urge to cry.

But, in spite of Maggie's snooping, it was what wasn't hidden that was terrible.

A couple of weeks after the shouting, Maggie's mother had left for work just before Maggie went to school, as she usually did. She'd kissed her forehead, said, 'Lock up, won't you?', grabbed her bag and keys from the kitchen counter and stepped out of the house in a wave of Poison perfume. The usual moment – the moment Maggie realised that she could, in fact, stay at home and watch television all day and no one would be any the wiser, came and went. Maggie, already in her coat and shoes, picked up her cold toast from the table and took a bite. She was about to pull open the back door when a cream-coloured envelope on the top of the fridge-freezer caught her eye. It was addressed to 'Darling', the letters written in her father's long and looping style. Turning it over, Maggie saw that it was open. So she removed the contents – a short letter – and read.

Darling Fiona,

I am so happy that we have sorted everything out and that we can move forward together. What I said was true, my love. I CAN forgive and forget. When I return, I hope we have a life together as a family.

Ever yours,

Alan

That day, Maggie recited the letter to herself again and again. *Forgive and forget. Sorted everything out. Move forward.* Walking home from school, she deliberately dawdled, taking the long way and walking round the park. Her mother had trespassed and her father was forgiving. That was not the way round Maggie had thought it would be. All her life, she'd been ready to forgive her father. Her mother had often said: 'Leave Daddy alone. He's having one of his moods.' Or: 'Don't mind your father. He hasn't slept.' As a family, they were always making allowances for Alan, for his silences, his blankness, his periodic inability to participate in their lives. Many Sundays were spent

Being Quiet So Daddy Can Sleep. Many evenings were spent wondering what Daddy was doing in his 'study' (a book-lined box room at the top of the house). Many family holidays, spent in a stuccoed holiday bungalow on Anglesey, took the same format. Each day Fiona would ready the picnic, get the two children into the car and drive to the beach, where she would unpack Joe's dinghy and Maggie's bucket and spade and reassure them both that their father would be joining them later, that he was just catching up on an hour's sleep; he'd been under pressure at work and it would take him a few days to recover. Just give him some time, then he'd be all theirs. Usually, Alan would not join them until the last couple of days of the holiday, when he would often completely over-rule their mother's plans in favour of something 'more suitable for these young 'uns'. Out would go Conwy Castle and in would come the pier at Llandudno. On one such day, Maggie's father bought her everything she asked for: a plastic cane full of Smarties, a candyfloss on the pier, a hot-dog from a stinking stall for lunch, chocolate éclairs in a damp, fern-encrusted tea-room in the afternoon, a can of Coke on the beach and, when they got back to the bungalow, a fish-and-chip supper. That night, she'd vomited violently, all over the queen-sized bed she shared with her brother. The next day, the family had picnicked on brown-bread sandwiches and tangerines at Newborough Warren and, despite the overcast skies, her mother had worn a large pair of sunglasses, which flashed blank accusations in Alan's direction. Maggie had been careful to hold her father's hand whenever possible, not wanting him to feel that he'd been wrong to indulge himself and his only daughter.

During that particular holiday, when she'd been ten and her brother twelve, Joe had sunk into full, if not fully open, warfare with his father. To Fiona's reassurances that their father would soon be there, Joe's response would often be a dramatic rolling of the eyes. And when Alan was actually with them, Joe walked a few steps behind the group, either staring at the ground or mimicking with fearsome accuracy the way his father moved and talked. Joe highlighted the things that to Maggie were so everyday as to be barely noticeable: the way her father stroked his earlobe as he thought of what to say, the lift in his voice when he spoke her name, the slight lag in his right foot as he walked. By the end of the holiday, Joe had stolen all these things and made them his own.

When she finally reached home, the words of her father's letter still beating in her head, Maggie saw her mother staring out of the front window, waiting for her return. Maggie considered walking past, heading straight down the road and on and on until she came to a stop somewhere – anywhere – else. But her mother had opened the door and was calling to her.

'You're late. Where've you been?'

Maggie shrugged. Her mother was wearing a new dress, blue and tightly fitted. She looked strange, her eyelids bruised with silver-grey shadow, her hair deliberately tousled and sprayed in a way that suggested she'd spent many hours in front of the mirror. She followed her daughter down the hall, saying, 'Your father's staying away tonight. Last-minute thing.'

Maggie hung her school bag over the back of a kitchen chair. To her surprise, Joe was standing by the back door. He'd changed out of his school uniform into a pair of jeans and a hooded top and was glaring at the floor tiles. Maggie opened the fridge, noticing that the envelope had been removed.

'So I thought we could go out,' her mother continued. 'Just the three of us.'

Very slowly, Maggie poured herself a glass of apple juice. After she'd drunk most of it, she wiped her mouth with her hand and asked, 'Isn't it a bit early?'

'How about a bit of enthusiasm?'

'Get your glad rags on, Maggie,' said Joe. Gesturing towards his own jeans and trainers, he added, 'I have.'

They parked on Broad Street and headed, as Maggie had known they would, for Browns. It was six o'clock and the huge restaurant was quite empty. The large windows, potted palms and dark wooden tables gave the place a vaguely continental feel, which impressed the three of them less than it would have done a few years ago. They'd recently been on holiday to Brittany and knew this sort of thing was ordinary, and much cheaper, in France. Still, when a young waiter showed them to a table, Maggie's mother thanked him too many times.

They'd never before shared a night out without Alan. Maggie feared that her mother wanted to 'open up', as they said on the talk shows, to her and Joe. Wishing to avoid this at any cost, she became sullen in a way that was new to all of them. When Fiona exclaimed over the size of her glass of wine, the delicious smell of frying steak, the whiteness of the napkins, Maggie looked at her lap, and it was Joe who responded with the necessary sounds. Her mother's strange dress, the way she kept touching the gold hoops in her ears and smiling at the waiter, were too much for Maggie to bear. When their food came (flaky fish pie for Fiona, herbed turkey escalope for Maggie, steak for Joe), Fiona held up her half-empty glass.

'A toast.'

Maggie watched as Fiona took a long drink. 'Your dad and me have been talking. We both think it's time he – had more of what he wants.'

Maggie thought her father always had what he wanted, but she said nothing. She looked at Joe, whose eyes were fixed on the Specials board above his mother's head.

'And he wants to move,' Fiona continued, 'to Wales.'

Joe said, 'What the fuck?'

'Language!' warned Fiona, rather half-heartedly.

Maggie said, 'Why was Dad so angry, the other night?'

Fiona put down her glass and sighed. In the minutes' silence that followed she seemed to deflate, ruffling her hair so it resembled her usual style once more, kicking off her heels under the table, pushing up the sleeves of her dress. Maggie felt a moment of reassurance: this woman was more recognisably her mother.

Then Fiona said, 'Listen.' She looked from Maggie to Joe and back again. 'Do you think you're old enough to understand something, if I tell you?'

There was no right way to answer this, so Maggie nodded. Joe did not move.

'I made a mistake. Marriage can be a difficult thing . . . I was seduced by a younger man.' Fiona blushed deeply. 'There. I'm not proud of it. Now you know what your father was so angry about.'

Maggie said nothing. She was trying to understand the full significance of the word *seduced*.

'His name was Calum. But you don't need to know that.' She took a breath. 'He is – was – my driving instructor. He's actually not a bad guy.'

Was there a small smile on her mother's lips as she said this?

'Jesus . . .' said Joe.

'But it's over now. And your father and I both think we should have a new start.'

Maggie tried to catch Joe's eye, but he was staring at the polished table in silence.

A month later, their house was on the market.

They moved to an old farmhouse on the outskirts of a village not far from where Fiona was born. Its walls were thick stone, its doors heavy wood. Its small windows looked directly onto the road, and, beyond that, the Snowdonia mountain range was visible. Inside the house it was dark and cold, even in the summertime. Although the village was quiet, the house was noisy. The ancient boards creaked, the iron latches clacked, the windows rattled. Alan said the move was worth it for the views alone. They had five small fields and, a mile away, a tiny, ramshackle one-storey boathouse on the shore of the Menai Strait. Fiona had left the island as a child, when her whole family had moved to Birmingham; no one currently living in the village had any memory of her. But, as Maggie's father said, this only increased the cleanliness of their slate.

Joe had it on good authority that in The Groeslon, the pub two doors from their house, the regulars talked of the English idiots who had bought the farmhouse and seemed to be trying to use it as a smallholding. It was, they agreed, utter folly: the place hadn't been worked for decades. Catherine Jones, its last owner, had made a beautiful lawn of the first field, and turned the pigsties into an ornamental feature. The old dairy she had used to house her much-envied sit-on mower, and the cattle sheds had long been a patio area. The English middle classes had a special kind of stupidity when it came to the land, though. They thought they could play on it, create a lifestyle of it, and it always, always came back to bite them. Joe particularly relished relating this bit to his sister.

Ignorant of such talk, Alan enjoyed himself immensely. He enrolled in Welsh conversation classes at Llanfairpwll, made a point of using the village Spar store whenever he could, and greeted anyone who would meet his eye. If they returned his greeting, he would lose no time in telling them that his wife had grown up in the next village, much to Maggie's embarrassment. Alan was ready for hostility and welcomed the challenge of bringing the locals round. The important thing, he told Maggie, was to show willing in the life of the community. That was why he'd tried to join the local chapel's congregation. He'd discovered, however, that the preacher was running a skeleton service these days; there was only one meeting a week, and that was in Welsh. If he wanted to worship, he'd have to go two miles down the road to the English church. Thinking it might be better than nothing, he'd made some investigations, and had been dismayed by the sound that greeted him as he approached the place: not close-harmony singing or the fiery oratory of a preacher, but the confident ticking of Mercedes engines as they cooled beneath the surrounding yew trees. The same cars were always parked outside the Baron Hill golf club during the week, or at the Tre-Ysgawen hotel and health spa on a Saturday lunchtime. This wasn't the sort of community life Alan had envisaged and, to his disappointment, he set foot in neither church nor chapel.

Once they had arrived on Anglesey, it was no longer Maggie's father who spent long hours alone in his room, refusing to join the family for meals or weekend trips. It was her mother. Maggie could tell whereabouts Fiona was by following the scent of Poison and Nescafé, but she seldom found herself in the same room as her mother for more than a few moments. As Maggie and Joe were eating, Fiona would slip through the back door and gaze at the fields. Whilst Maggie was getting ready for school, Fiona would watch morning television in the gloomy sitting room, a small bowl of Alpen balanced on her knees. She didn't talk about the move, or about what she did all day whilst her children were at school. And even though she was the only member of the family who spoke Welsh, Fiona made no friends in the village.

Joe, however, became friendlier towards his sister. There was a sense of solidarity. They were in this together, and even if the locals weren't very welcoming, even if Joe and Maggie didn't speak more than a few words of the language (they both knew how to say *Diolch yn fawr*, but hardly dared risk it), wasn't this the place where they'd spent all their childhood holidays? During those first few weeks, it seemed to Maggie that they went everywhere together, and that Joe – the Joe who'd once needed her more than anyone else – had returned to her.

Neither one of them would venture to the Spar to face Glen alone. Glen didn't work in the shop, but he was always there, leaning on the counter, chatting to Cheryl, the owner. He was, Maggie estimated, in his thirties. His cheeks, chin and neck were covered in burnt-looking stubble. His voice was low but forceful. Ordinarily Maggie loved the distinct and precise undulations of the language; they reminded her of the times her grandmother, who had died the year before, had used to call at the weekend and her mother's voice would find this new, startling territory of halting rhythms and noises made from the back of the tongue. Fiona seemed suddenly to be full of opinions and force when she spoke Welsh on the phone; there was little room, it seemed, for the sliding hum of indifference, the mumbling sounds of ambivalence. When Glen spoke it was the same, only more so, and Maggie found her face reddening with the frustration of not knowing what he was talking about. Was it the weather? Some profound comment on local politics? Or something about her? Whatever it was, she stood close to Joe then, both of them pretending to be unashamed by their own ignorance. At these moments she half-expected to feel Joe's hand on the small of her back as they paid for their magazines.

And at Ysgol David Hughes, Maggie was delighted to find that Joe made no protest whenever she sat next to him on the bench behind the sports hall. The other kids watched them, and they watched back, and Maggie wondered if her brother might need her again. She even began to listen for that click in his mouth, to be ready to help him, if necessary.

Not long after they moved, the family spent a Sunday afternoon on the beach at Llanidan, by the boathouse. Maggie followed her brother down the long shady lane and emerged onto the shore with a feeling of elation: after the darkness, here was the glitter and glare of the water; after the damp smell of fallen leaves, here was the breeze of the sea. They stood together, grinning. Then her father told them how treacherous the strait actually was; he described how the current could change in a heartbeat because there were actually two tides, one at either end of the strait. Whirlpools, he said, often formed near the rocks. It was a churning, unpredictable channel, the sandbanks forever shifting beneath the water. Maggie found it hard to believe that such an apparently tranquil stretch of blue could be so full of danger. It looked so safe; this was not even the sea, after all, but only the strait, and just across the water there was always a house, a road, a mountain to be seen.

It was autumn and the wind was stiff enough for her and Joe to need windcheaters and for her mother to hold herself tightly as they sat around a wood fire, cooking sausages on skewers. After they'd eaten, Maggie's mouth still smarting from the hot fat, she and Joe went crab-fishing on the stone groyne. Their father showed them what to do. First, find a long stick. Second, tie a piece of string around it, attaching a small stone as a weight. Then, kick a limpet off the groyne, scoop it from its shell and tie it to the end of the string. Dangle the limpet in the water and wait for your crab to come to you.

It sounded simple, but she soon found that her kick was neither swift nor stealthy enough to surprise the limpets welded to the rock. A few bashes would break their shells, but then the bait was no good. 'You need a whole limpet,' their father said, 'to be in with a chance of tying the thing and dangling it.' Joe developed a talent for asserting his authority, booting the slimy creatures from the stone and releasing them from their shells with a flick of his penknife, and she was grateful when he tied one to her line. But catching a crab – which happened startlingly quickly – was a shock: suddenly there were the rusty brown shell and spot eyes of the alien creature before her, its claws frantically gripping the air, and all she could do was toss the thing back into the sea. Joe laughed, but not long after he caught another, so large that even their father stepped back. Maggie and Joe exchanged glances, and that was enough for Joe to grasp its body between an outstretched finger and thumb and shove the crab into his sister's face. Their father tried to push Joe's hand away from Maggie, but she didn't flinch; instead she reached up and took hold of the crab's cold, hard body. Together, Maggie and Joe examined the creature. 'Look at its eyes,' Joe said. 'Looks dead already, doesn't it?'

Maggie nodded. Then something caught her; perhaps the intoxication at their tangible power over the crab. 'Let's pull its legs off,' she said, grinning.

But he shook his head. 'No point. Throw it back.'

'We should eat it,' said their father. 'Take it home and put it in a pot. It'll be delicious.'

'No,' said Maggie. 'Throw it back.' And with one flick of Joe's arm, the crab was returned to the sea.

'Your loss,' said their father. He shrugged and picked his way back across the slippery mass of seaweed that covered the groyne.

Maggie and Joe watched him go. Then they looked at one another and laughed. As they negotiated the seaweed, Maggie almost fell and her brother clasped her hand. When she was upright he held onto it for a few seconds more than was necessary, before laughing again. The warmth of Joe's approval flooded her body, and Maggie was suddenly glad they'd moved to the island.

Joe did not attend his sixth form for long. One lunchtime he wasn't in his usual position on the bench. Maggie knocked on his bedroom door that evening and was allowed in. Joe's bedroom had the look of a place that had not yet taken shape, even though they had been in the farmhouse six months already. In one corner was a pile of paperbacks, in another a stack of cardboard boxes with his name inked on the side, still unopened after the move. On his desk was his most prized possession: a Nikon camera and several rolls of film. He had saved up and bought it just before they'd moved to Wales. There were also several books about photography on the table, with scraps of paper protruding from their pages. Joe refused to show anyone his pictures, but Maggie had looked at them once when he wasn't there. To her surprise, he'd obviously spent a lot of time poking around the local lanes and gardens. His pictures were all close-ups of plants: intricately textured leaves coated with frost, dew-touched stalks, spiders' webs strung between skinny twigs.

'Where were you today?' she asked.

Upstairs the whole house was uneven, with slanting floors, bumpy ceilings and sloping walls. Joe's room seemed to lean to one side. His wardrobe doors hung open, displaying many empty hangers.

He didn't look up from the bed. He was lying across the duvet, reading a copy of *Practical Photography*, which he'd started buying recently.

'I didn't see you at school.'

He turned a page. 'This island is full of natural riches. It's a shame to waste them, sitting indoors.'

It was what their father often said at weekends.

'I've come to the conclusion,' said Joe, 'that education – at least of the sort offered to the likes of us – is largely pointless. So I'm exploring my environment. Which I think is a better use of my time.'

'Isn't that a bit – nihilistic?'

He raised his black eyebrows. 'Nihilists don't explore their environments, stupid. They don't believe in exploring. Or in environments.'

*

68

A week later, Joe came home on a motorbike. It was red and silver, like a toy spaceship. The wheels looked like jewellery to Maggie, the spokes were so intricate and shiny. The tank was bloated, like a pregnant fish. Sitting astride it, he waited for a few moments before taking off his helmet and looking towards the house. Maggie and her mother and father had gathered at the window, alerted by the long, loud gurgle of the engine.

'Good God,' said Fiona.

'We've been expecting it,' said Alan. 'Let's not make a meal of this. It's a bit of freedom for him. And the roads here are so much quieter.'

Maggie watched as her father strode out into the road. Joe cut the engine and grinned. Alan touched the handlebars, stood back. 'It's a beaut,' she heard him say. 'Almost as good as the one I had at your age.'

Even this comment didn't wipe the smile from Joe's face.

Fiona gripped Maggie's shoulder. 'I'd prefer it,' she said, 'if *you* didn't go out on that thing.'

Every afternoon, after he had apparently been to school, Joe would roar off on his bike, his camera slung across his body. He'd bought a new helmet without a visor and a pair of goggles that were too large for his face, giving him an insect-like appearance. Maggie watched him kick away the stand and wobble down the road until he'd gained enough speed to steady himself. Maggie's mother watched with her, one hand over her mouth, the other on Maggie's shoulder.

Then one afternoon Fiona was out shopping and Maggie watched her brother alone. Just before he was about to kick the stand away, she ran out into the road. He lifted his goggles. 'Take me with you,' she said.

He took a long time over getting her helmet done up in the right way.

'Hurry up,' she warned. 'Mum'll be back soon.'

He lifted his chin. 'Hold tight,' he said, 'and lean the way I do.'

The seat was surprisingly comfortable. She held onto his second-hand leather jacket, which he'd bought in a gas-fume-filled shop on Little Clarendon Street before they left Oxford. As they accelerated down the road, past The Groeslon and the English Church, she found herself laughing. Soon, though, she was only able to gasp as her body was pummelled by the wind, the machine roaring beneath them. The road slipped away and the view blurred. Trees, sky, sea – all passed at tremendous speed. It seemed to Maggie that they were going ridiculously, terrifyingly, gloriously fast. The icy wind rendered her fingers useless, even beneath their mittens. She kept shouting at him, telling him to slow down, but knew her voice was useless against the din of the engine. When they stopped in Beaumaris, her legs were shaking. 'You went too fast!' she said, unsure if she was angry or exhilarated.

'We were only doing thirty,' he laughed.

They turned their backs on the genteel façades of the town's Victorian villas and went down to the beach. Together they leaned against the cold sea wall, helmets in hands. The tide chucked white foam and stones in their direction.

'Do you miss Oxford?' Maggie shouted over the wind.

Her brother shook his head. He looked across at the snow-capped mountains, the view of which was startlingly clear at this time of day. 'This place is sort of getting to me,' he said, 'now I've got the bike.'

Joe took a few photographs, sloping off on his own along the shore, whilst Maggie searched for stones with holes in them. She'd been collecting these since they moved to the island, and had six at home already; there seemed to be no shortage of them here. She'd heard they were lucky, but it wasn't this that made them interesting to her. It was the strange way they were formed, the way stone could give way to air, so suddenly and completely. The way the holes might be hidden, on first sight, and then reveal themselves. Such a void could transform a very ordinary, grey pebble into a piece of sculpture.

Just as Joe came back, she found another. 'Here,' she said. 'Have a holey stone. It's supposed to be lucky.'

He brought it to his face and examined the strange buckled shape. 'Thanks,' he said, with a flicker of a smile. 'If it isn't, then I'll blame you.'

By the time Nula was ready for work in the mornings, Maggie had usually succeeded in involving Samuel so deeply in a game of trains or cars or tractors that he seemed to find it an irritation to have to stop whatever he was doing to kiss his mother goodbye.

Some mornings Maggie could see the pain on Nula's face as her son failed to protest enough at her departure. Other times she saw only Nula's relief at being free to leave the house alone. After she had gone, Maggie would always make an extra effort to get Samuel excited about the day to come. 'Let's go to the park and take this DIGGER!' she would say. Or: 'Shall we go to the music group and see who can sing the very LOUDEST?' Even so, occasionally Samuel wouldn't come away from the bay window, where he propped himself up against the back of the armchair, Leggy Monkey deep in his mouth, to watch his mother leave. 'Mummy will be back, Sammy, I promise,' said Maggie. 'She'll be back very soon.' On bad mornings, the mention of the word *Mummy* would be enough to cause Samuel's face to fall, and tears to drip on Leggy Monkey's head. As she held the boy, his wet cheek against her chest, Maggie thought: at least he lets me comfort him. He doesn't push me away. Other children she'd looked after had, in this situation, kicked her, hit her and screamed in her face. Samuel, however, always surrendered to her embrace, and in the end he would quieten, and allow her to take him away from the window.

Maggie's contract stated that she was expected to *shop for and prepare healthy meals for the child, planning weekly menus as appropriate*. But, more often than not, Nula would leave a rushed note on the fridge about what Samuel should eat that day. Usually it involved warming up some leftovers from the night before.

One teatime when Samuel was almost a year old, Maggie reheated the chicken risotto he had refused at lunch. When she'd first fetched it from the fridge it had been thick with butter and cream, flecked with bright-green parsley. Now, as she stirred, it turned into a pallid grey stodge. Nevertheless, Maggie waved the spoon towards Samuel's mouth and made encouraging noises.

Then the front door opened. Without warning, his mother had arrived home early and she bustled into the kitchen, her face flushed from the wind, her oversized cardigan hanging open. Smiling, she rushed towards Samuel with her arms flung wide, but then came to an abrupt halt. 'What's that?' she said, glaring at the risotto.

Samuel held out his arms to be lifted from his chair.

'Didn't he have this for lunch?' asked Nula. She was standing very straight now, one hand on her hip. In the other, her car keys rattled.

'He wasn't very interested in lunch . . .'

'So it's been warmed again?'

'Mama! Mama!' Samuel shouted.

'I didn't want to waste it.'

Nula lifted Samuel from his chair and cradled him to her

shoulder, rocking him back and forth, kissing his curls and saying nothing.

'Is there a problem?' asked Maggie.

Nula gave a heavy sigh. 'That rice has been heated up three times now.' Balancing Samuel on her hip, she emptied the risotto into the bin, banging the bowl firmly on the metal rim. 'It's a bit of a health risk.' Then she looked her son in the face and said, 'You didn't eat any of it, did you, Sammy?'

'Not one single mouthful,' said Maggie.

'Please don't heat things too many times, OK, Maggie?' said Nula. 'Now, what else can we give you, Sammy . . . ?'

Maggie pushed back her chair. Snatching the loaf from the breadbin, she hacked off a thick slice. Then another.

'What are you doing?'

'Giving the child a healthy meal,' said Maggie, throwing the bread onto a plastic plate and presenting it to Nula and Samuel with a fixed smile.

Nula took the plate. 'Thank you,' she said. 'Maggie—'

'I made a mistake,' said Maggie, aware of the crack in her voice.

'It doesn't matter.'

'It shouldn't have happened.'

'I'm going to give Samuel his tea now,' said Nula, plopping the boy back in his chair, which prompted him to shout in dismay. 'Let's not make a big thing of this, all right?'

'I hope you know it won't happen again.'

'I'm sure of it,' said Nula, straining to make herself heard over Samuel's escalating cries. 'Why don't you go home early?'

That night, Maggie spent a long time googling the phrase 'reheated risotto health risk'. She went to bed only when she was satisfied that she'd presented Samuel with no more than a minimal amount of danger. Minimal, that was, compared to the risk from his exposure to childcare by a non-immediate-family member for more than forty hours per week at such an early age. To reassure herself further, she looked up one of her favourite papers on this subject, which argued – very even-handedly, in Maggie's opinion – that childcare was best performed by a parent until the child was at least three years old. Second-best, the paper went on to say, was one-to-one care by a non-parental figure (a grandparent, or a qualified nanny, for example). On the one hand, Maggie found it comforting to think that she was a step up from a nursery environment. On the other, it was never nice to be called *second-best*.

Rain and butterflies. These were the things that made Maggie fall in love with Samuel.

It was a wet day, the rain beating at the large windows, and all her plans (park, bakery, back for lunch) were in ruins. The wind blew water into the house. Nula had told Maggie that Greg wouldn't replace the 1930s back door because it was vintage. 'You know,' she'd said. 'Capital *V*.' It didn't fit, though, and wind and rain would seep through the gaps on gusty days. Some of the sash windows had a similar problem, and there were regularly small puddles of water on the sills in the bath-room and the back bedroom. Maggie liked this; she was glad the Shaws' house had these obvious, material imperfections. It made her feel more at home. But every time Greg saw a hint of dampness, he tutted, loudly.

Maggie and Samuel were in the sitting room, watching the rubbish truck. She held him about the middle as he balanced on the back of the armchair. He was beside himself with excitement, not because of the rubbish truck but because of the rain, which obscured their view, fracturing the truck into hundreds of glinting droplets. 'Whoo,' he shouted. And he pressed his nose to the glass, as if hoping to feel the rain. Someone rushed by with a multicoloured umbrella, causing him to laugh loudly. He gripped Maggie's hand as he stood and pointed at the weather for a good ten minutes, enraptured by the sight of water pelting down the glass, thundering through the trees outside. What wonder, she thought, to see rain and love it so. She said, 'Let's go and get wet' and they both put on their raincoats and wellies – Samuel's red and shiny, Maggie's decorated with goldfish – and stood outside the back door, welcoming the rain onto their hands and faces. Samuel said, 'Uh-OH!' when Maggie stamped in a puddle on the path; he laughed and copied her, pushing her out of the way and stamping first one foot and then the other in the water, until they were both soaked up to the knees and Maggie was weak with the joy of being rained on with a thirteen-month-old boy.

Afterwards she made him toast soldiers, dried his hair and hands with a towel and sat with him on her lap, watching with quiet glee as the rain battered the windows and seeped under the door.

And butterflies. One stormy summer morning they sat together at the table, the light outside so thin that she had to flick on the lamps. Samuel bent his head over the cardboard wings she'd cut out the night before. His mother had provided poster paints in primary colours, but Maggie wanted to introduce Samuel to cerulean blue, magenta, burnt umber, vermilion, aquamarine. And so she brought her own tubes of acrylic to the house. They were left over from her GCSE art course and the caps had dried on and were hard to shift, but once she'd managed, the oily smell rose up and she was back in the overheated art room, Miss Bagshawe standing behind her, earrings jangling as she pressed her bony fingers into Maggie's shoulders and said, 'Very *expressive* work, Maggie.' In those days painting had been something vital to Maggie. There had been no art on the walls of her family house apart from a mountainscape, faded and framed in dusty glass. When she had asked her father who'd painted it, he'd said, 'Debenhams' and laughed. But in the school library Maggie had found a book of Impressionist landscapes and, most lunchtimes, went to look again at Van Gogh's baked south, those yellows so sickly and alive, those crows so childlike and important, and she experienced an unnameable, physical sensation right in the pit of her stomach that made her breathing alter. She hadn't known, before, that it was possible to have a physical reaction to a page in a book.

Samuel trailed his fingers through the thick colours, then examined them at close range. 'Don't lick,' she said, knowing vibrancy like this would be impossible for his mouth to resist. What else can you do with such red but eat it? 'Here,' she said, guiding his fingers instead to the white paper. 'And then we fold it like this.' And – hey presto – a butterfly! Samuel was so delighted with the bleeding blobs of colour that he wore the butterfly on his head, streaking his hair yellow, blue and pink. They made dozens, then flew them around the room, letting them drop from the table to the floor and batting them at the kitchen windows as if they had their own will to be free.

As she fell in love with Samuel, she thought of all the other children she had loved. Theo. Charlotte. Amy. William. They had all been loved, and were all lost. Maggie had been careful, when she'd started nannying, to keep an emotional distance. She had tried her best not to become involved. But she'd soon realised that emotional distance is not an option with children under five. To look after them well – and Maggie had always liked doing things well – involved love. Changing filthy, noxious nappies. Sterilising endless bottles and preparing formula to strict instructions. Reading the same boring story aloud until you knew it off by heart. How could you do these things without love? And Maggie had learned early on that the thing all very young children, especially babies, needed most of all was physical contact. Maggie counted herself lucky to be someone who cuddled babies and toddlers for a living. It was the best part of her job. Charlotte, Amy, Theo, William: she had lifted them all crying from their cots, cradled them to her chest and rocked them back to sleep, sometimes for many hours. She had blown raspberries on their soft naked tummies until they squealed with pleasure. She had nuzzled their malleable ears and patted their perfect bottoms. She had pretended to eat their fingers and toes.

Between the ages of four months and three years, William, the little boy she'd looked after before Samuel, had spent five days a week in Maggie's care. Maggie now did her utmost not to think of William too often, because she could no longer touch or hold him, and when she'd seen him in the street a few weeks ago his mother had stopped for the very briefest of chats before hurrying her son away. It was as if, Maggie thought, she'd wanted William to forget that it was Maggie who was there when he had first walked from chair to sofa; Maggie who picked him up when he'd tried to extend his reach to the door and had fallen on his face; Maggie who had heard him say his first word – *car*; Maggie who had comforted him when he wet himself over and over again as she'd potty-trained him.

But Maggie had grown tired of being careful. She'd decided it was pointless, really, to try to stop herself falling in love. And, she reasoned, Samuel was different. Samuel was family.

'Samuel's vests are too small.'

Falling in love meant that Maggie began to speak her mind.

When Maggie tackled Samuel's mother about his vests one Friday, Nula smiled. Maggie often wondered why Samuel's mother smiled so much when she was obviously so unhappy. They were in the kitchen, having tea. Nula was working from home that day, because, she claimed, she was feeling under the weather. Samuel was napping and Nula had come down from her study, apparently to get a drink. But Maggie knew Nula was checking up on her, wanting news of Samuel's morning. On this particular morning, though, Maggie didn't feel like assuaging his mother's guilt and fears by reassuring her that Samuel was just fine, they'd had so much fun in the park and, yes, he ate all his lunch. She felt like telling Nula that his vests were too small. She added, 'I could buy him some bigger ones. The next time we're in town.'

'I can do it.'

Maggie ducked her head, as if avoiding a blow. She wanted to ask: when? Soon? Instead she said: 'I noticed they have three-for-two. In Boots.'

Nula observed Maggie with a steady gaze. Then she said, again, 'I can do it' and went back to her study.

*

79

It was easy to imagine, during the daytime, that he was hers. She was alone with him for ten, sometimes eleven, hours. And everyone she met immediately assumed she was Mummy. Maggie always denied this, but often enjoyed the compliments that followed: 'You're so natural with him! He's obviously very bonded with you!' And once: 'Does he cry when you hand him back to his mother?'

It hadn't come to that, yet. William had cried, sometimes, and then his mother had cried, too. But Maggie knew that Samuel was sad whenever she said goodbye. She could tell by the way he refused to say the word back to her. Instead, he would silently bury his head in his mother's lap. It was as though, she thought, he could not face their parting.

Some nights Maggie would wake in a sweat, alone, wondering where his little hand was. Then she would remember that he was at home, with his parents. And she would lie awake for the rest of the night, imagining different scenarios, none of which involved Greg or Nula in Samuel's life.

Most weekends, after she had done her weekly supermarket shop, Maggie found herself wondering what Samuel would be doing.

Nula had once mentioned that she and Greg had taken Samuel on a Sunday outing to Waddesdon Manor. The following Sunday, Maggie drove out there herself. As she crunched up the tidy gravel pathways and admired the elaborate topiary, she imagined the wheels of Samuel's pushchair dragging through the stones, how he would moan to get out, then moan to get back in again. She sat in the café in the old stable buildings, ordered herself a latte and tutted audibly at how unsuitable the menu was for children. Coffee-mocha cakes and meringue towers were so wrong for pre-schoolers. What would Samuel have eaten in here? She hadn't asked his mother. But it was difficult to picture the boy managing to do anything in the place apart from crawling under the tables, getting plastered in cake crumbs and irritating the hell out of the white-aproned waiters.

A couple of weeks later she'd bumped into the Shaws on a Saturday. It was a warm, windblown afternoon and they were shopping on the High Street. Greg was pushing the buggy with one hand, and Nula was looking in the windows of Hobbs. They greeted Maggie enthusiastically, embracing her and asking what she had managed to buy so far. 'Nothing,' was her reply. 'I've been in the Ashmolean.' Nula pulled an impressed face, then said to Samuel, 'Look! It's Gee-Gee!'

Samuel eyed Maggie suspiciously.

'Hi, Sammy,' Maggie said, kneeling beside the buggy.

Samuel turned his face away.

'He's tired,' said Nula.

'He was up bloody early,' added Greg. 'As usual.'

Maggie tickled Samuel's chin and he giggled. Then she leaned close to his ear and whispered, 'Are you tickly?'

'No!' he squealed, going pink with delight.

Nula said, 'Don't be rude to Maggie, darling.'

'It's all right,' Maggie smiled. 'It's just a little joke we have.'

'How sweet,' said Nula, with a frown.

'Let's get a coffee,' suggested Greg, looking at Maggie as if to include her in the invitation.

'Good idea.' Nula took hold of the buggy and pushed off. 'See you Monday, Maggie,' she called over her shoulder.

Greg shrugged, winked, then followed his wife.

*

Greg liked ironing. Every Wednesday afternoon he worked from home, and by half-past four he was usually in the kitchen, assembling the board and preparing the basket of clothes for his oncoming attack. As Samuel needed his tea around this time, Maggie had no choice but to watch as Greg filled his sleek weapon with distilled water and reached for another shirt. He would shake the fabric vigorously before arranging it on the board, then pause before lifting the iron. Puffs of steam would rise around his face as he nudged the hot steel into corners, occasionally causing the board to shake as he pressed the iron onto collars, along cuffs, across shoulders.

From his high chair Samuel would gaze at his father, mesmerised by the steam. Greg would laugh and say, 'Watch and learn, Sammy boy, watch and learn. One day you'll be a man, my son.' This always made Maggie laugh, and then Samuel would laugh, too. Greg would often try to strike up a conversation whilst he worked, but Maggie usually managed to keep their discussions focused on Samuel's development. Greg's face was a little too open when he asked how she was, a little too encouraging when he enquired whether there was 'Any gossip?'

Maggie had been working for the Shaws for over a year before the conversation developed any further. One afternoon, Greg set up his ironing equipment as usual, but said absolutely nothing as he did so. Maggie was supervising Samuel as he ate a bowl of pasta with his fingers. As usual, they both watched as Greg ironed. But Greg said nothing to his son, or to Maggie.

He was stretching the shoulder of another shirt over the board's nose when something compelled Maggie to ask, 'Have you always ironed?'

Greg did not look up. 'God, no.'

Using his whole hand, Samuel stirred his pasta so hard that several tomatoey tubes flew from the bowl and landed on the table. 'Splod!' he said. 'Splod!'

Maggie was about to begin clearing away when Greg said, 'I started doing it to annoy my ex-wife, actually.'

He straightened a collar, fired a jet of popping steam and added, 'She refused to do anything domestic. So I started spending Sunday afternoons ironing. At first it was a joke, I suppose. I didn't want to pay someone to do our ironing, and she didn't believe me when I said I'd rather do it myself. So I went out, got all the gizmos, got stuck in.' He examined the bottom of the iron for a moment – Maggie wondered if he might actually spit on it – before attacking the collar. 'And after a while I got really into it, you know? I find it relaxing. A simple task, well done. That's rewarding, isn't it?' He looked at her.

Maggie wiped the sauce from Samuel's hands. 'And was your ex-wife annoyed?' she asked.

'Absolutely livid,' Greg said with a smirk. 'Madeleine hated it when I did anything better than her.'

'I didn't realise you were married before.' She glanced at Samuel, wondering how much of this conversation he was taking in. But the boy was enjoying splatting new patches of tomato sauce on the table, then rubbing them hard into the grain of the wood.

Greg sighed. 'We were both very young.' He put his iron down, carefully folded his pristine shirt and added it to the pile. 'And what about you, Maggie?'

'Nothing to tell,' she said, wiping Samuel's hands again, but making no real attempt to stop him playing with his food.

'Oh, now,' said Greg, stepping out from behind the ironing board, 'I don't believe that. Not for one minute.' He leaned against the kitchen table, arms folded.

Samuel looked at his father. 'More!' he demanded, slapping the table.

Maggie set about clearing up. 'You can have a yoghurt, Sammy, OK?'

'I'll get it,' said Greg, fetching a pot from the fridge and sitting next to his son.

Maggie hovered by the table as Greg opened the yoghurt and handed Samuel a spoon.

'I'll watch him,' said Greg. 'You don't mind, do you?'

Maggie was so surprised to see Greg helping with teatime that she let a moment pass before she said, 'Of course not. You don't have to ask.'

'I don't want to step on your toes,' he said.

Maggie busied herself with stacking the dishwasher.

'So . . . there must be something to tell,' Greg persisted, wiping yoghurt from his son's mouth.

Slamming the dishwasher shut, she laughed, despite herself. 'Nothing serious.'

It was the truth, in a way. Even during her time at Jesus, where she'd managed to get through several parties by becoming drunk on warm white wine, Maggie had had very few sexual encounters. There had been a memorable night spent with a Biology undergraduate named Vern, who talked about the Revolutionary Communist Party, kissed her in the morning and told her he'd like to have sex with her. She'd consented; it had been painful. She'd spent the rest of the term avoiding him.

'Well,' said Greg, again cleaning Samuel's mouth with a baby-wipe. 'That's a very great shame, because you're an attractive woman, Maggie.'

'I find it's better to give him a big wipe at the end, rather than wipe him between mouthfuls,' said Maggie.

Greg didn't flinch. Instead he said, 'So what do you do when you're not performing miracles with our boy? What does Maggie do for fun?'

Still standing by the dishwasher, Maggie stared at him. If he was mocking her, his face showed no sign of it: his expression was one of frank interest.

'Actually, I like to paint.'

'Is that so?'

'But I don't do it very often . . .'

'Well, I'd love to see something,' said Greg, opening another yoghurt for Samuel.

'I haven't got much to show.'

'I *knew* you were artistic,' he said. 'Artistic Maggie, that's what I thought. And I was right, wasn't I?'

'More!' Samuel demanded, holding up his spoon.

'Samuel,' warned Maggie, coming to the table, 'be nice.'

'That's all right,' said Greg, 'isn't it, Sam-Sam? Daddy doesn't mind, does he? You're only little . . .'

'I think he's probably had enough,' said Maggie. 'Nula doesn't like him to have more than two. Those yoghurts are actually full of sugar.'

Greg held up his hands. 'I'd better get back to work, Sam-Sam.' Before leaving, he stood and ruffled his son's hair. 'You didn't know you had an artist for a nanny, did you?' he said.

Back at her flat that evening, Maggie poured a glass of red and pulled out an old sketchbook. While she flicked through, she imagined herself sitting at the Shaws' kitchen table, Greg turning the pages slowly as he quietly appreciated her pen-and-ink drawings of Port Meadow, the canal bridges and the covered market. He wouldn't know, she thought, how clichéd and weak they were; he wouldn't be appalled by the wholly expected views, the laboured lines and the unimaginative use of colour washes. He would look at them and think: here is someone who can do something I cannot.

Maggie decided she wouldn't show him the book in which she kept her best drawings. Every couple of weeks she tried to complete a picture of Samuel. She longed to draw his eyes – to capture their arresting clarity – but the only way she could get him to keep still for long enough was to draw him whilst he was asleep. And so she would sit close to his cot and peer through the bars, her book balanced on her knees, and examine his flushed cheeks, his open mouth, his sweaty hair, the pouchy flesh of his chin and neck. She loved the way time would fall away as she concentrated only on the contours of Samuel's sleeping face. Something told her Nula would not be comfortable with the idea of Maggie keeping a pictorial journal of Samuel's development in this way. And so she had never mentioned it.

The television was on, with the volume turned off, as it always was. Maggie didn't wish to hear the voices coming from the screen, or to get involved in the stories rolling out across the channels, but she did like the flickering presence in the room. Whenever she came back from a long day's work at the Shaws', Maggie's flat reminded her of her brother's bedroom on Anglesey: it had that same sense of impermanence, even though she'd tried to make it hers with the Paula Rego print on the wall, the purple Welsh quilt thrown over the second-hand sofa and the beautifully solid oak coffee table, an expensive impulse buy after she'd landed her first nannying job. But the flat resisted her efforts, stubbornly remaining uncluttered and unlived-in. Even in the kitchen, where Maggie's collection of chintzy unmatched teacups, picked up from charity shops, was displayed, everything remained clean and in its place, as if no one had ever used it. Every Saturday morning Maggie cleaned the flat thoroughly, whether it needed it or not.

Some evenings, sitting at her computer scanning news sites or looking up advice on childcare, she stopped clicking the mouse for so long that she thought she heard the machine breathing in time with her own lungs.

Maggie took a large swig of wine. Outside the window, a student shouted, 'I bloody love you!' Looking out, she saw a girl passing by, books clutched to her chest, a bewildered expression on her face. Was she, like Maggie, unable to believe in the role she was expected to play in this city, the role of the Oxbridge student? Occasionally Maggie regretted still living in the centre of town, where she was often reminded of her failure to capitalise on becoming such a highly regarded entity.

Once it had seemed like fate. Her teacher had said: 'Apply to Jesus. They have a Welsh thing.' And, given the circumstances, it had appeared the right thing to do. Her family had, as Joe put it, imploded. Sometimes it seemed to Maggie that the whole island had imploded.

Having gained a place despite saying next to nothing in the interview, Maggie didn't stay long at Jesus. She simply failed to turn up for the second year. What she remembered most, now, was the cold. Sitting up in her single bed, the duvet pulled around her chin, a hot-water bottle burning her feet, trying to stay awake to read the book gripped in her freezing fingers. At first she could not grasp what she was expected to do as a student here at Jesus College, Oxford. It had seemed such an overwhelming thing, to be an Oxford student at last, to be getting what her mother and teachers had referred to as a 'proper education'. 'You won't want to know us after that,' they'd said, gleefully, and she wondered why they sounded so happy about it, even though it made her feel proud and clever. She was leaving for Oxford; it was what all successful people did. In the stories she'd read of difficult or poor upbringings this was often the happy ending: an Education. Which was to say, an Oxbridge Education.

This great thing, this education, seemed flimsy and difficult to grasp, though, and Maggie found that it was possible to disappear in college, to lose yourself so completely you ended up avoiding all mealtimes in Hall, even breakfast.

She'd got her own supply of sliced bread and a toaster in her room, and kept butter on the windowsill. That seemed to be enough, along with the oranges she bought from the covered market. She loved their luxurious colour; her room and hands always carried their scent during her time at Jesus. She limited herself to two a day – one at lunchtime and one in the evening – and during the hours in between she looked forward to breaking into that lively flesh, to tasting the sweet juice. A bitter orange was a terrible disappointment, enough to convince her that nothing good would happen in the twelve hours following its unpeeling. Instead of thinking of her home, of the strait, of Joe, of Nula, she thought of her next orange and slice of toast, and how many hours there were until she could again indulge in these luxuries. At the end of each month, Maggie's mother sent her a ten-pound note in an envelope, telling her to buy herself something nice. She put this money aside to pay for her weekly visits to the café in Allders department store, where she could sit and order a coffee and a slice of cake without the threat of bumping into any other student. Whilst there she would allow her feet to defrost in the warm breeze coming from the café's electric heater, spending ten minutes studying the laminated list of beverages, even though she ordered the same cappuccino and carrot cake each week. She'd seldom look up from her book, but she enjoyed hearing the voices of other human beings who were not from the university: old ladies treating themselves to a toasted teacake, mothers asking their children to 'Please behave' and 'Aren't you going to eat that, now I've bought it for you?' And the children themselves, who would sometimes lean up against her table, smile and ask whose mummy she was.

The sketchbook was still open on her lap when she reached for her mobile, found Greg's number and sent the following message: *Shall I bring pictures tomorrow?*

Almost immediately her phone vibrated in response: *Hell, yeah x.*

The next morning, Maggie wrapped her sketchbook in a plastic bag and placed it on the back seat of her car. She told herself that she wouldn't mention it, or even take it into the house, unless Greg said something first.

As she drew up outside the Shaws' Greg was in the driveway, about to leave for work. He raised a hand in greeting and she found herself immediately reaching into the car's back seat for the sketchbook. She was thinking about waving the thing at him, even calling out that she'd brought it with her, but when she straightened up he was already reversing out of the drive. From the window he called, 'Have a good day, yeah?' and winked.

Maggie watched him disappear. Then she placed the sketchbook back on the seat and faced the house, where Samuel was waving excitedly to her from the sitting-room window.

*

That evening, as she was about to unlock her car, Greg's Golf came round the corner. She tried to pretend she hadn't seen him, but he flashed his headlights at her, wound down the window and shouted, 'Maggie! Hold on a sec.'

She waited, keys still in hand, as he parked in the driveway. Heart FM came to a sudden stop, there was an abrupt slam of the door and then he was there, standing near her in the evening light.

'So,' he said. 'Did you bring them?'

'What?'

He smelled of something lemony and overpriced. 'Weren't you going to show me your artwork today?'

She stared at the Tesco bag on the back seat and said nothing.

He gave a soft laugh. 'Come on, Maggie,' he said. 'I've been looking forward to it.'

'I've got to get back . . .'

'We could go round the corner for a quick drink, if you like. My treat. You deserve it, after all your hard work.'

Maggie looked towards the house. The curtains were open, but there was no sign of Samuel or Nula. They must still be in the kitchen, she thought, looking at a book together. She hoped they weren't reading *We're Going on a Bear Hunt* again. She'd already read that to him several times today.

'Nula won't mind,' said Greg. 'She's always saying we should take you out, as a reward.'

'I didn't bring anything,' she said. 'I forgot.'

There was a pause.

'It doesn't matter,' Greg said, moving closer to her. 'Let's go anyway.'

She pressed her key fob and the car's locks jumped in unison. 'Sorry,' she said, opening the door. 'I've got other plans.'

He stepped back. 'No problem,' he said. 'Another time, yeah?'

He turned away and started walking back to the house before she could answer.

Maggie avoided Greg as much as possible after that. She was even relieved when she didn't receive an invitation to Samuel's second birthday party. Maggie had expected to be invited, not because Nula and Greg thought of her as a friend, but because she'd assumed they would need her help. Several times, whilst they were discussing the plans for the celebrations, Maggie had thought Nula's next sentence would be, 'You *are* coming, aren't you?' or 'You do know you're invited, don't you?' She'd had her excuse prepared: an unavoidable visit to an old friend who was having relationship problems.

But the invitation never came, and on the afternoon of the party Maggie sat at home watching Robert Redford in *The Great Gatsby* on Film4 and trying not to think of the confidence in Greg's voice when he'd said, 'Another time.'

Samuel was almost two when Nula started sending the texts on leaving the house for work. If she knew she'd be able to take a long lunch, she'd type: PLEASE. Moments later, usually, his reply would be: THANK YOU. It had been so easy, and she had thanked God for him, for the hour she would spend in his company. For that hour, she would not have to think about anything but what was unfolding right then and there, what was happening between her and this man.

Walking to the café, only ten minutes from her office, had been almost the best part for Nula. Because it was May, of course, with the birds singing crazily and the cherry blossom bursting and the sky racing from grey to blue to white and back again, and the sun warming her face as she pushed her way down the High Street and along Carfax to get there, feeling that it was possible to experience again this lightness in her limbs at the thought of his eyelashes and the way they curled, for Christ's sake, curled up and round like a doll's. His eyelashes! What was wrong with her?

It struck her as essential, at this point, to think of how she had followed Greg along this street years ago, essential to face it and to smile at the thought of it, simply to smile and carry on in the direction her legs were carrying her, which was towards the café where she would meet Sean.

On their first lunch date she'd had fifteen minutes to kill

before they were supposed to meet, and she'd slipped into the café alone. Along the wooden counter all sorts of delicious treats were offered up on pieces of slate: slabs of salted caramel shortbread, stacked like Stickle Bricks, carrot cake heavy with cream-cheese topping, loaf cakes glistening with the sweet ooze of expensive chocolate. Strange to put food on a slate, she thought, and was reminded, briefly, of Anglesey and of Joe; she stopped shaking her purse for the right change and stared at the black rough-hewn surface of the slate, picturing the mudflats in the strait, where each day the water left and then erased its mark. Her eyes blurred and she jolted a little when the man behind the counter asked what it was she wanted.

She sat in the corner with her espresso, her phone ready on the table. She knew Greg wouldn't come here; he never took lunch breaks and, if he did, it was to entertain clients in restaurants, not to eat sandwiches in cafés. She hadn't thought, however, of the possibility of bumping into one of her NCT friends, and when Anne Peasemore came in with her son Jacob, Nula's heart jumped. She'd last seen Anne at Jacob's second birthday party, throughout which Jacob had either screamed or sulked. All afternoon Anne had looked deeply furious. The other parents had been sympathetic, but Nula had picked up on a certain feeling of quiet triumph from some quarters. *See how spectacularly all this fuss can backfire*, the apparently consoling faces said. *By giving him too much, see how ungrateful you have made your child.*

Jacob was shouting about wanting chocolate and was beginning to bang loudly on a table with a flattened palm whilst his mother tried to find the right change in her purse. Nula watched as Anne wagged a finger at her garrulous child, and prepared herself to explain to Anne that she was on a lunch break and, yes, she was still working full-time, and, yes, she missed her boy every minute, but it was nice to have a change of scene. How she would explain Sean's presence, if he turned up on time, was more problematic. After a few moments, though, Nula realised that Anne would not even look her way. She had too much to look at already and, if Jacob's behaviour continued to deteriorate, she would leave the café pretty soon. Moments later, Anne was handed a brown paper takeaway cup of cappuccino and a massive chocolate brownie, which she passed to Jacob. Nula watched Anne leave, confident in her look-no-child disguise, and smiled to herself. It was still possible, then. Still possible to be a woman drinking coffee alone, waiting for a man. Still possible, here in this café, to smell the good coffee, expensive perfume, fresh newspapers and toasted bread. She sipped her drink, felt the caffeine twitch along her veins and gave the man behind the counter – ridiculously young, she saw now, young enough to wear thick specs and look cool – a long look, happy to think that, once she was home, Samuel would be there to kiss her and she could be his mother once more. But, for now, there was the café. And there was Sean.

She thought of buying him a piece of shortbread in readiness, but she was anxious not to play the role of sugar mummy. Sean had his own money; as a freelance director with no family, he made plenty. This flirtation could so easily be taken to its logical conclusion, during those weeks when Sean was between jobs. And there was little danger, she told herself, of falling in love with him. He wasn't even handsome, not really: he was too gangly and strange-looking for that. His jaw was crooked; there was a large gap between his front teeth. There was only five years between them, but when he looked at Nula a boyish glitter would appear in his eyes so that she expected him to blush and duck his head, as though she were the sexy teacher and he the inexperienced head boy. That he did not only increased his appeal. In fact, she had been surprised by his boldness when he'd started the whole thing by leaving the note on her desk last week: *Lunch? S x.*

Lunch. S x. So many possibilities lit up in Nula's heart.

He arrived early, greeting her with a big smile and such a chaste peck on the cheek that Nula began to wonder if she had misinterpreted his intentions. Whilst he ordered an espresso at the counter she tried not to watch him digging for change in the pocket of his jacket. He always wore the same tweed jacket and jeans, a white shirt, pointy brown brogues.

Then he planted himself on the chair opposite her, emptied two packets of sugar into his drink and said, 'You look a bit gorgeous today, don't you?'

She couldn't stop laughing; she laughed at the clunkiness of his opening line, but she also laughed with sheer pleasure. Sean laughed, too, displaying his white throat.

Then there was a pause. Nula looked into her cup.

'So,' he said.

'So.'

Sean gave another laugh. 'What's going on with you?'

The things she couldn't talk to this man about flickered through her head: her son, her husband, her house, her nanny. 'The usual. Tight budgets and grumpy camera operators,' she said. 'And good coffee, now.'

He knocked back his espresso. 'Great coffee.'

'Coffee is important,' said Nula.

'Oh yeah. You should never put anything not-delicious near your mouth.'

'You've learned that, have you?'

'Through bitter experience,' he said.

'Hey, you!' A woman in her late twenties appeared at their table. She was carrying a pile of books under her arm and was grinning broadly at Sean.

'Georgia,' he said, a small frown passing across his face. 'How's it going?'

The woman told Sean she was looking forward to seeing him at that weekend's film festival, and Sean nodded. He didn't introduce her to Nula. Instead, as he exchanged a few pleasantries with the woman, he put a hand on Nula's forearm as if to keep her there, as if to reassure her that this was a momentary distraction. Was he showing the other woman that he had some claim to Nula, that she belonged to him in some small way? Nula glanced down at Sean's fingertips, flat and cool on the naked length of her forearm, and smiled at the woman.

Sean and Nula started meeting three times a week, always at lunch, always in the same place. They drank coffee and shared the occasional brownie. Sean talked a lot about his job, about the difficulties of getting anything but 'shit TV by the yard' to direct, and Nula liked listening to his humorous, brisk tone. She watched him swallow and couldn't stop herself wondering what it would be like to unbutton his shirt and slip a hand around his warm side, couldn't stop herself picturing his head between her legs. But they hardly touched.

Still, Nula bought the underwear. She had a meeting in Soho one afternoon, and when it was over she went into a tiny, expensive lingerie boutique nearby. It was very warm inside; she was the only one in the shop and there was no sign of the assistant. It had been so long since she'd been in such a place that she closed her eyes and took a deep breath, inhaling the perfumed silence. In the window there was a silver torso sporting a white bra and knickers with blue lace threaded through the seams; the sort of faux-virginal stuff Greg liked. Inside were the more grown-up items: padded black silk plunges, red lacy thongs, pink satin camiknickers, elaborate lace basques and suspenders. Nula bought a satin bra and knickers and suspender belt, all in black with pink trimmings, spending over two hundred pounds. The assistant, who had ruby-coloured hair and a massive bosom, said nothing to her apart from asking if she wanted the items wrapped. Thinking Greg would notice the box and bag when she got in from work, Nula declined, and stuffed the lot into her handbag. She resisted the temptation to look at the set whilst she sat on the train, distracting herself with emails on her laptop, and when she arrived home she left the underwear in her bag, ready for the next day.

She put the underwear on in the company toilets before going out to meet Sean, grazing her hip on the toilet-roll dispenser as she bent to pull up her stockings. After a month of lunches she'd decided it was time to take the lead. As she adjusted the padded balcony of her bra, she planned to put a hand over his and say something like, 'Shall we go somewhere else?' She'd cleared her afternoon of all meetings, and Sean's flat wasn't far away.

As soon as they had settled in their usual place Sean said, 'So I'm going up to Edinburgh this weekend . . .'

Nula smiled and smoothed her skirt across her knees. She could tell Greg she was needed on a shoot. Maggie would probably come and help out with Samuel. She could save the underwear until then.

'You've been, haven't you? Any recommendations?'

This was something they often discussed: the relative merits of various city-break destinations, whether Stockholm was superior to Amsterdam, food-wise; whether it was better to explore Rome's churches or Paris's galleries; how much you should expect to pay for a decent night's sleep in these places. Like Nula, Sean was convinced of the importance of large beds with solid mattresses.

'My girlfriend's left it to me to organise the whole bloody thing,' Sean continued.

For a second, Nula couldn't speak.

'When I say girlfriend – well. It's on and off. You know.'

'But at the moment it's on?'

'Seems that way.' He smiled, in what could have been an apologetic manner.

She knew she should reel off a list of places – decent restaurants, interesting cafés, little-visited but fascinating museums – but all she could manage was: 'It's been years since I've been. I wouldn't know.'

'I'm disappointed,' he said, pouting a bit. 'You're usually such an expert on these things. I was relying on you.'

She looked away.

'Of course,' Sean continued, 'she might go off me again before we make it up there . . .'

Nula glanced at her watch.

'Have you got to get back?'

'I think I'd better.'

Nula had talked about *balance* to Greg. She'd said she needed to regain a little more balance in her life, and in Samuel's life, too. She wasn't uncomfortable, she said, with Maggie's closeness to her son – on the contrary, she was glad of it. Samuel was happy, and wasn't that what mattered?

Of course she said nothing about wanting to limit the

number of times she might see her own humiliation reflected back at her in Sean's young, eager, attractive face.

She didn't mention, either, the day she had arrived home from work and found Maggie reading a book about forest animals to Samuel. Standing in the hallway, listening to their voices in echo, Samuel trying out each of the phrases Maggie offered him ('Big bear! Red deer!'), Nula found herself frozen to the spot, keys and bag still in hand. It seemed impossible to announce her presence. Instead she listened as Maggie imitated the voices of a cockney squirrel and a West Country owl with such relish that she could not stop herself giggling. Maggie giggled, and Samuel giggled right back at her.

Nula didn't mention any of this to Greg. Instead she said that it would be better for all of them to have more balance, wouldn't it? Going part-time at work would be the perfect solution.

After she had given these reasons to Greg, she realised she'd been reluctant to disturb Maggie and Samuel's perfection together. Was it a failure of desire, then? Had she failed to *want* to be included enough to take that step into the room? Perhaps she'd been content to let the two of them be. And, as a result, that was how it was. Their voices in echo, and Nula standing in the hallway, listening. The idea haunted her, and she made a private vow to reclaim her son from Maggie.

Not long after Samuel's second birthday, Nula bought a *Sachertorte* on her way home and insisted that Maggie stay for a slice. Greg was upstairs, getting Samuel ready for bed. Sometimes Nula did this: arrive home late with some offering for Maggie, sit at the kitchen table and, after her suggestion of a glass of wine had been refused, make a pot of Earl Grey and ask Maggie how she was getting on.

This time, she started things off by telling Maggie how good it had been to see Samuel running around with his friends at his party, how irritating Lilly had been with her jam tarts, how Greg had eaten so much cake that he'd had to lie down afterwards.

Maggie watched her cousin fiddle with her new necklace – a silver bird on a long, delicate chain. It reminded Maggie of the one Nula had worn when she'd first arrived at the farmhouse on Anglesey. She listened to her cousin's chatter for a while, ate her cake in a few large mouthfuls and then found herself interrupting. 'It must be very healing for you,' she said, 'having Samuel.'

Nula spluttered out a half-laugh. 'What do you mean?'

Maggie studied her teacup. Didn't Nula realise that Joe would have told her everything? Of course not, she thought. Of course not.

'Maggie?' Nula said. 'What do you mean?'

Maggie hesitated. She didn't want to think about her own part in what had happened – she still blamed herself. But ever since she'd arrived at the Shaws' she had wanted to talk about her brother. She wanted to say his name aloud to someone who had also loved him. And so she said, 'I mean, after everything with Joe – you know.'

Nula pushed her plate away. 'It wasn't that big a deal,' she said. 'I don't know what Joe told you, but – well, it was just a teenage fling.' She focused her gaze on the kitchen window. 'It was bound to end, you know? One way or the other.'

'Of course,' said Maggie.

Nula gave a tight smile and reached for Maggie's plate, clearly anxious to end the conversation.

Maggie continued, 'It was a shame, though, wasn't it? I mean, it ended so badly . . . I was very upset—'

'It had nothing to do with you, though, did it?' Nula said, sharply.

Maggie said nothing.

'Sorry,' said Nula. 'It's just . . . I know Joe was a bit cut up about it, but . . .' She twisted the bird so its beak pointed at her neck. 'These things happen. I've put it all behind me. I don't think about it.'

'I don't think Joe ever got over it,' Maggie said.

Nula stared at Maggie, her eyes glassy, her cheeks pink. Maggie couldn't be sure, but she thought this idea was slightly pleasing to Nula.

The long silence was eventually broken by Samuel running into the room in his pyjamas and flinging himself at his mother's legs.

'I'd better get going,' said Maggie. 'It's getting late.'

'Yes,' said Nula. 'You'd better.'

*

That June, Maggie's flat became uncomfortably humid. Leaving the windows open at night meant that the sounds from the street kept her awake. She began to spend hours at the computer, trying to tire her eyes enough for them to close as soon as she climbed into bed. It didn't work, and she often found herself awake at three in the morning, writing lists of the following day's activities and menus in an effort to remove these things from her wakeful brain.

Despite this lack of sleep, she was late for work only once. She'd finally dropped off and then overslept, waking after eight and leaving the house without breakfast or a shower. The traffic was clogged by the time she got on the road, and as she reached the Shaws', an hour late, she was aware of the smell of her own sweat. She jogged down the path and didn't take the time to wave to Samuel, who was, as usual, watching from the sitting-room window as she approached. Before she'd managed to get her key in the lock she could hear him in the hallway, shouting 'Gee-Gee!'

As soon as Maggie made it into the house, Nula appeared and placed her hands squarely on Samuel's shoulders, bringing him to an abrupt halt.

'Sorry I'm late—' Maggie began.

'You look tired,' said Nula.

'I'm fine.'

'Come and have a sit down. There's something I want to talk to you about.'

She was smiling, almost, as she said it. And, now that Maggie had a chance to take a breath, she saw that Nula was wearing a denim skirt and a T-shirt. 'You're not going to work?' Maggie asked.

'I've taken the morning off,' said Nula. 'Sammy, why don't you watch TV for a while?'

Samuel said, 'YES!' and stumped into the sitting room.

Nula rolled her eyes. 'Would you mind turning it on for him? Then we can have a proper chat.'

Maggie did as she was asked, leaving Samuel chewing on a Lego brick and standing an inch away from *Bob the Builder*.

In the kitchen, Nula poured tea from the pot. Maggie glanced around the room, searching for some clue to what this was about. Had Greg said something about their – what had it been? She might have described it, if pushed, as a *brief exchange*.

'I've got a bit of news,' Nula said, opening the patio doors.

Was she pregnant again?

'Let's sit outside.'

Maggie looked towards the door to the hallway. 'What about—'

'We'll hear him,' Nula stated.

The sunlight was already strong. Before sitting, Nula dusted off the patio chairs with a tissue. From where she was sitting, Maggie could hear the sounds of next door's baby crying, a car crawling along the street, a distant siren. She sipped her tea and ran through the previous few weeks in her mind. Apart from the thing with Greg, everything had been going smoothly. Samuel had, on the whole, been happy. And he was, as she had reassured Nula just the other day, hitting all the expected development landmarks for his age: he could put two or three words together, he could kick a ball, he could point to parts of his body when asked.

'We've been so happy with your work, as you know,' Nula began. 'Samuel has absolutely blossomed under your care. And I hope you've been happy here with us.'

'I love being with Samuel,' said Maggie, unable to keep the enthusiasm from her voice.

'Greg and I had a talk last night.'

Maggie shaded her eyes with a hand. The bright sunlight was making it difficult to look at her cousin's face for too long without squinting. Everything in the garden glared: the leaves on the apple tree, the recently mown lawn, the spray-cleaned patio bricks, Nula's bare but yet-to-be-tanned legs.

'We want to make some changes.' Nula put down her mug and took a breath. 'I'm reducing my hours at work,' she said. 'I'm going part-time, in fact, so I can spend more time with Samuel.'

'What about your career?' Maggie blurted.

Nula gave a light laugh. 'It can wait, can't it? But Samuel can't.' She ran her hands through her hair. 'You see, I've realised that I'll never, ever get this time back. And I'm missing so much . . .'

'But he's fine,' Maggie said, quickly. 'He's fine with me.'

'I know that. But I'm not fine, Maggie.'

'I thought you were – better.'

Nula eyed Maggie for a moment before nodding. 'Oh, I am! I am. But what I mean is, now that I am, I can see what I'm missing.'

Part-time, she'd said. Which would mean Maggie was still wanted, half of the time. Which wouldn't be intolerable.

'So,' said Maggie, trying to keep her voice even, 'which days will you work?'

'I need to talk to my boss—'

'When do you think this will start?'

'It'll be another month, at least.'

'If you can let me know which days you want me here, then I can start to look for other work—'

'The thing is,' said Nula, cutting her off, 'we think this might be a good time to start Sammy at nursery.'

Maggie swallowed.

'Please don't misunderstand this, Maggie. It's absolutely not because we're not happy with your work – we are. It's because we think it's best for Sammy. He needs more socialisation, now he's two . . .' A flush was working its way up Nula's throat as she gabbled. 'And this way we can make all the changes at once – it won't be so unsettling for him.'

A short silence passed.

So it was to happen again. Maggie thought of William, of his mother's tight face as she rushed on to the nursery, not stopping long enough for Maggie to speak to the boy. She'd thought with Samuel it might be different. But every time it was the same.

Nula sighed. 'I'm so sorry, really I am.'

Maggie could only look at the ground and repeat, 'I love being with Samuel.'

'We'll give you glowing references, and we'll leave it a couple of months, shall we? So you've got plenty of time to find something else . . .'

Maggie pushed back her chair and stood up.

Nula caught her arm. 'Maggie? Are you OK?'

'Of course,' Maggie said, shaking her off. 'I understand. I understand completely.'

'I was so worried about telling you,' said Nula. 'We'll all miss you.'

Maggie stared down at her cousin's pleading face. 'I'd better go and check on him,' she said, making for the house. 'Too much telly tends to make him fractious at this time of day.'

Back at her flat that night, Maggie took some paracetamol for the headache that had plagued her all day. Then she opened the file on her computer named 'S'. There was eighteen months' worth of reports there, each one saved by the day's date. Every file had several headings: *Activities. Outings. Meals & Snacks. Nappies. Naps. Other.* When she'd first started working for the Shaws, Maggie had emailed these reports to Nula at the end of each week so that Samuel's mother could get a full picture of her son's development. She had been careful to write them in a factual, detached manner. OUTINGS: *We went to the park. Samuel enjoyed the swing, but was reluctant to use the slide.* MEALS: *Lunch: Puréed butternut squash. Snacks: bread sticks. Tea: Puréed banana. Baby rice.* OTHER: *Samuel was unsettled when his mummy left, but we played with the trucks, which distracted him, and he coped well with the rest of the day.* After a couple of months Nula had said, 'There's no need for these weekly reports, Maggie. Just talk to me at the end of each day, OK?'

Maggie had agreed, but had secretly continued to write the reports. And as they progressed, they became more personal in tone. *Friday, April 10th.* ACTIVITIES: *We went to the singing group. Sammy sat on my lap for the first half of the session, refusing to join in. But for the second half he sang and danced with the others. Proud of him!* MEALS: *Snacks: In the newsagent's I bought S a bag of buttons. He'd been so sweet all morning. Our little secret!* NAPS: *1.30–2.30 p.m. Today S wouldn't go to sleep in his cot. Wanted cuddles. So I let him snuggle in my lap. When he woke he was very happy. Glad I did it. Didn't mention it to Mummy, who thinks he should always go to sleep on his own.*

Maggie read through several entries like this. With each new entry the pain in her head seemed to twist a little tighter. Nula was so wrong about her son's needs.

Every mother who'd employed Maggie had been the same. Unwilling to carry out the job of childcare themselves, but very clear on how Maggie failed to do the job correctly.

What the boy needed, Maggie had always told Nula, was more fresh air. A freer environment. Not a nursery place. When she'd been between contracts Maggie had worked in a few nurseries, and she'd been chilled by some of the things she had seen. Babies left to cry for hours because it wasn't time to be picked up. Children forbidden to play outside because the grass was too wet. Television used as a substitute for care, due to staff shortages. The best of games interrupted because it was Snack Time. Or Circle Time. Or Story Time. The managers of such places seemed concerned only with rigid schedules and tight financial margins. No child could flourish in such an environment.

She saved all the documents together in a file named 'For Nula'. They would be there, should she decide to send them to his mother.

Outside, the bells of some college or other began to peal. The echoing sound seemed to press its way into the flat. It made her feel queasy. She closed her eyes, trying to stop the pain that was now digging its way from her head to her neck and shoulders.

She took some deep breaths.

Every time it was the same. Theo. Charlotte. Amy. William. All loved, and all lost.

And the other child, too, the one she hadn't been able to save.

Standing, she reached up to the shelf and found her book of sketches of Samuel. She flicked through the most recent ones. They were snatched, hurried things; she had conjured him with a few soft lines, some hasty shading. But their quickness gave them energy, and her feeling for Samuel – the way she knew and loved every nook and cranny of his face – gave them life.

Then she saw that several of the early pages had become strangely warped. In one drawing, Samuel's nose was smudged; in another, his left eye was a grey smear. The dampness in her flat must have seeped into the paper, damaging her best work.

Rage shot through Maggie's body, making it tremble. She had to leave this place. The drawings were imperfect, now. They were ruined. They were no longer enough.

She took some more deep breaths.

A picture began to form in her mind. A picture of the boathouse and the shore at Llanidan. A picture of her brother, grabbing her hand to save her from falling. A picture of herself, holding Samuel around the middle to keep him safe as he gazed into the shifting waters of the Menai Strait.

Not everything was broken. Some things could be put right.

She opened her eyes. The bells came to a stop, but their iron sound lingered. She listened until the last reverberation had faded into the June evening, and then she made her decision.

She would not be parted from Samuel.

She might not take him tomorrow. Or the next day. But she would take him.

III

The summer Maggie was sixteen, her cousin came to stay.

It was 1991. The cousin was seventeen and her name was Nula, which was a name out of a pop song. She had long limbs and black patent pumps. Because she was at private school, she arrived a couple of weeks before Maggie and Joe's summer holiday had even started. Her father waved her goodbye from the gate. Maggie had met Nula and Uncle Ralph a few times before, in Oxford; but generally the families didn't socialise. Ralph was to bunk up in the boathouse by the strait for the next month, using it as a studio. Maggie didn't understand why Nula wasn't staying with her father, but her mother had sighed and said Uncle Ralph needed the space to paint. It was good for him to have all that light, probably. Her father had laughed and said his brother had always been a selfish bugger.

After she'd taken her suitcase upstairs, Maggie watched as Nula stood by the gate next to the disused pigpens, playing with the gold chain around her neck. A delicately filigreed butterfly hung from the chain, and occasionally Nula placed the butterfly between her lips and sucked on it.

In the yard was a small barn for the goats and pony, a chicken coop and the old dairy where Maggie's parents kept a lawnmower and various garden tools, and Joe kept his motorbike. Maggie's mother often said, 'We're living the dream of self-sufficiency, kiddos', with an unmistakable grimace. Alan actually still worked as a part-time accountant, despite planning to make enough money from his smallholding to live on.

Joe was in frayed jeans and trainers and Maggie wore an old tracksuit. The two of them kicked a football against the pigpens. They hadn't kicked a football together since they were small, but – faced with the vision of their cousin – something compelled them to begin a physical game. Surrounded by the grey concrete of their back yard, her shoes spattered with rain, Nula wasn't exactly pretty, but she was shiny, like money. Maggie did not want her shoes or her polished hair for herself, but she found her cousin's stillness distracting. Without movement or expression, Nula watched, her thick eyebrows knitted together. She was able to stand and watch until Maggie and Joe tired of football, and of being watched. The two of them went indoors, leaving Nula by the gate, silently twirling her necklace around her finger.

That evening Maggie's mother said they should help themselves. On the large oak table there were egg sandwiches, a bowl of crisps, a heap of crumbed ham. She'd made a cake, which was unusual. She'd recently insisted that Alan have the Aga ripped out ('Why do I need the bloody oven on all day?') and replaced with a new gas stove, so perhaps she felt she should use it. The sponge had sunk on one side, but all afternoon Maggie had smelled baking and the sight of the actual cake, dusted with caster sugar, was so exciting that she let out a little yelp and then hated herself for sounding so childish. Whilst Joe and Maggie reached for sandwiches, Nula went straight for the cake. She took a slice and broke it into tiny pieces on her plate, before eating a quarter and leaving the rest. Joe looked at Maggie and Maggie looked at her mother, but Fiona said nothing, which was more than her daughter could take. 'Aren't you going to eat—?' she began, but Fiona interrupted her. 'Concentrate on your own tea, Maggie,' she said, and carried on sipping her coffee.

Before getting into bed Nula brushed her hair for five minutes, eyes steady in the mirror. Maggie pulled her blue dolphin duvet up to her chest, pretended to read her novel and said nothing. Then Nula slipped her slim body, clothed in cerise pyjamas that reached right down to her ankles, into the camp bed on the other side of Maggie's room. Maggie reached over to turn off the lamp and the two girls lay in the darkness for a long time. An hour, maybe more, passed.

Maggie listened to Nula's movements – turn, cough, sigh – until her cousin seemed to be asleep. But still she was unable to relax, or to move. It seemed very important to Maggie that she appeared to be asleep; otherwise Nula might know that her every breath was being monitored. She might know how important her presence in this room was.

Just as Maggie felt herself on the edge of sleep, Nula suddenly sat upright in her bed. Maggie watched her in the half-dark, unable to tell if her cousin was looking at her or staring at the wall. Nula gave a huge sigh, then threw back her pink eiderdown, swung her legs around and stood up. Maggie clicked on the light and saw that Nula's face was waxy and pale, her eyes open. First smoothing down her pyjamas, she headed for the door.

'Nula?' Maggie whispered. 'Nula?'

There was no response. Scrambling from bed, Maggie followed Nula as she walked steadily down the sloping landing towards the stairs. Nula's hand momentarily felt the air before finding the bannister, and Maggie lunged forward, thinking her cousin would fall to the bottom and she would be blamed for her early, tragic death. But Nula took the stairs slowly, carefully, without a wobble. Maggie kept close behind, telling herself she was ready to catch her. Maggie's mother had once told her never to wake a sleepwalker. But she hadn't elaborated on why this was. Did sleepwalkers fall into a coma if wakened? Was the shock so great that they risked falling to the floor and seriously injuring themselves? Or would they become violent and lash out at whoever had woken them? Maggie imagined Nula suddenly reaching for her hair and pulling her to the floor. That had happened once at school when a girl called Tina had cornered her in the cloakroom. 'Give me your bag, snob,' she'd demanded. 'Swot,' Maggie had said. 'You mean swot. There's a difference.' Bam! She was on the tiles, her hair in Tina's sweaty fist. Her scalp yanked from her skull. 'Don't. Tell. Me. What. I. Mean.'

Nula floated through the kitchen and made straight for the fridge. Maggie wondered how she knew where the fridge was, let alone how to reach it whilst apparently asleep. Pulling the door wide, Nula leaned towards the glow of the electric light and her sleeping face sprang into colour.

'What the fuck is she doing?'

Maggie had been so engrossed in watching Nula that she hadn't heard Joe come in. He was standing behind her in his blue pyjama bottoms, one hand in his thick hair. 'Is she asleep?'

Maggie nodded.

'Wild!'

It was one of the American phrases he'd picked up recently. He had been reading the Beat poets.

Nula took a slice of ham from a plate in the fridge, folded it neatly and popped it in her mouth. Maggie and Joe watched as she took another, then another, then another.

'She didn't eat any tea,' Maggie said.

'She had loads of chocolate on her,' said Joe.

'How do you know?'

'She gave me two Mars Bars.'

Nula hadn't given Maggie anything.

'Let's wake her up, then.'

'No,' Maggie said. 'It's dangerous.'

Joe looked at his sister.

'Mum said so. The shock can make them . . . violent.'

He laughed. 'What's she going to do?' Nula walked past him and he stepped back, then watched her make her way steadily out of the door and towards the stairs.

'She's just a girl,' he said.

'Like me,' Maggie said.

Joe shook his head. 'Not like you, little one. Not like you at all.'

Maggie hadn't made many friends since moving to Anglesey. At school she tended to sit next to Ceri, who wore a black hairband and tortoiseshell glasses, which she had a habit of pushing back up her nose with one long, precise finger. Ceri wore a lot of make-up and some of it ended up on her lenses, obscuring her eyes and making it difficult to concentrate on what she was saying. Maggie enjoyed sharing Ceri's crisps, but she focused on what she was really good at: pleasing the teachers and passing her GCSEs. She figured that it was useless to start trying to please the other kids. It wouldn't be long before she'd be doing her A-levels, and then everything would change anyway. Not speaking Welsh wasn't helpful, but Maggie suspected that even if she had, it would have been difficult to overcome the scrutiny of the others.

Maggie had never liked being alone, but being with lots of people was worse. Two or three had always been good numbers for Maggie. With two or three, you can be almost sure you'll be heard when you speak, and if you do something stupid not too many people will notice. She counted Joe as her two, and thought perhaps Nula could be her three. So, despite her cousin's shining impenetrability, Maggie liked having Nula in the house and decided to do her best to become her friend.

For those first two weeks Maggie wondered what her cousin did all day whilst she and her brother were at school. Nula always had plenty of fashion magazines, and she'd brought some videos with her, too: she hated teen films, but loved anything with Audrey Hepburn. Sometimes, after school, the two of them would settle down to *Breakfast at Tiffany's* or *Roman Holiday* and Nula would laugh in what Maggie assumed were all the right places.

Some nights Nula came into Maggie's bed after sleepwalking. She lay perfectly still, as still as on that first day when she'd stood in the back yard playing with her necklace. Maggie tried to be as still as Nula. She listened to Nula's stomach as it consumed the food of that night's roaming – perhaps some cold sausage or some cheese. It whirred and mashed, plopped and shuddered, and Maggie listened, unable to sleep. Nula gave off so much heat that Maggie had to kick the duvet from her own legs and feet. In the morning Nula would wake and creep back to her own bed. Maggie pretended to be asleep too, knowing that she must not let on that she'd been aware of the other girl's presence or mention anything about the two of them sharing a bed.

'It's all about food,' said Nula, one morning. 'The sleep-walking. Did I look in the fridge?'

Maggie confirmed that she had.

'What did I eat?'

'Nothing.'

'Thank God.'

'But you drank half a pint of milk.'

Nula covered her mouth with a hand and pretended to retch. 'Milk,' she said. 'Vomit.'

'You could have died.'

Nula seemed to take this statement in her stride. 'Do you think I need therapy?'

'You could have died.'

Nula laughed. 'Did you save me, then?'

Maggie nodded. 'I followed you. To make sure you didn't fall.'

'That's it then,' said Nula. 'I owe you.'

Walking arm-in-arm with her new friend along Llangefni High Street, Maggie thought of those words. *I owe you.* But what? Maggie wanted to ask. What, exactly, do you owe me? She wasn't sure that she altogether liked the idea of being owed something.

It was the Saturday before her school broke up, and the sun had yet to show itself. Nula was looking chicly practical in her red windcheater and matching wellies, whilst Maggie was in a black sweater and jeans. The stink of the chicken factories that lined the town's outskirts wafted by now and then. Maggie had apologised for this, and for Llangefni in general. Her cousin had suggested this trip to the island's capital, saying she wanted to explore the place properly. Maggie knew that the shops in Bangor were much better, but to please Nula she had agreed. She'd been careful not to talk too much, though, having learned from watching her cousin during the previous week the value of a quietly superior attitude. Maggie would have liked to stop occasionally to look in a shop, especially at the art supplies in W.H. Smith, but Nula ploughed on. As they walked, Nula's habit was to catch everyone's eye, then glance away in a manner suggestive of her utter indifference. Occasionally she nudged her cousin in the ribs at the sight of someone particularly ugly. Most men in baseball hats warranted a nudge, as did most women in short skirts, especially if they were over thirty. 'Fat knees,' Nula would whisper. 'No one wants to see a fat knee.'

Maggie had the feeling of being let in on some sort of magnificent conspiracy, the true nature of which was, as yet, a mystery to her.

On their third lap of the same street Maggie risked suggesting checking out the paints in Smith's. Nula shrugged and said they could, despite her complete lack of interest in art.

As they entered the shop Maggie said, 'But your dad's a painter. And he's pretty famous, isn't he?' She had wanted to bring this up ever since Nula had appeared at the house, and felt her heartrate increase as she uttered the word 'painter'.

'It's all a bloody sham,' said Nula, picking up a copy of *GQ* and glaring at it. 'Art's for people who can't grow up. Artists are all totally self-obsessed. All they can do is make pictures. What actual *use* is that? And he's not even *remotely* famous.'

Maggie said nothing. Her cousin slammed down the magazine. 'Know what I want to do? What I *can't wait* to do once I leave my shitty school?'

It was clear to Maggie that an answer was not required.

'Work in the media.'

Maggie nodded, but dared to ask, 'Isn't that all a bit – shallow, though?'

Nula laughed. 'Probably. The main thing is my dad *hates*

it. Hypocrite! He says he hates the media, but he can't get enough of those foreign fucking films. Especially anything French.'

'But French films *are* art!' Maggie said, feeling herself flush. She wanted to add, Haven't you seen *Manon des Sources*? Haven't you felt the heartbreaking significance of Daniel Auteuil's stubble?

Nula looked at her. 'Dad only watches them for the women. Anyway. The media is more honest. People buy it, enjoy it, dispose of it. It's a much purer relationship.'

'Joe says it's capitalism at its worst.'

'Does he?' said Nula, interested. 'Maybe he's right.'

They'd reached the rows of paint, and Maggie crouched down to inspect the colours. In the Smith's in Bangor, she'd done this every Saturday since they'd arrived on the island. She usually allowed herself one new tube per week.

'What else does Joe say?' Nula asked.

'About what?'

Maggie glanced at her cousin, but Nula was apparently absorbed in studying the shelves above her head.

'About what he likes.'

'Joe doesn't like much, really,' Maggie said, selecting a tube of burnt sienna. 'Except his camera. And his motorbike . . .'

'Has he got a girlfriend?'

Maggie stood. At eighteen, Joe had had a couple of girl-friends already, but he'd been so open about meeting them and talking about them that Maggie had known they meant very little to him. Back in Oxford, both Suzie and Flick had been brought home to tea and spent lots of time chatting with her mother whenever they'd come round to go out with Joe.

'No,' she said. 'Why?'

'Just wondering.' Nula kept her eyes on the shelves. Then she gave a little giggle. 'Sometimes he looks at me funny.'

'Funny how?'

'As if he's scared, or something.'

Maggie could think of nothing to say to this. She could hardly imagine such a look on her brother's face.

'Maybe I'll just ask him,' said Nula. 'I'll just say: *Joe, are you fantasising about me, or what?*' She laughed, and Maggie tried to laugh back.

There was a pause.

'So,' said Nula. 'Shall I buy you that?' And she snatched the single tube of paint from Maggie's hand and strode to the till.

Ever since Nula had mentioned the word 'girlfriend', Maggie had wanted to tell her about Rhod. But each time she thought about how to do so – of what the story of Rhod actually was – it seemed there was nothing to say.

Rhod was tall and blond with big pink cheeks. He was known to be the school purveyor of good weed, and as such he was held in high esteem by most of the girls in Maggie's year. During lessons he spent a lot of time tapping out beats on one knee or drawing rather accomplished pictures of breasts. His mother owned the one trendy hairdresser's in Menai Bridge and as a result he sported a head of complex and subtle highlights. His cuffs and nails were always clean.

It had started one afternoon towards the end of term, whilst she was on her way to Geography. Maggie became aware of the pungent smell of Rhod's deodorant beside her in the corridor. Then his voice, very close to her ear: 'I love the ones who don't even know they're sexy.' Maggie turned to face him.

He smiled. '*Terminator 2*'s on in Llandudno on Saturday night. Fancy it?'

'No, thanks,' said Maggie.

She walked on, congratulating herself on her decisive, yet polite action. But he followed, skittering in front of her like a puppy. 'Why the fuck not?' he asked, palms open, eyes wide. 'You'd love it. I guarantee it.'

'Not my thing,' she said, trying to move past him.

'What is your thing?'

To her deep shame, what came out of her mouth was, 'French stuff. I like French films.'

'Not many of those round here,' he said, grinning.

They looked at each other for a moment. Sensing she was in danger of smiling back at him, Maggie pressed on.

'Let me know,' he called, 'if you change your mind. Yeah? Maggie? Yeah?'

Maggie had no idea how to tell this story to Nula. It seemed the sort of thing her older, more sophisticated cousin would like to hear, the sort of thing that she might advise Maggie about. But Maggie hardly dared to believe that Rhod's interest was real, let alone utter her suspicion out loud.

The day after their school broke up for the summer, their mother suggested Maggie and Joe take Nula on the bus to Llandudno. It was a warm Thursday, the bus was full and they had to stand. Somehow Maggie became separated from her brother and ended up at the back, hanging onto a seat and gazing down at the greasy parting of an old man's hair, whilst Joe and Nula stood together near the driver. Occasionally Maggie caught a glimpse of her brother leaning over to hear something Nula said, and heard him laughing in a manic way that was very unlike him.

When they got there, Joe looked around the wide bay, already busy with holidaymakers, and suggested they walk along the pier, but Nula smirked and said she'd rather go for lunch. 'Seems like a popular place,' she said, 'there must be somewhere half decent?' Maggie and Joe looked at each other doubtfully. Maggie was glad when Joe suggested Burger King, and Nula said they should forget it and get ice cream instead.

They walked together along the prom, Maggie's attention caught, as it always was, by the old ladies who sat on benches, some of them knitting, some of them working their way through bags of chips or doughnuts as they watched the kids and the mums and dads dawdle along the tarmac. The traffic and the sea roared as one; the seagulls whirled and whooped overhead. Nula was wearing a short skirt and her flat pumps; her long legs were already tanned. She walked close to Joe and, next to her, Joe seemed to become taller, his back straighter, his strides longer. Maggie hurried to keep up with them. They stopped at an ice-cream kiosk and Joe bought Nula a Cornetto and Maggie a 99 cone. When Nula offered Joe a lick, Maggie said, 'Actually, *I* want to go on the pier.'

'OK,' said Joe, turning round to face her, wiping ice cream from his lips. 'You go.'

'What are you going to do?' Maggie asked.

'Sit on the beach,' said Nula, answering for him. 'Work on my tan.'

'But you haven't brought a towel,' said Maggie.

'We'll get deckchairs!' announced Joe.

Maggie stared at him. Joe had never hired a deckchair in his life. It was the sort of thing their father hated: only idiots, he said, would waste money on a folding chair when the sand would do. And deckchairs were, surely, strictly for the over-sixties.

'Great idea,' said Nula, biting into her cornet.

'See you back here in an hour?' said Joe, with a slightly apologetic look at his sister.

'I won't need that long . . .' Maggie began. But Joe and Nula were already descending the steps to the beach.

Maggie didn't let herself stand and watch the two them. Instead, she pushed on along the prom towards the pier. When she felt she was out of her brother's sight, she stopped and sat on a bench, silently fuming. She could see no evidence of Nula's suggestion that Joe was scared of her. All she could see in her brother's face when he looked at their cousin was some kind of dog-like anticipation. It was as if, she thought, he was begging for a treat.

A few yards from the bench, a tall red tent was surrounded by children, all frowning up at Mr Punch as he tricked the hangman into his own noose. Mr Punch's voice was amplified over a tannoy, and every time he shrilled, 'THAT'S THE WAY TO DO IT!' several children covered their ears. One toddler started to cry, standing up and looking around frantically for her mother. When no one came forward to claim the child, Maggie found herself standing and approaching the girl, holding out a hand. But a man wearing only a pair of long beach shorts thrust himself before her and scooped the child into his arms.

She thought she might cry at that moment, with the man scowling at her and Mr Punch screeching and her brother and her new friend nowhere to be seen. She might just stand there and burst into tears, as the child had done. But then she noticed Rhod.

He was with a couple of friends, hanging about beside a burger van. She recognised one of them as his mate Matt, who wasn't nearly as revered by her classmates as Rhod himself. Matt wore the wrong trainers, and his pale cheeks were splattered with acne. She watched Rhod as he chewed carefully on a chip and nodded at something Matt was telling him. Then the group moved off, chucking their food wrappers in or near the rubbish bin as they swaggered towards the beach.

Maggie followed them. They took the steps down to the sands, and she was suddenly hurrying to get close to Rhod, to be seen by him. A large family was also coming down the steps, squabbling about who should carry the buggy to the beach, and Maggie found herself pushed in front of Rhod, who had paused to light a cigarette. As he saw her, she was horrified to realise that, ever since he had first spoken to her, she'd been waiting to hear his whisper in her ear once again.

'Maggie,' he said.

To hide her smile, she turned away and took another step towards the beach, thinking she could look back and say something amusing and perhaps even flirtatious when she'd gathered herself sufficiently. He shouted something in Welsh to Matt, then he followed her, his body so close behind that she was sure she could feel his breath on her hair. And as he finished his words, his hand was suddenly between her legs. For a couple of seconds Rhod's fingers pressed on Maggie. Right there. She stopped on the step, unable to move or speak, whilst the family's buggy finally crashed onto the sand. Rhod stepped past her, onto the beach, the offending hand now raised in a jaunty wave. A great blush bloomed all over her body.

On the bus home, whilst Joe and Nula sat together at the back, Maggie leaned her forehead on the grimy window, closed her eyes and dared to go over the whole thing again. After she had rejoined her brother and cousin she'd spent the afternoon sitting dumbly on the beach, scanning the scene for any sign of Rhod. And she had managed almost to dismiss it as the sort of thing every girl found herself subjected to from time to time. He was an imbecile, obviously. He'd behaved atrociously, without a doubt. Perhaps she should tell someone what he'd done. But, equally, shouldn't she be able to shrug it off? A pat on the arse. That was all it was. A bit yucky. A bit stupid. It hardly counted as abuse. Did it?

As she relived the moment – his fingers pressing, one, two, three – she found herself unable to ignore her first reaction to Rhod's touch. Before she'd had time to think, before she'd had time to understand anything about what was happening, her response had been one of undeniable pleasure. He had touched her somewhere he shouldn't and, despite finding him unattractive, what she had felt was joy.

She wanted to cry with the shame of it. She wanted to report him to someone, just so she could convince herself that she had felt something – anything – else. Before the bus pulled into their village, Maggie had decided what to do. She would tell her brother. She would put an end to it.

'I need your help.'

That evening she stepped, uninvited, into Joe's room. He was sitting on his bed, his back against the wall and his hands behind his head, watching *Naked Video* on his portable. Nula was next to him. When they saw Maggie, Nula swung her legs from the mattress and looked at her fingernails. Joe cleared his throat. It took a moment for him to turn the television's volume down and glance at his sister. 'Yeah?'

'Can I talk to you – alone?'

Nula gave a small laugh. Joe did not. Looking from Joe to

Maggie, Nula nodded. 'Understood,' she said. 'Brother–sister thing.' And she slipped out of the door.

'Well?' asked Joe.

'Someone's sort of – harassing me. A boy.'

He sat up, patting the bed to indicate where she should place herself.

'What's he done, then?'

'Nothing. Not much. He just – won't leave me alone.' Maggie took a breath. 'And he's a complete dork.' A shrill laugh.

Joe frowned. 'Has he hurt you, or what?'

The concern in his voice made it tempting to lie. But Maggie shook her head. They both looked at the television for a few moments before Joe said, 'I could have a word with him. If you like.'

He'd got the point much quicker than she had expected. Nevertheless, she said, 'I'm not sure' and examined her hands. 'Do you think that would be a good idea?'

He touched her shoulder. Squeezed. 'You'd better tell me his name, hadn't you.'

Since Joe didn't disclose what he was going to say to Rhod, exactly, or when he might tackle him, Maggie assumed almost nothing would happen. When she found herself worrying about what Joe might do, she told herself that she had gone to her brother for advice, rather than action, and anything that happened now was, therefore, not her responsibility.

Two nights later, there was the familiar farting engine sound in the street. The back door slammed. Joe passed by the sitting-room door in a streak of leather and helmet. Neither Maggie's mother nor her father made any comment, although, like Maggie, Nula watched the door for a moment after Joe had passed, as if expecting some atom of him to remain there.

Maggie waited until the ad break before going upstairs. Joe was sitting on his bed, still wearing his leather jacket. His back was towards her and he didn't turn round when she said his name. The overhead light, which still didn't have a shade, made the slanting room horribly bright. He held the buds of his earphones in one hand. A tinny sound, which Maggie recognised as 'Tangled Up in Blue', escaped his fist.

She closed the door behind her. It took her a moment to realise that her brother was crying. Very quietly, but absolutely openly. She sat beside him and he continued to cry, allowing the tears to gather on his chin and drip onto the battered collar of his jacket. She said his name again and he hung his head, wiped his face with his sleeve. 'It's OK,' she said, but still he did not look at her or stop crying. She thought, for a second, of fetching her mother, but instead found herself reaching up and stroking the side of his head. It had been many years since she'd grasped his beautiful curls in a fight, or in play, and his hair was stiffer than she remembered. He didn't move, so she continued to push her fingers through his hair, inhaling the outdoor smell of his jacket, keeping her hand on his head until her arm ached and her brother had stopped crying.

'What happened?' she asked.

He looked at her. She'd expected to see a bruise, or a cut, on his face. But there was nothing.

'Was there a fight?' she asked.

He closed his eyes and hung his head.

'Are you hurt?'

He gave a miserable nod.

'Oh, Joe—'

Then Joe looked at Maggie and said, 'Could you ask Nula to come up?'

It took Maggie a moment to register what he'd said, but once she had, she got out of Joe's bedroom as quickly as she could. Then she went downstairs and informed her cousin that she was wanted. What really hurt was that Nula didn't even appear triumphant as she brushed past Maggie on her way to comfort Joe. She just looked as though getting what she wanted was an everyday occurrence, and perhaps, Maggie thought, even something of a burden.

Maggie had heard, many times, about her uncle's failings in life. According to her father, Ralph lived off his wife's family's money, ignored his own children and had betrayed their mother. And all for what? To sell a handful of mediocre paintings. 'He's always been the same. Insists on being *different*,' Alan would say. 'Showing the rest of us up. Bloody attention-seeking, I call it.'

But when she'd been told he was coming to stay for the summer, Maggie had gone to the library in Bangor and managed to find an article on R.V. Wichelo in a copy of the *Artists' Newsletter* from the mid-1980s. She'd read that Wichelo's work was 'excitingly visceral' and 'excoriatingly real'. There was a reproduction of his work *Untitled (Domestic Scene)*. It showed a small naked woman with tired eyes reclining on an unmade bed. She held a lily in one hand, and at her feet was a large, grubby-looking Highland terrier. In the background an open window looked out onto a grey city sky. Everything about this picture gave Maggie a not-unpleasant feeling of disquiet, particularly the caption, which read, 'One of Wichelo's many canvases of his latest muse and suspected mistress, Sandy Jenkins'.

Maggie's art teacher had recently told her that her own work was 'quietly excellent'. Not 'dynamic' or 'sophisticated', which were terms she applied to Marc Griffin's pictures. Marc looked a bit like George Michael and painted portraits of homeless people on very large canvases. But still. 'Excellent' was thrilling, even if Maggie wished her teacher had dropped the 'quietly'. Maggie knew that Miss Bagshawe had talked about art school to Marc and his friend Avril, who had piercings in her eyebrows and hair dyed the colour of blackcurrant juice; she knew that the three of them often spent lunchtimes together in the art room, drinking coffee and painting whilst Maggie and Ceri stood by the tennis courts, looking in at the lighted windows of the craft block, eating crisps and discussing how much they hated physics. Miss Bagshawe sometimes called Marc and Avril 'cariad'. All she called Maggie was 'Margaret' in a faux-English accent, which only increased Maggie's longing to be called 'cariad' and to be asked if she was looking forward to starting her art A-level. If only she could drink coffee in the art room and sit on the desk, and make Miss Bagshawe cross and uncross her legs and laugh, these things might happen.

After he'd dropped his daughter at the farmhouse, it took Ralph two weeks to return. Nula said this was because her father was engrossed in his work. It was always like this when it was going well; you learned to be grateful for the silences, the absences, because then you knew that Ralph was succeeding. Maggie thought of her own father's silences and absences and how these signified, in their house, something quite different.

He came for Sunday lunch. It was a breezy, sunny day and, in preparation for his appearance, Fiona had decorated the kitchen with bunches of cornflowers. The floor tiles shone bright red, and the small windows sparkled in the sunlight. Fiona had applied her plum-coloured lipstick, something she'd stopped doing since they'd arrived on Anglesey. Cooling on the dresser was a gooseberry pie, and already on the large table were dishes of exotic-looking salads of roasted peppers and mozzarella cheese. Fiona had sent Alan to Bangor yesterday to find such things and had berated him when he'd failed to acquire any bottled artichokes.

Alan had only just emerged from the back field, where he'd spent most of the morning busying himself with something or other.

The knocker sounded, and before Maggie or Fiona could get to the door (Nula stayed on the sofa next to Joe, her eyes glued to the *EastEnders* omnibus), Ralph was in the kitchen. Alan met his brother with a handshake and a brief touch on the shoulder. Ralph was a man of medium height, his large chin defined by a dark, closely cropped beard, his blue eyes fierce behind his metal-framed glasses. He was wearing a plaid shirt and jeans, and a pair of battered workmen's boots. Sweat shone on his forehead. He looked like a sturdier, darker, hairier version of Alan; perhaps, Maggie, thought, this was how her father would have looked had he run away to join the circus.

'Fiona!' Ralph said, holding his arms out wide.

She submitted to his bear-like embrace. He held her for a long time, patting her back as if she were a child, and Maggie was surprised to see her mother beaming once she'd been released. 'I've said it before and I'll say it again,' said Ralph. 'You've got a *woman* there, Alan.'

Fiona tittered and Alan looked to the floor.

'They're all mysteries, aren't they?' continued Ralph, viewing Fiona through narrowed eyes. 'Don't understand any of them. Wouldn't want it any other way.'

'What would your wife say to that, I wonder?' asked Alan.

Ralph laughed in an uninterested way. 'What's for lunch, Fiona? I've existed on nothing but beans for a fortnight.'

Joe came in. He ignored Ralph, and Ralph ignored him. Then they all seated themselves at the table and waited for

Nula to join them. Both Fiona and Alan told her that lunch was ready, but achieved no response. Eventually Ralph went into the sitting room to fetch her. Maggie tried to hear what he said, but only caught Nula's voice, suddenly loud, saying, 'And I've been waiting for *you* for a bloody fortnight.'

As she sat down next to him, Ralph caught his daughter's elbow. 'You look well, love,' he said. 'Must be all this fresh air.' Nula bent forward to receive his kiss on her cheek in silence.

Nula refused everything barring the salads, which she ate slowly and dutifully, picking out all the pips from the first of Alan's home-grown tomatoes.

Ralph enquired whether the lamb was Welsh, and Maggie was embarrassed to hear her mother say that it was. She'd been sent to the Co-op in Llanfairpwll to buy the meat – a leg from New Zealand – herself.

'You can tell,' said Ralph, audibly swallowing a mouthful. 'It tastes of grass.'

'Alan's trying to raise livestock,' said Fiona. She'd already drunk a glass of the Rioja that Ralph had supplied.

'Not so much livestock as a few chickens . . .' said Alan. 'Couple of goats . . .'

'For the cheese,' interjected Fiona. 'There's a growing market for the cheese.'

Ralph put down his knife and fork and rested his tanned hands flat on the table. They seemed to Maggie to be reaching right across the wooden surface to where she was sitting. A large, scratched digital watch hung loose at his knobbled wrist.

'Goat's cheese,' he said. 'That's so – great. Wish I'd got into goat's cheese.'

'People will always need cheese,' said Maggie. 'It's a good thing to get into.'

Nula laughed, very loudly. 'Unlike art,' she said.

Ralph raised his eyes to Maggie. 'And how old are you now?' he asked.

'Sixteen,' she said.

'Is that right? And what is it you want to *get into*, sixteen-year-old Margaret Wichelo?'

Maggie looked at the flat black hair that covered her uncle's forearms. 'I want to be a painter,' she said.

She'd thought he would laugh; he did not.

'What about university?' Alan said. He turned to Ralph. 'Her predicted GCSE grades are very high.'

'Aren't you trying for Oxford?' asked Fiona.

'She could go to art school there,' said Ralph. 'If she wanted to. Although she'd be better off in London. Or Glasgow.'

Every face around the table turned to look at Maggie.

'And what is it you want to paint?' Ralph asked.

Until he asked the question, she didn't have an answer.

'People,' said Maggie. 'Families. I'd like to paint families.'

Joe smiled at her. 'Good subject,' he said. 'Nice and gory.'

'Doesn't she remind you of Aunt Georgina?' said Ralph to Alan. 'The one who lived alone? Had all those paperweights and that amazing garden? Wide cheekbones. Small mouth. Something very vibrant about her. Whatever happened to her?'

'I've absolutely no idea,' said Alan, standing to clear the plates.

'Maggie's like me,' said Fiona. 'Everyone says so. She's just like me.'

'Oh, she is,' said Ralph, filling up Fiona's glass. 'She certainly is.'

Nula and Joe asked to be excused. No one seemed to notice the two of them slipping through the back door and out into the sunshine. No one except Maggie.

*

133

The next day, Maggie visited the boathouse. As he'd left, Ralph had suggested she pop over, if she wanted to, just to have a look at how things work, and Maggie had said she might, and her mother had said *of course* she would. Her daughter would love to take Ralph up on such a generous offer. Alan had said nothing at all.

It was two in the afternoon, a time she'd calculated as the least offensive: he wouldn't feel obliged to offer her something to eat, or even a cup of tea; he would probably still be on his lunch break and so she wouldn't be interrupting his work. It was the first really hot day of the summer, and before coming Maggie had toyed with the idea of wearing a sundress; encouraged by her cousin, she'd bought a new one recently and quite liked the way the spaghetti straps fell off her small white shoulders. But at the last minute she'd changed her mind. In her black jeans and T-shirt, she walked the mile along the lane, thickly shaded by oak and elm, to the boathouse.

Halfway down was the tiny church of Llanidan. She had first walked here with Joe on a gloomy autumn day. A row of ruined arches looped up from the grass like a gigantic stone caterpillar, but the central part of the church remained roughly intact. A grey-green sheen covered the crumbling brick and windows so completely that it seemed to Maggie moss and lichen would grow inside, too. At home they would never have entered a church voluntarily, but this mysterious building offered itself to them, the rusty gate hanging open, the broken door gaping. Joe went in first, leaving Maggie shivering outside. On hearing him exclaim, 'Bloody perfect!' she went in and saw what had pleased him: a glass box containing a few assorted bones. On a typed label were the words 'SACRED REMAINS', followed by something in Welsh. Joe had photographed that box for a long time while Maggie waited, breathing in the mould that bloomed up the walls and along the pews. She asked Joe whether he was becoming obsessed with death, and he said he just liked the idea that someone had bothered to keep the stuff there, in a box, labelled.

She rounded the corner. In the next field, the sheep sounded like quad bikes. The strait glittered deeply. The sky was faultlessly blue in a way Maggie found suspicious. Such a perfect summer's day could end only in a storm.

The whitewashed walls of the boathouse stood, small and squat, just above the shore. Today the tide was out, revealing a beach that looked to Maggie like the floor of a messy bedroom, littered with driftwood, mudflats, straggly rugs of bladderwrack, flocks of squawking seabirds.

She crunched along the stones, dried seaweed cracking beneath her trainers. Then she mounted the steps, took a breath and knocked hard.

Ralph came to the door in a pair of denim shorts and his work boots. His chest was muscled, speckled with grey-and-black hair. Maggie swallowed. He looked puzzled, as if he had forgotten his niece was visiting.

She pushed her hair back. 'You said I should come.'

He nodded, waved her in. Once she was inside he looked her up and down, dragged a hand across his face, sighed deeply and said, 'You're sure you want to be here?'

The smell of turps and paint, sweat and seawater. She nodded.

'You can watch, then. Sit there. I won't talk. I'm in the middle of something. So there's no talking. Understood?'

The front door opened directly into the kitchen and living area. He'd cleared away almost all the furniture in the room, apart from the sofa, which he'd covered with a dust sheet. The rug was rolled and propped in the corner. Maggie wondered if her mum and dad knew that the floorboards in their boat-house were now smeared with paint. Even the kitchen table had gone; on the floor by the sink was a kettle and a couple of dirty mugs; an open packet of PG Tips. Whilst he positioned himself behind the easel, which was turned away from her, she sat on the edge of the sofa.

It was clear from several small studies propped against the wall and tens of photographs tacked around the place that he was painting the strait. This surprised her; from the article in the *Artists' Newsletter* she'd gathered he painted mostly portraits. Each study was painted with loose, vigorous brushstrokes, which made the water appear gloomy and threatening and alive.

After the initial shock of quietness (she noticed a small transistor radio beneath the window, but it was turned off), Maggie began to enjoy listening to the tiny noises of Ralph's makeshift studio. Apart from the whisper of the sea and the cry of the terns, there was the ever-present backing track of the moans of sheep. Ralph's brush made all sorts of sounds on his canvas: light taps, rhythmic swooshes, gunfire rattles, a dry grinding. He'd regularly stalk over to the window, his boots clomping on the floorboards, look out and grunt. After a while, though, she realised she'd tuned out from even these noises and was listening instead to the sounds of Ralph's body: his nails scratching at his own scalp, the groans he made as he drove his brush into the paint, the occasional sigh of either frustration or satisfaction at the marks he'd made and – an hour in – the gloopy calls of desire from his stomach. She could have sworn she heard the breath rolling in and out of his lungs, and perhaps even the smack of saliva as he stretched his mouth into a horrified gawp at whatever it was he could see taking form before him.

At first these bodily broadcasts made her blush. But after a while she was fascinated by the way Ralph seemed deaf even to the loudest of them.

Hours passed. Stiff from sitting for too long, desperate for a pee and a glass of water, she cleared her throat in the hope that he would notice her discomfort. He did not. She sat for a further half-hour, shifting constantly, but failing to find a comfortable position. Still Ralph did not speak or look her way. Eventually she looked at her watch and made a small exclamatory sound. Ralph continued to scrutinise his canvas. Unable to bear it any longer, Maggie stood. 'I have to go,' she announced.

Without a glance in her direction, he said, 'Cheerio, then.'

She hesitated, thinking that perhaps this was a joke. But he carried on with his work, his face a mask of concentration.

Seeing she had no choice, she pulled open the door.

As she stepped outside, she heard his voice. 'Please come again, Margaret Wichelo,' it called.

For the next week, Maggie visited the studio every afternoon. She told no one where she was going. If anyone asked, she said she was going to the library in Bangor to get ahead with her A-level reading list. No one questioned this. Her mother had taken a cleaning job in Llanfairpwll despite Alan's protests, and was out most evenings. Alan seemed happy working on the 'farm', as he'd begun calling his couple of fields; his face was starting to tan and at mealtimes he talked about the rejuvenating power of the land.

Nula and Joe were spending most of their afternoons together now. Maggie had asked, once, to join them, but the look on her brother's face had been enough to prevent that question escaping her mouth ever again.

Maggie knew that Joe was in love. It had been there in the way he'd asked for Nula, that evening after the incident with Rhod. It was there in the way he fell silent whenever Nula came into a room, the way he blushed when Maggie uttered her name. In the past few days, this blush had been replaced by a visible sheen on his skin, coupled with a deepening of his darker moods.

And so Maggie continued to go to the studio. If Nula and Joe were going to disappear, she could, too.

Nula was pleased when, a week after appearing at the house for Sunday lunch, Ralph had said she should come with him to Newborough Warren, for a picnic. It was another bright, warm morning and she put on a turquoise minidress. Unlike her mother, her father never commented on anything she wore – even when her skirts were extremely short. Occasionally, though, he did admire the effect of a particular colour on her skin. She also went into her aunt's kitchen and stole a round of Brie from the fridge, as an offering for the picnic.

Arriving at the boathouse, Nula found the door ajar, and voices coming from inside. She stopped for a moment to listen and heard her aunt say, 'Are you sure?' and her father answering, 'Of course. She won't mind.'

Nula gave a loud knock.

'Darling!' Her father ushered her in. 'Aunt Fiona popped by, and I was just saying – wasn't I ? – what a good idea it would be to have her join us.'

Nula stared at her aunt, who was waving a hand in front of her pink face, as if to brush Ralph's words away. Her dark-blonde hair, which was usually held in the tight grip of a plastic clip, hung around her face and curled at her shoulders. She was wearing lipstick. 'No, no, really, I've lots to do . . .' she protested.

Ralph caught her round the shoulders and squeezed her to

his side. 'Rubbish! Come on. You spend too much time in that house.'

How did he know that? Nula wondered. And was it even true?

'And it's a glorious day. How often do you get those, up here? Tell her, Nula. Tell her she should come.'

Nula smiled weakly. 'If she wants to, then she should.'

Even Nula stopped, once they'd battled to the top of the dunes, and gasped at the vast expanse of brilliantly coloured shore and sky. Across the water, white clouds danced over the mountains, and on the beach, creamy sand swept on for miles. Despite the gusty wind it was very warm, and Ralph immediately suggested a game of bat and ball. Although he generally loathed sports, once on a beach Ralph would produce a couple of battered tennis bats and a ball and proceed to punish anyone who would compete with him. Nula declined to join in, and instead sat on her father's old towel to watch. At first Aunt Fiona seemed reluctant, too; but soon she removed her shoes, rolled up her flowered shirt sleeves and was skittering about with her bat, laughing at Ralph's exclamations. 'Come ON!' he shouted, jumping into the air to retrieve a ball. 'He smashes another one right on the line! It skims the net! Oh, I SAY! I SAY!'

Nula closed her eyes and tried to listen to the birds rather than her father's voice. Joe had told her their names: oyster-catcher, lapwing, curlew, meadow pipit. She didn't know one song from the other and, she suspected, neither did he; but the names themselves were enough to make her smile. In her bag, the stolen Brie would be softening. It would just have to stay there until it stank, now that Aunt Fiona was here. Why had she ever believed she might actually have a day alone with her father? She should have stayed with Joe. That morning he'd appeared, as usual, with the spare helmet. Nula didn't know why she hadn't told him where she was going. It had seemed necessary to have a secret. Joe always looked at her with such intent that it was, in some ways, a relief to be away from him.

She heard her father's voice again – 'It's a perfect drop shot! Just look at that backspin!' – and remembered another holiday, when she must have been about five. Ralph had taken her and her sister, Hester, riding on a sandy beach. He'd lifted her into the saddle and then hauled himself into position behind her. There was a warm smell of leather and horse shit, and the sun like a hot hand on her head. When he said, 'Go on now, girl', his voice was so gentle she wasn't sure if he was addressing her or the animal. They trotted along the shore whilst Hester rode on ahead. Nula looked back at him, at his prominent chin and his lips, full and red in the midst of his dark beard. 'Turn around,' he said. 'Look at that magnificent view. The best way to see a landscape is on horseback.' She nodded and held the reins tighter. Her father kicked the horse to quicken their pace and Nula's bare legs began to chafe on the animal's prickly sides. The speed with which the beach flashed by was exhilarating for only a few moments; soon she wanted to squeal. Knowing how much her father despised such girlish reactions, she managed to control her voice until the words came into her mouth: 'Daddy! I want to stop.'

To her astonishment, her father pulled the reins and the horse immediately slowed its pace. 'You did very well,' he said. 'That was very fast, and you did very well indeed.' When Hester looked round for them, Nula had the special delight of knowing that her sister could see their father kissing the top of her head. It had been one of the happiest moments of her childhood.

When she opened her eyes, her father was standing with his hands folded behind his head, displaying a feathery fan of black armpit hair to Aunt Fiona. He was wearing a very tatty pair of greyish shorts and nothing else, having removed his shirt and tossed it onto the towel beside Nula during the game. Nula was used to seeing her father's body – slight but muscular, always tanned – and wasn't at all surprised by his near-naked state. Fiona seemed to be listening intently to Ralph's monologue. 'That's the thing,' he was saying, 'with Klimt. He can be very sensual, but his work is also, to my mind, rather brittle. It's erotic art as interior decoration.'

Nula had heard this evaluation before. Fiona, however, seemed impressed and was nodding rather wildly. Struggling to her feet, the warm sand giving way beneath her, Nula approached the two of them. On reaching her father's side, she found herself immediately encircled by his strong right arm.

'Hello, lovely daughter,' he said. 'Look at her, Fiona. Don't you think she's lovely?'

Fiona said, 'That's a very striking dress, Nula.'

Nula plucked at her hemline. 'Shall we start the picnic? I'm hungry.'

'In a minute, love. Bat and ball? Your aunt's pretty good. Fiercely competitive.'

Fiona smiled. 'No point in playing otherwise.'

'You girls pretend to be above such things, but I've never known a woman who didn't love to thrash the living daylights out of a man.'

Fiona tittered, and Nula said, 'Dad. I'm starving.'

Ralph rolled his eyes and consented. The three of them

walked back to the towel, and Ralph made a show of struggling with the zip of his rucksack, before tipping its contents onto the towel. Stepping back with a flourish, he urged them to tuck in.

'Is that it?' asked Nula. There was half a baguette, two bruised apples, a bag of crisps and a bottle of cider.

'Not a great feast, I know. But I thought we'd have a drink,' he said, offering the bottle. 'To celebrate.'

'Celebrate what?'

'The summer. My work going well. Being here with family . . .' He smiled at Fiona, who looked down at the faded towel.

Nula took the bottle, aware of Fiona's gaze as she tipped it to her mouth. Her aunt was probably trying to work out if this was normal for Ralph and his daughter and, if it was, whether that was OK. Nula had the occasional drink of cider in the park with some girls from school on a Friday or Saturday night, but she had never before drunk alcohol with her father. Ralph actually drank very little, preferring tea, or iced banana milkshakes on hot days. Nula had seen her mother drunk – her face flushed and damp, her words coming too fast – but never her father.

'You're enjoying it up here, then,' Fiona said.

'Oh, I am,' said Ralph. 'Loving it. Menace and mystery in equal measure.'

'How about you, Nula?'

Nula noticed that her aunt's nose was already sunburnt. 'It's . . . interesting,' she said. 'Quiet.'

'It's great that you're getting along with Joe and Maggie so well. Isn't it, Ralph?'

'Really great,' said Ralph. 'Good for her to get out of the city. Not that Oxford's much of a city. People call it a seat of learning, but to me it's more of a . . .'

'. . . damp pit,' finished Nula.

Ralph laughed. 'She knows me,' he said, shaking his head, 'all too well.'

'Joe seems much happier, since we got here,' said Fiona. 'I worry about that bike, but I suppose he needs his independence . . .'

'Christ, yes,' said Ralph. 'Let the boy spread his wings.'

Fiona looked at Nula, her eyes seeming to invite some kind of revelation from her niece.

Nula said nothing. Instead she took off her sandals and buried her toes in the sand. Ralph joined in, sprinkling his daughter's feet with a heap of fine, warm granules. When he'd covered them entirely and placed a seashell on each one, he asked Fiona, 'Is Alan happy here?'

Fiona gave a shrill laugh. 'Why don't you ask him?'

'He doesn't tell me much,' said Ralph. 'Never has.'

Fiona sighed and rubbed at her reddening nose with some force. 'Happi*er*, I would say.' She took up the bottle of cider and pressed it to her lips. 'When I married him I had no idea that he longed to *escape to the country*, as they say.'

Ralph ripped off the end of the baguette and offered it to Nula, who refused. 'I don't think any of us knows who we're marrying,' he said. 'How can you know? You're just lucky if it turns out they're not as bad as you are.'

Fiona raised her eyebrows. 'Are you bad?'

'Not as bad as some.'

Nula drank some more, enjoying the acidic thump of alcohol in her stomach.

Fiona snorted. 'Do you know what I heard, about you?' she asked Ralph.

'How could I?'

'I heard that you hated women.'

Ralph looked at his daughter. Nula looked at the sky. The

thin clouds had a scattered appearance, like talc spilled on a carpet. She could hear the hurt in her father's voice as he asked, very quietly, 'And who told you that?'

Fiona shrugged. 'It's what people say, isn't it?'

'Which people?'

'I don't know . . . feminists, I suppose.'

'But who said it to you?' He flicked a small, tight smile in her direction. 'My brother?'

She paused. 'Look. It's not what *I* think.'

Ralph drilled a hole in the sand with his index finger. 'But why would anyone think that?'

Fiona brushed her fringe from her eyes and laughed. 'Oh, Ralph. You know why. You must know why.'

He waited, his face unmoving.

She sighed. 'It's how you paint them.'

Ralph withdrew his finger and very slowly wiped sand on the towel. 'Why would I spend my career – my *entire* career – painting something I hate?'

Fiona held his gaze. 'It's a good question,' she said.

Without looking at his daughter, Ralph said, 'Nula, you don't think this, do you? You don't think I hate women, do you?'

Nula continued to look at the sky, and to drink her father's cider.

'It's probably how you present them,' said Fiona. 'So uncompromising, so honest – look at your paintings of Eleanor.'

Nula knew those early portraits of her mother, and she loved looking at their teased surfaces, at the mystery of the woman in them, small, grey, pale, with her legs wide open and her hair so wild and curly it looked like a strange wig. This woman, who was not yet her mother, looked out of the canvases with an inviting kind of sadness.

'I paint what I see,' said Ralph. 'That's what people don't understand. I don't decide. I just look.'

'I understand,' said Fiona, placing a hand on his knee and shaking it gently, as though he were a sulky toddler in need of bringing round.

Tired of this conversation, Nula reached into her bag and retrieved the round of Brie, which had gone floppy in the heat. The ripe contents bulged against their plastic wrapping. She threw it into the centre of the towel, where it landed with a soft *plud*, and said, 'I borrowed your Brie, Aunt Fiona.'

Fiona stared at the cheese.

'I hope you don't mind. I was going to replace it.'

Ralph said, 'Excellent! Let's eat.'

Nula allowed her father to scoop some of the Brie onto a piece of baguette for her. The two of them had almost finished the entire packet before Aunt Fiona said, with a tight smile, 'What's mine is yours, Nula.'

On the afternoon Nula went to visit her father, Maggie joined Joe on the sofa in front of the TV. It was clear to her that Nula hadn't told him where she was going when he looked up and said, in a disappointed tone, 'Oh. It's *you*.'

He appeared to be engrossed in *Neighbours*, his long legs dangling over the arm of the sofa, the remote cradled to his chest. Every few moments he would look either at the door or at the side of Maggie's face. Then he began to switch channels. As he hit the remote, each pop of the television seemed to increase his agitation. It was only when they were nearly at the end of *Going for Gold* that Joe demanded of his sister, without taking his eyes from the television, 'Why have *you* sat here all afternoon, watching this crap?'

She didn't reply.

'Shouldn't you be at the library? Working on getting a bit cleverer?'

'I'm taking a break,' she said.

After a while he asked, in a softer voice, 'Not seeing Nula this afternoon, then?'

He'd cleared his throat before he said her name, as if it caused him physical difficulty, and Maggie knew that he was utterly lost. This knowledge filled her with a sudden rage.

'Nula's visiting Uncle Ralph,' she said, in what she hoped was an even tone. 'Didn't she tell you?'

'She told *you* that?' he asked.

Maggie ignored the question. 'She also told me you freak her out,' she said. 'Staring at her all the time.'

Joe flinched. 'No, she didn't,' he said, but his eyes slid towards his sister.

'Nula tells me everything,' Maggie continued. 'We're best friends.'

Joe gave a small laugh. 'I doubt that. I doubt that very much indeed, little one.'

Tears pricked Maggie's eyes. She snatched the remote, hit the Off button and left the room.

Something of a routine was established between Maggie and Ralph. He would leave the door of the boathouse open from about 1 p.m., and she would let herself in without a word and go about making them both tea. When they'd got their drinks, Maggie would sit on the sofa and watch. Sometimes Ralph would ask her to pass him something – a clean cloth, a different brush, a new tube of paint from the drawer – and she began to anticipate what he wanted by the shape of his frown or the way his hand moved when he reached up to touch his hair, which he did often. Ralph's hair looked a little like a black felt cap, worn tight to his skull. Maggie found herself imagining what it would be like to touch it, despite not being sure she would like the way it might feel.

One afternoon, Maggie broke this routine by taking with her a tin of home-baked biscuits. She'd made them that morning, telling her mother that she wanted to learn more about cooking. On testing one she'd been disappointed; both greasy and hard, the biscuit failed to melt on the tongue or crumble on the lips and she'd considered making another batch. There wasn't time, though, so she'd placed them on a piece of kitchen towel in an old Roses tin and held them out to Ralph on her arrival. He looked at the tin, then at her, then at the tin once more.

'What's that?' he asked, blinking.

'Biscuits.'

He took off his glasses and frowned at the tin.

'Shortbread.' When he didn't respond, she added, 'I made them. This morning.'

'Did you?' He sounded surprised, if not pleased.

There was a pause. 'Thank you,' said Ralph. And, replacing his glasses, he took the tin and put it next to the kettle. Then he picked up his brush and began work again.

After about an hour Maggie got up to make them more tea, having decided that she would say nothing further about the biscuits. Perhaps her silence would prompt a comment from him.

However, she found it hard not to stare at the unopened tin as she sipped her drink. As usual, Ralph didn't stop work, but drank his tea whilst standing at the easel, using the break to survey what he'd done, occasionally standing back and grunting.

She waited, thinking he might suddenly clasp a hand to his forehead and exclaim, 'Your biscuits! How could I forget?'

Instead he gulped his tea so audibly that, in her irritation, she stood and said, 'I have to go.'

It took a moment for him to look at her. 'You only just got here, didn't you?'

'Two hours ago.'

'OK,' he said. His gaze returned to the canvas as he readied himself to make another mark.

'Shall I come again?'

He lowered his arm. 'Of course you should.'

'It's just, I'm not really learning anything.'

'In that case—'

'What I mean is, you're not really teaching me anything. I've been coming here for almost two weeks and you haven't taught me anything.'

'There's so little I can teach you. Really.'

'How can that be true?'

He sighed and moved away from the easel, towards her. 'It's all about looking.'

'I know that already.'

'And looking is what you've been doing, isn't it?'

He was standing in front of her now, his arms folded across his chest, still holding the paintbrush.

'Isn't it?' he demanded.

'I suppose so.'

'Then you've learned something.'

She glanced over at the unopened biscuit tin.

'There's nothing to tell you, Maggie. It's just about the doing. That's what's so good about it. It's just the doing. That's how you learn.'

'But all I've been doing is sitting here . . .'

'OK,' he said. 'OK.' He went back to the easel and checked the canvas, as if it might have changed during the few seconds in which he hadn't given it his attention. Then he put the brush down and returned to where she was standing. Hooking his thumbs into the top of his shorts, he surveyed her in a way that made her skin feel horribly alert.

'You want to do more than just sitting there, watching?'

'Yes.'

'Then sit for me. Look at it from the other side. Then you'll see how paint can transform something.'

She stared at him, her mouth open.

He stared back. 'You'd have to be naked, of course,' he added.

Maggie didn't return to the boathouse for three days.

Each evening she would sit on the steps of the old dairy, watching the sun go down and thinking about Ralph's proposal. The sunset made everything glow, even the chicken coop and the rusty water butt.

Of course she had walked away after he'd made his suggestion, thinking she should immediately register her deep and utter outrage. On reaching the ruined church, though, she'd burst out laughing and had giggled all the way home. It wasn't that she thought Ralph was joking, although part of her hoped he was. She laughed because she was shocked, but she also laughed at herself, because she could not believe she hadn't seen it coming. Of course he was going to ask her that. Hadn't the *Artists' Newsletter* mentioned his mistress? She had remembered the name. Sandy Jenkins. Such an ordinary name. Something old-fashioned about it. Something that suggested to Maggie school dinner ladies, or girls who walked dogs to make a living. Why wouldn't he ask her too, then? And wasn't his art all about bodies? All about flesh? Wasn't that why she had found it interesting?

To Maggie it had always seemed that the best way to think about sex was as a project she had yet to tackle. Privately, she'd set aside an age – eighteen – at which she would make an effort to experience the full thing. Up until then, she decided, she would read about sex. It would be a sort of research project. If she researched it thoroughly, she would be ready when the time came, and would not be found wanting. Perhaps she wouldn't even find sex itself to be wanting. Certainly she did not want to repeat her experience with Rhod. The research, such as it was, had been a frustrating business, however. She had looked to literature first, dipping into D.H. Lawrence. Heart thumping with anticipation, she was disappointed to find the actual sex to be rather opaque. Anaïs Nin was much more enlightening, but the richness of her prose was distracting and a little overdone for Maggie. Reading *The Color Purple* aged fourteen, she'd confirmed the position and function of her clitoris. That had been very useful.

Posing naked for her uncle had not been part of the plan.

Sometimes she imagined herself flinging his paints across the room, demanding a full apology and proper instruction from this moment on. Did he not realise how inappropriate his behaviour actually was? Did he not realise she was *sixteen*, for God's sake?

Sometimes, however, she imagined herself arriving at the boathouse in silence, smiling a lopsided smile, slipping her dress from her shoulders as he looked on, aghast. And one night she dreamed he was moving his face close to hers, his stubble prickling her cheek. His hand was on the small of her back as he whispered in her ear that he was sorry, but she was perfect. *Perfect.*

Then, on the third evening, Nula came out of the house, placed herself on the step beside Maggie and opened a can of Diet Coke.

'All right?' she asked.

It was the first thing she had said to her cousin for days.

Maggie looked towards the back of the house. She had expected her brother to be following Nula, but there was no sign of him. 'Where's Joe?' she asked.

'Indoors.' Nula took a long drink and pushed her hair out

of her eyes. It was an elegantly frustrated gesture, one that Maggie had tried, privately, to emulate. Since Nula had arrived on the island, Maggie had made a decision to let her own hair grow longer so that she, too, could toy with it in expressive ways.

'Your brother can be fairly intense,' said Nula. 'He seems to think he's some kind of Celtic warrior.'

This was news to Maggie.

Nula stretched out her long legs and examined her toenails, which she'd recently painted bright blue. 'He keeps going on about Plas Coch,' she said, pronouncing *Coch* to sound like *cock*.

Maggie had heard of the place, but knew little about it.

'It means red place,' explained Nula. 'Because of the blood. There was a big battle near there. The Romans trying to invade. The Celts holding out for ages, looking very scary. Woad and everything. And a lot of blood.'

'What's that got to do with Joe?'

'Direct bloodline to the Druids,' said Nula, swigging her Coke. 'Apparently.'

'But he's English,' said Maggie. 'He was born in Oxford. Like me.'

'Your mum's Welsh, though,' said Nula.

'Kind of,' said Maggie.

Nula rolled her eyes, but Maggie could tell by the little blush that had appeared on her cousin's cheek that she was slightly impressed by all this.

'Have you seen your dad lately?' asked Maggie, aware that her question was abrupt, but unwilling to witness any more evidence of Nula's deepening relationship with her brother.

Her cousin shrugged. 'He's pretty busy. That's what he came here for. To work.'

'He paints a lot of – women, doesn't he?'

'Uh-huh.'

'Doesn't it bother you?'

'Why would it?' asked Nula, looking up at the windows of the house.

Maggie said nothing.

'Oh,' said Nula. 'You mean because they're naked.' She twirled her butterfly necklace around her finger. 'Contrary to popular belief,' she grinned, 'Dad doesn't fuck all his models.'

To her annoyance, Maggie found herself looking away in embarrassment.

'I mean, he's painted me. And my sister. Loads of times.'

'What, without your clothes?'

'Do you think that's weird?' Nula laughed. 'If you think about it, it would be much weirder if he *didn't* paint us. I mean, if he made some sort of special exception for us, then that would be weird.'

Maggie tried to digest this idea. 'Right. Sure.'

'The thing with Dad is – what you have to understand about him – is that the work comes first. Always. It has to be like that. So it doesn't really matter who he's painting. What matters is the painting itself.'

For someone who'd claimed to hate art, Nula sounded curiously proud of this idea.

'If you're going to succeed,' she said, 'it has to be like that.'

The back door opened and Joe appeared. He was wearing his leather jacket and was carrying two helmets. Another jacket was slung over his arm.

Nula jumped to her feet, pushed a hand through her hair and smiled.

'Hi,' said Joe.

'Hi,' said Nula.

Unable to stand the way her brother was glowing in Nula's direction, Maggie also jumped to her feet. 'Nula thinks you're a Celtic warrior, Joe,' she blurted.

Joe laughed. 'Does she now?' he said, with a sly look at their cousin.

But Nula completely ignored the comment, and instead reached out to touch the leather on Joe's arm. 'You didn't, did you?' she gasped, with a small jump in the air.

Joe nodded and handed her the spare jacket.

'You got it!' Nula cried. And she immediately pushed her arms into the sleeves of the thing and twirled around in the evening light, hugging the jacket to her body like a favourite cuddly toy.

'I went back to the shop, afterwards . . .' Joe said.

'Oh, Joe, you're so sweet!'

Joe didn't argue with this. Instead he held out the spare helmet and said, 'Come on, then. Let's try it out.'

After they'd gone, Maggie sat back on the step, drank the rest of Nula's Coke, then crushed the can beneath her foot until it was completely flattened, like the roadkill that was such a common sight on the lanes around the island.

That evening, Joe took Nula down to the shore near Plas Coch.

She wore the jacket he'd bought for her, even though it was too heavy, even though it smelled of someone else's perfume and made her sweat. She liked the feeling of containment it gave her, the feeling of being protected from the outside world by its tough leather shell. Joe parked his bike by the big crenellated house that was now a hotel and they walked across the lawns, Joe showing her the way, ignoring the stares of guests enjoying pre-dinner drinks on wooden-slatted sun loungers. He led her towards the water, past the strangest tree Nula had ever seen. It was wide and low, its branches almost scraping the earth, its rippled bark and dark, waxy leaves suggesting a solid, complex construction that seemed more like a house than the house itself.

As they walked towards the shore, the sun was going down over the strait, depositing a pinkish sheen on the water. On the mainland, the mountains had flattened to shadow. The tourist boats had all gone now, and Joe said that the strange electrical *pleep-pleep* they could hear was actually an oystercatcher, searching the shallows for food. Nula rewarded him for this insider information with an impressed look.

They picked their way along the grassy, uneven headland. Joe grabbed her hand and she didn't protest. His fingers were softer than she had imagined. He led her to a patch of red earth, right down by the strait, sheltered by trees. Then he turned and looked at her and she smiled, expecting a kiss. There had been many charged looks and flirtatious exchanges over the past weeks, but, so far, no actual kiss. Instead of kissing Nula, however, Joe began to recite the lyrics to 'Personal Jesus' in the nasal wheeze of his father, complete with shoulder tic, dancing with his elbows up round his ears. She laughed, as she always did at this joke. Then, with a flick of his chin, he became his mother, complete with her unsure, sliding eyes. Nula laughed again. Next it was her father's turn. Ever since Ralph had turned up at the farmhouse for lunch that Sunday, Joe had been perfecting this speech. 'The thing about Rothko,' he said, barking out a sudden cough that sent Nula into giggles, 'is that the colours LIVE. Absolutely LIVE.' A shake of the head, a furrow of the brow. He was in full flow. 'And the thing about ME is that mine DIE. They just DIE on the canvas.' He swooned, took off his jacket and threw it and himself onto the earth.

After a moment, she sat next to him and said, 'Dad *is* a really good painter, you know.'

'I thought he just DIED on the canvas . . . That's the thing about WICHELO—'

'No,' interrupted Nula. 'Dad's actually good.'

Joe coughed, then managed to compose himself. 'And what makes him actually good?' he asked.

'His vision, I guess,' said Nula. 'His way of seeing the world . . . His masterly use of paint as an expressive medium.'

Joe pulled a face.

'You may know about oystercatchers,' said Nula. 'But *I* know about art.' She was only half-joking.

'Doesn't he paint a lot of naked women?' Joe asked, with a snigger.

'Yes,' she said, leaving a pause before adding, 'including me.'

Joe gaped at her. She stared back, taking the opportunity to examine him. His dark hair had been flattened by his helmet, but still it curled up at his long neck. There was something feminine about his face – his brows were fine and perfectly shaped, his nose thin, his lips full – but she noticed that his large hands were red and chafed around the knuckles.

'He paints everyone naked,' Nula said. 'It's fascinating, really. Naked, we're exposed – but we're also levelled. We're like animals, I suppose. Just flesh and blood.'

Joe was still staring at her, his eyes black.

'What?' she said, smiling.

He put his hand inside her jacket, slipping it past the zip and onto her waist.

'What?' she said again, softly.

'I could never do that to you,' he said. 'I'd never make you an animal.'

Then he pulled her to him, found her mouth and kissed her. She straightened up, briefly, and laughed, but his expression was so wounded that she put her fingers on his hot neck and kissed him back.

Maggie was sitting in the library at Bangor, an unopened poetry anthology in her lap. She'd already read her A-level set texts (*Far from the Madding Crowd*, Heaney's *North* and *The Tempest*) and so had moved on to this collection, which promised to explain to her what life really was for 'modern women in our hectic, eclectic society'.

A returns-trolley squeaked past and she looked, again, at the clock: 3 p.m. A youngish woman with a yellow complexion shouted at the smallest of her three children to please stop throwing videos around the room. In the far corner, someone was winding the microfiche at an alarming speed. Behind the desk, two librarians watched with dark expressions, apparently unwilling to show the man – again – how it was supposed to be done.

Maggie made a decision. Maybe what Nula had said last night was true. Perhaps Ralph didn't care who his models were. But maybe it was better that way. Whatever the case, her cousin and brother had once again roared off in their matching jackets that lunchtime, and all her mother had said about it was *Take good care of Nula on those roads, Joe.*

It was four-thirty by the time she got there, having taken two buses. As she hurried along the lane it started to rain, water dripping heavily from the oaks and down the neck of her T-shirt. At the boathouse door she smiled. He'd left it ajar for her, as usual. She was welcome still, then. Nevertheless she hesitated, wondering if she should knock to get his attention.

Having decided against it, she stepped into the room and found Ralph sitting on the sofa. His easel had not been assembled and he was wearing an old blue dressing gown. His feet were bare. She noticed each of his elegant toes was perfectly even. Glancing towards the sink, she saw that her Roses tin had been opened and was now empty.

'Uncle Ralph,' she said.

He looked up at her. 'Have you come to tell me off?' he asked. 'If so, I think I should be the one to tell you off first. I haven't been able to do a stroke of work since you stormed out like a bloody drama-queen. I've been worried sick about it.'

She stared at him.

'I mean, you're an artistic young woman. I can tell that. You know that. What goes on in here is between us, isn't it? You haven't gone blabbing to your dad, have you? Eh? That'd be the last thing I need. Is he coming here to kick the shit out of me?'

She studied his face. He hadn't shaved and his eyes were surrounded by black moons.

'Uncle Ralph . . .' she tried again.

But he was in full flow. 'Get it over with. Tell me what an old lech I am. Come on. Do your worst. You young girls are all the same. So fucking sanctimonious—'

'I've come to say that I'd like to do it,' she said.

There was a long pause. Maggie listened to the rain battering the roof. Then Ralph let out a great huff of laughter. 'You would?'

She brushed the wet hair from her eyes. 'Yes. I would.'

'That's . . .' He hung his head for a moment. 'Well. Thank Christ for that,' he said. 'I think you'd better call me Ralph from now on, don't you?'

He was up on his feet, first dragging a huge sketchbook out from under the sofa, then running his fingers through a box of charcoal he'd fished out from the kitchen cupboard.

'Are we going to start now?'

'No time like the present.'

Maggie looked around the room. Shouldn't she have some-where to undress, at least? She'd imagined a screen, her own clothes draped seductively over its edge as she emerged from behind its panels wearing only some sort of kimono-style dressing gown.

'You can undress through there, if you like.' He was gesturing towards the bedroom.

She hadn't thought that she would have to walk across the room naked. She had thought it would be a question of just lying on the sofa and untying her gown. Instead it was Ralph who was unknotting his dressing-gown cord to reveal his usual naked torso and shorts. Maggie watched as he sat on a chair to pull on his work boots. He ran a hand over his thatch of hair. Then he put on his glasses and said, 'Look. If you're not comfortable, just tell me—'

'No. I'm fine.'

'Good.' He placed his hands on his knees. 'So what we'll do is: you take everything off in there, and then we'll get the position right.'

He waited for her to move.

'OK,' she said.

'OK,' he said.

'OK,' she said. She wanted to laugh, to tell him she'd been joking; perhaps he would laugh too, and they could carry on as before. She imagined herself running back home along the lane, still sniggering. She could say to Nula, 'Guess what, I nearly posed naked for your dad', and Nula would probably just roll her eyes and say, 'Who hasn't?'

Instead she went into the bedroom and closed the door. She was thankful there was only one small mirror above the chest of drawers. She didn't want to watch herself doing this. With one fluid movement she unpeeled her damp T-shirt and threw it to the floor. For a minute she stood looking at it. XS, the label read. Through the rain-streaked window, the strait was full, its grey water almost lapping the walls of the house. Perhaps she could crawl out of the window and swim away on the tide. Or hide beneath the bed. Or start to cry. Ralph's bed was unmade, and on top of the small stool by its side was a framed photograph of Nula, aged about six, sitting on a horse, wearing a too-large riding hat and a flowered vest. She was laughing, and looked happier than Maggie had ever seen her. The frame was Sellotaped together at one edge. She took off her jeans. Could she enter the room in her bra and pants, both dirty grey, with lank bows attached to the elastic? No. He would send her right back into the bedroom. Maggie turned Nula's photo face-down, removed her underwear and pulled open the door.

He let her walk across the floor before he looked. He sat on a chair, readied his sketchbook. As he flipped over a page she felt the breeze brush her knees. She plopped abruptly onto the sofa, from which Ralph had removed the dust sheet. The old velvet prickled her legs and bottom, and she folded her arms across her chest. Her feet were icy, but an awful heat filled the rest of her body and she knew she would be blotched with raspberry blushes from her forehead to her stomach.

'Make yourself comfortable,' he said, still not looking directly at her. 'We'll go with whatever position you like, to start with.'

So it was clear that just sitting was not enough, that she wouldn't be able to hold herself like this, shoulders and knees almost meeting. He was waiting for her to do something else, to show him something else. Keeping her eyes on the ceiling, she lay back, stretched both arms above her head and hooked one ankle across the other. She concentrated on the irregular beat of the rain on the windows.

Holding the sketchbook, he walked up and down the length of the sofa, surveying his new subject. Then he smiled very brightly and said, 'Perfect. Maggie. That is perfect.' Only then could Maggie let her gaze rest on his face. His eyes were narrowed, serious; his lips pressed in a thin line.

Maggie was surprised by how quickly posing for Ralph came to seem normal. It felt deliciously grown-up, lying naked in the boathouse for hours with Ralph stalking the room, taking in her every angle, as she listened to the strait reaching for the house, and the gulls crying for food. All she had to do was turn up and take off her clothes. Speaking, even thinking, was not necessary. The sight of her body was enough to please Ralph, enough to spark him into creation. She found herself enjoying being naked on the slightly rank sofa, the closeness of the air warming her flesh, the seams of the cushions digging into her skin so that when she unpeeled herself from them at the end of a session, her body was imprinted with their strange lines and creases, like one of Joe's botanical close-ups. Without making any effort, she felt herself to be fully in the room. She had never before known such pleasure.

Every afternoon for the next fortnight, Nula and Joe went some-where, usually the shore near Plas Coch, laughed together and then made love. No one else seemed to notice what was going on. Alan was always working, and Fiona was often out – where, Nula didn't know. Even Maggie seemed to have vanished.

As they lay together on the red dirt and explored one another's bodies, Nula told herself that Joe wasn't so special, that this was one of those summer flings that everyone seemed to have at this age, and it wouldn't last. She knew, though, that he felt differently, and there were moments when she believed she would never again experience anything quite like this. His dark eyes watched her. What she'd said to Maggie about him looking scared was true. He was careful with her in a way other boys had never been. It surprised and delighted her, this nervousness of his. She'd had to take Joe's hand and guide him to where she liked to be touched, that first time. She'd loved that she was the one showing him what to do; it was a new power, like the power she had discovered weeks ago when she'd realised she could halt Joe's laughter by showing him a certain kind of smile, or an exposed thigh or shoulder.

Once they had become used to one another's bodies, the power she'd felt was quickly replaced by something much more unsettling: the knowledge that she found it impossible not to give in to the sheer joy of touching Joe and being touched by

Joe. Very soon she found herself being careful, in return; she found herself wanting to please him, asking him what he would like her to do, how he would like her to be. That was when he started to take photographs of her. He did not, to her slight bafflement, ask her to remove her clothes, or to pose in any way. Instead he would suddenly produce the camera and take a few snaps whilst she was talking. Once she dozed off beneath the tree after they'd had sex, and woke to find him pointing the camera at her face. She put her hand over the lens, and he took a photo of that, too.

One night she had a dream that she was in the bath at home, with locks of Joe's hair floating around her. As she ran her fingers through it, she thought they'd been found out, that everyone knew their secret, but she didn't much care. She was glad he'd been there, in her house, which, she somehow knew, was no longer her home.

He took her to the ruined church at Llanidan, to show her the box of bones. It was almost the end of August.

The air was heavy as they walked slowly along the lane, stopping occasionally to look up at the ancient shapes of the trees and touch each other's fingers.

Outside the church, graves were piled up like abandoned books. The doorway was partially obscured by a yew bush, on which Nula scraped her bare arms as they went inside.

But Nula was not thinking much about her surroundings. She was thinking about Joe's body. He liked her to kiss the small of his back until he groaned. As she walked between the dusty pews, she wondered whether this church would be private enough for them to use, whether Joe would like that. Whether that was actually his plan.

But he was pointing to a small wooden box on the altar.

'Whose bones are they?' Nula asked, peering in at the discoloured heap of crumbling matter.

Joe said he'd read about them in a local guidebook, and they belonged to someone called St Nidan. But, better than that, he said, there was a local belief that this church once contained a thigh bone which, no matter where it was taken, would always return home.

'Isn't it insane?' he laughed. 'I mean. A bloody thigh bone with a homing instinct.'

Nula smiled, shivered. It was dark and cool inside the church, and smelled of mould. 'Shall we go?' she asked, hoping they would take their usual trip to the shore near Plas Coch.

'Wait,' he said. 'I got you something.'

And he produced a thin silver ring, decorated with a tiny Celtic cross.

She laughed, nervously, and thought about saying *It's not really my style*, but instead she took the ring and slipped it on her middle finger.

'So you come back,' said Joe, taking her hand and holding it, very tightly.

The next afternoon, Uncle Alan insisted that Joe go with him to choose a birthday present for his mother and, with Maggie also out of the house, Nula found herself heading down the lane to the boathouse. She'd barely seen her father all month.

The door was closed, which was unusual. Her father hated closed doors, especially on warm days, saying that they blocked creativity and smacked of English middle-class modesty of the worst kind.

Instead of knocking, Nula peered through the side window.

The strength of the sun outside made it difficult to see clearly, but she recognised her father's booted feet beneath an easel and, reclining on the sofa directly opposite the window, a thoroughly naked – and rather beautiful – Maggie.

Instinctively she ducked down, her heart racing. Maggie. Could it have been?

She peeked through the glass again, to check what she'd seen.

Walking slowly back to the house, Nula took some deep breaths and told herself that she didn't feel shocked. Her father painted almost every woman in his life. Why shouldn't he paint his niece?

She also told herself that she wasn't jealous, and that the whole thing was only amusing. So that was what Maggie had been up to! Nula had wondered, if only mildly, where her cousin went every afternoon, and it all made sense now.

Except it didn't. Maggie, with her library books and her quiet watchfulness, seemed like the last person who would end up posing naked on a sofa.

Then, rounding the corner by the church, Nula remembered the look of rage on Maggie's little face after Joe's ridiculous scrap with that local boy. She'd looked close to tears as she'd announced that Joe wanted to see Nula. Perhaps claiming Ralph's time and attention was Maggie's twisted way of getting revenge.

As she dawdled beneath the shade of the trees, it crossed Nula's mind that she could inform Joe, or her aunt, and put an end to it all. But what would happen then? Her father would be livid. Nothing depressed him more than an interruption to his work. He'd probably insist they packed up and left the island immediately, robbing Nula of her last few days with Joe. And, even if they didn't, Joe would again become protective of his little sister. Although Nula wasn't altogether sure if she believed his story, he'd told her that he'd given as good as he'd got in that fight, and he'd seemed proud of it, too.

By the time she reached the house, Nula had decided that she wanted Joe all to herself, at least for the remainder of the holidays. She would do Maggie the favour of keeping this particular secret.

IV

Samuel is snoring and Maggie cannot believe how long he's been asleep – three hours now – and takes this as a sign that she has done the right thing. Not that she needs a sign. Not that there is any doubt in her mind. But this long, deep sleep is obviously what he needed. A complete rest, after what must have been a terrible night. No wonder his mother looked so tired this morning. And where better to rest than in the safe, enclosed world of this Fiat, driving towards Anglesey?

She's played her Billie Holiday CD three times now. She skips to 'I Cover the Waterfront' again and begins to sing, confident the sound of her voice will not disturb the child. When he wakes they will have gone through the mountains. They can stop in the centre of some small town, she can let him have some fresh air, perhaps go to a café and feed him a muesli bar and a yoghurt. She has Bangor in mind. It's the kind of place that's small but still anonymous; no one will think twice about a girl dressed in black pushing a little boy in his buggy. In fact, if there is one thing she has noticed since doing this job, it's that young women with children in buggies and slight frowns on their tired-looking faces are pretty much invisible. The only people who look at you are other women with buggies, and they are mostly too preoccupied with their own children to notice much else.

But they are away now; they are on the road. She has

deliberately chosen to drive through Snowdonia, even though it's the slightly longer route, wanting the contrast between the glowering mountains and the windblown flatness of the island. The road in front narrows and becomes steeper as she rounds another bend. Her hire car labours up the incline in screechy second gear. It seems necessary, though, to approach Anglesey from this side, to earn its comforts after the terrors of grey peaks, twisted trees, fallen granite and – worst of all – scarred mountainsides, their sides sheered away by slate-mining.

She imagines arriving at Llanidan with the sun going down. She will lead Samuel by the hand to the boathouse, up the steps from the shore and through the wooden side door. He'll look at her, a little confused, as she says *Welcome home*, and his lip will drop as if he is about to cry, but she will take him in her arms and show him everything that was once Joe's.

The sky is the colour of washed-out vests and summer rain lashes the car. The sound makes Samuel stir. His head thrashes from side to side, eyes flickering, and Maggie begins to coo: 'It's all right, Sammy, Gee-Gee's here, we're in Gee-Gee's car, and everything's all right.'

His eyes snap open and he stares at the rain-washed window and lets out a howl. 'Hand!' he demands. 'Hand!' She tells him she cannot give him her hand, she's driving and she needs both her hands, but she will do so as soon as she can, and his response is to shout, louder, 'Hand! Hand!' A sign says: HOLY-HEAD 25. It is half-past four, almost his normal teatime, and this will have compounded his misery. His cries have become screams now, his legs are thrashing, and he starts to cough with the effort of so much distress. But Maggie does not increase her speed, does not look at his red, wet face in the rear-view mirror. She concentrates on the traffic and finds the road into Bangor. It is not as she remembered, perhaps because it's raining so hard that the streets themselves look smeared. She follows the one-way system and, before she knows it, the town itself is disappearing behind her without ever having materialised. When she performs a hasty U-turn, several other drivers blast their horns. She pulls into Morrisons car park near the university, switches off the engine and turns to look at the boy. His face is flaming with rage and his cries have become so wild she fears he may vomit. And so Maggie ducks out of the car into the rain. She has given up trying to console him with her voice, and it is a great relief to release his car seat's aggressively tight belt and pull him to her. Samuel pushes his fists into her chin and stretches his neck back as far as it will go and lets out a last wail, so loud and desperate that she almost shouts back at him, almost says: 'Don't you know what I've risked, for you? Don't you know?' But instead she holds him tighter and runs into the shop.

The glare of the supermarket lights and the beautiful swoosh of the automatic doors are enough to surprise the boy out of his tears. He gulps, shudders, relaxes his head on her wet shoulder. She knows better than to try and cram him into a trolley seat. Instead they stand for a few moments, Maggie cradling and shushing Samuel, her summer raincoat and bag dripping water to the floor, his nose beginning to run. A voice comes over the tannoy, 'Donna to checkout four please', and Samuel looks at Maggie and says, 'Talking.'

She wipes his nose, puts him down and lets him run to the apple display so that he can choose one. 'This!' he says, grabbing the shiniest, reddest of the Jonagolds. 'Are you sure?' she asks. 'This!' he says again, dropping the first and picking a second, larger apple. 'OK, let's get that one,' she says, but he's hit his stride now and is letting apples fall to the floor faster than she can retrieve them. 'Samuel,' she says, 'Sammy—'

'Challenging age, isn't it?' asks a voice from behind.

Keeping one hand on Samuel's shoulder, Maggie turns to face a man in a green Morrisons apron. 'I'm NEIL,' his badge announces.

'Sorry,' she begins. 'We'll pay for them . . .'

'No need,' he says, crouching down to look Samuel in the face. 'What's your name, then?' he asks.

'This is Samuel,' says Maggie, then covers her mouth with a hand. A ridiculous slip. She'd decided on another name: Stevie. She must remember these things.

'And how old are you, Mr Samuel?' Neil asks.

Samuel looks at the floor.

'Just two,' Maggie answers.

'Oh dear,' says Neil. 'Terrible twos, is it? Poor Mummy.' He pats Samuel on the head. It's not done forcefully, but Maggie finds herself yanking Samuel away from this stranger's touch. In such situations she often says: 'I'm not Mummy, I'm the nanny' and this is enough to wrong-foot whoever is trying to strike up a conversation. It is hard not to use this tactic on Neil, and she knows her actual reply – 'Best get on' – won't deter him for long.

'You're a lucky boy, Mr Samuel.' Neil straightens and addresses the comment to Maggie, who pretends not to have heard.

'Mummy?' asks Samuel, his face hopeful.

Maggie picks him up and heads for the door, dimly aware of Neil calling something after her about forgotten apples. She presses on, out into the rain, praying that Samuel will not repeat that word.

Back in the car she does everything she can to distract him, letting him sit in the driver's seat and grasp the steering wheel as she feeds him yoghurt from a plastic spoon. He opens his mouth and shuts it again, opens and shuts, opens and shuts, never once taking his eyes from the windscreen as he mimes driving, occasionally exclaiming BEEP, sometimes standing up with excitement, but always returning to a crouch when she tells him to do so. She watches his hands on the steering wheel, the way he grips the thing as if his life depends on it. She has long known the strength of this boy's will, but for the first time she finds its power a little unnerving.

A knock at the window. She jumps, but Samuel hardly notices, so engrossed is he in his driving. It's Neil, holding a wet bag of apples. Through the rain-smeared glass she can see a worrying light in his eyes. It's something she has seen before. He is a man looking for an opening, a way in. Perhaps he thinks she's a single mum who would kill to have a man – any man – in her life.

Reluctantly she winds down the window. 'I really don't want a whole bag,' she says.

He doesn't flinch. 'They're almost out of date. They throw them out. It's a waste.'

A pause.

'Your little boy really wanted one, didn't he?'

'I can't take them,' she says, winding the window back up.

Neil straightens so that all she can see are the ties of his apron digging into his waist, but he doesn't move away from the car. He stands straight, and she sees now that he is lean. His body is younger than his face, which she had estimated to be past thirty-five. Minutes pass and still he does not move. Samuel shouts BEEP-BEEP once more, but then looks at Maggie and demands, 'APPLE!' She offers him yoghurt or juice, but 'APPLE,' he shouts. 'APPLE.'

Her heart starts to pound and she instructs herself to get a grip. Neil is just a man looking for a way in. Desperate, perhaps. But not threatening. Not necessarily. She is about to relent and wind down the window once more when she hears a dull thud on the car roof. Through her side window she sees Neil walking back to the shop. She sits for a moment, her head in her hands, listening to Samuel's ever-escalating cries for APPLE, and feels an urge to chase after Neil and thank him profusely for his gift. Instead, though, she opens the door and looks on the roof. Resting there is the 'family bag' of six small apples, 'perfect for lunchboxes'. And underneath the bag is a card. Picking it up by its slightly sodden edges, Maggie sees it's a business card of the type people once got printed up in post offices.

Back in the car, she peels an apple, cuts it into thin slices and gives one to Samuel. Only after she's fed him the entire thing does she read the card. NEIL JONES, it says. HOUSE MAIN-TENANCE, DECORATING, BUILDING. NO JOB TOO SMALL. BANGOR 302978.

She stuffs the card into her pocket, then peels and slices another apple and eats it herself.

Once she is out of Bangor, Maggie starts a song.

'OH! The grand old Duke of York, tiddly pom!'

'POM!' echoes Samuel.

'He had ten thousand men, tiddly pom!'

'POM!'

'He marched them up to the top of the hill—'

'POM!'

They speed along the Holyhead Road and up onto the elegance of the Menai Bridge, its chains strung out before them like an industrial necklace. On either side of her now, the blue water opens up. All in a rush, it seems, they leave the rainy hillsides behind and drive towards the sudden sunshine of the island. CROESO I YNYS MÔN, a sign says. Just at that moment Samuel lets out a long, delighted raspberry. Catching his eye in the rear-view mirror, Maggie blows one back to him.

I know everything about him, she thinks. She has looked at the red book in which his parents have recorded weights, measurements, feeding and sleep patterns. She has opened Nula's laptop and seen every photo his mother has taken of Samuel, and has watched the video Greg made of his son coming home from the hospital – the wind outside the John Radcliffe's main entrance blowing Nula's light scarf into Samuel's screaming face. In the video, Nula stops waving and turns from the camera to shelter the boy from the sun, bundling his head against her chest and shouting something at Greg. Maggie can't make out the exact words, but they are irritated and impatient, perhaps, 'Get the car!' Or maybe, 'What are you doing?' And Maggie has read Nula's diary, a leather-bound book with creamy pages that Nula keeps in the bottom drawer of her desk. The entry for the week of Samuel's homecoming is scrappy, but memorable: *How can I do this? How can I bring this baby safely into the mess that is my own home, let alone the outside world?*

Even though she is aware that Anglesey has become gentrified in some parts, the new Waitrose on the roundabout at Menai Bridge surprises and disappoints her. She'd thought the island was resistant to such things.

Once they have found the right exit, Samuel is content in his car seat for roughly three minutes before he starts wailing, 'Get OUT!' Maggie has brought a bottle of milk in his changing bag, telling herself she would use it only in an emergency. She pulls over, hands him the bottle and is rewarded with immediate silence. He is too old for a bottle, but since starting work for the Shaws, Maggie has often been greeted in the morning by Samuel running around with a plastic teat gripped between his teeth. She'd suggested to Nula that they eliminate this morning bottle, reminding her that the prolonged contact with the sugars in milk was bad for the boy's teeth, but had been greeted with a hazy smile and the words, 'You're right, Maggie. But it's not so easy.'

By the time they reach Llanfairpwll, Samuel is still sucking on the bottle, and Maggie is beginning to regret giving him the thing. Still, it gives her time to think about what she should do once they arrive. There is a small hope inside her that Joe will actually be there to greet them, although it's more than she can allow herself to expect. So she makes a mental list of practical things: change his nappy; she'd meant to do that in Bangor, but Neil had distracted her. Put water on to boil for Samuel's pasta. Stash away the few clothes she's brought with her. She's brought no bedding, but she is sure he will prefer to sleep with her, at least at first. Everything will be strange and he will need the comfort. She'll have to make the trip to Llanfairpwll tomorrow for more supplies. She knows that the longer she leaves this, the more risky it will become.

It is only now that she has time to consider seriously the possibility of being followed by the Shaws' car. She quickly dismisses this idea as ridiculous: neither Greg nor Nula will have arrived home from work yet. It is usually six-thirty before they come in, and it's rare, these days, for Nula to call the house from work unless she is going to be late. Perhaps she can pick up a few toys in a charity shop. She has brought nothing save the monkey. But it's well known that children play with whatever is at hand. They don't actually *need* roomfuls of plastic rubbish to entertain themselves. At the Shaws', Maggie had never failed to be shocked by the number of new toys Samuel acquired – something appeared every week, to add to the wooden toy box in the sitting room, and to the large stocks that Nula kept in clear plastic boxes in his bedroom and in the cupboard under the stairs. Maggie had once suggested they rotate the boxes, allowing Samuel access only to one at a time. Nula had smirked. 'Let's just let *him* decide what he wants to play with, shall we?' she'd said. Maggie didn't back down. 'Wouldn't it be better to limit his choices, just a little?' she'd asked. 'Do you mean we should have some sort of toy *timetable*?' Nula responded, incredulously.

She takes a left turn, pointing the car towards Llanidan.

'We're home!'

Maggie applies the handbrake and turns to beam at Samuel.

'We're home,' she says again, trying to keep her tone upbeat. Samuel looks out of his window without repeating the word, a slight frown on his usually clear brow.

Maggie had fought her urge to stop the car at the top of the lane and walk Samuel down that long, beautiful path to the house. Instead she drove past the fields with their glimpses of the strait, under a canopy of oak and elm, winding down the windows to let in the sounds of sheep, birds, wind and sea, and parked as close to the shore as she could. She'd wanted to get him inside quickly, to show him their home, let him meet her brother, if he was there; make Samuel something to eat and settle him inside the place, before letting him explore outside. There would be time enough for that.

The boathouse, always ramshackle, now looks neglected. Its once-white paint is streaked with algae and bird shit. The front door is beginning to rot around the bottom. The small windows are covered with a film of salt.

She carries him along the beach and up the steps to the door. Samuel points towards the strait and shouts, 'Sea!'

'Yes,' says Maggie. 'We live by the sea.'

'Sam in sea?'

'Later, my love,' she says. 'We'll look at it later.' In all her years of nannying, it's the first time she's used the endearment. Usually she limits herself to *sweetie* or *pumpkin*. At the Shaws', *my love* had often been in her head, but she hadn't once let the term escape her lips for fear of being overheard by Nula or Greg. Tears come to her eyes on hearing herself speak the words, even though Samuel makes no acknowledgement of the utterance.

Blinking hard, she puts him down so she can turn her key in the lock.

'Here we are, then.'

He takes the hand she offers him, follows her inside.

It is cool and rather dark, but not, as she'd feared, musty. Joe has been here recently; she can tell by the smells of bacon fat and unwashed sheets. She calls his name, twice, but there is no reply.

'We're home,' she says again, perhaps addressing the house itself. Still her brother's voice does not sound out of the gloom. No one steps forward to welcome her, and the emptiness of the place causes her to scoop Samuel into her arms and kiss him on the cheek. He struggles away, eager to explore. She is not sure why she needs to cry; not sure she can stop herself from doing so for much longer.

Maggie had known that her brother hardly uses the house

any more. Her mother had told her so in a letter. But, despite herself, she'd hoped that bringing the boy here would somehow be enough to make Joe appear.

'What that?' demands Samuel, pointing to a mobile made of seashells. A new addition. It tinkles slightly in the draught coming from the window. To buy herself a bit of time to get the bags and make tea, she unhooks it from the ceiling. 'Shells,' she says. 'For you.' He grabs it in his fist and shakes it, creating a loud clacking noise and releasing a puff of dust. He seems satisfied by this act.

Coming back into the boathouse from the car with Samuel's bag, she worries briefly about its size. Will there be enough room to play here on a rainy day? Toddler groups are now out of the question. And there's a ladder leading into a tiny loft space. She hadn't, until now, thought of how dangerous that would be for Samuel. She will have to remove the ladder altogether, leaving them stranded downstairs.

She puts the bag on the bed, noticing the missing hooks on the curtains. On the wall hangs a poster for the film *Midnight Cowboy* – another new addition to the place, one that Joe must have hung recently. Back in the living area, she notices there are no photographs in sight. And now she's had a chance to look properly she can see that everything is oppressed by dust. The old stainless-steel sink and drainer, the Formica trestle table, the brown velveteen two-seater sofa – Maggie tries, and fails, not to picture herself naked upon it – the yellow rag rug, all need her attention. But cleaning will have to wait.

There are still streaks of paint on the floorboards, too. On the journey here Maggie had thought only of Joe in the boathouse, but now she pictures, very clearly, Ralph standing in the centre of the living area, one hand holding a paintbrush, the other touching the tight cap of his hair, whilst his eyes appraised her body. She finds herself blushing.

Samuel has tired of the shells. Throwing them behind him, he runs into the bedroom, grips her hand and demands, 'Cuddle.'

'Come on, then,' she says, lifting him onto her hip. 'OK?' she asks, attempting a smile. 'We're OK, aren't we?'

'Where Mummy?' Samuel asks.

She has already thought of how she will answer such questions, and it doesn't shock her to hear it. She is surprised that it has taken him this long to ask. 'Sammy, listen. Mummy's had to go away for a bit to work, OK? So you'll stay with Gee-Gee, at Gee-Gee's home, OK?'

After all, this isn't the first time Samuel has been told that his mother is away. Nula has travelled with work a couple of times before. On both occasions Greg had been officially in charge, which had concerned Maggie.

'Mummy work,' repeats Samuel.

'That's right,' says Maggie. 'Shall we do your nappy?' She hasn't changed him since leaving Oxford and his trousers are bulging.

'Gee-Gee home.'

'Exactly.'

It is enough, for now. He allows her to lay him on the bed and attend to his nappy, then reaches towards the radio alarm clock on the chair beside Joe's bed. 'What that?'

She sits him up and shows him how to turn the radio's bleeper on and off. When she is satisfied that he can entertain himself with this for a few minutes, she leaves him there while she prepares his pasta, trying not to notice the greasy state of Joe's pans. At the moment Samuel won't eat anything for tea other than pasta with tomato sauce, or couscous with boiled carrot batons. This is another thing she means to tackle.

It's almost six-thirty already, and as a way of bribing him to sit at the table she allows him to eat two more pots of yoghurt whilst he waits. He becomes very quiet as she drains and cools the pasta, and when she puts the plate before him he manages only three mouthfuls before resting his head on the table and closing his eyes. Wisps of his blond hair trail in the red sauce.

Maggie's shoulders release as she realises that the day – their first day home together – is over. She picks up the sleeping boy, wipes the sauce from his hair with a finger, carries him to the bedroom and carefully lays him on Joe's bed. She removes his socks and trousers before pulling the duvet over his legs. This will be the first time he has slept in a bed, rather than a cot, and so she places a pillow on either side of him in an attempt to ensure he doesn't roll off. The journey has exhausted him; there is soon a patch of wetness growing on the sheets from the trickle of saliva escaping his slack mouth. She touches his forehead, whispers, 'Sleep well, my love.'

Maggie paces the boathouse, unable to settle. She cannot fight the urge to give the place a clean, to make it nice for Samuel when he wakes up. Or perhaps to improve it for Joe. Her brother's cleaning products amount to one balding scouring sponge and an eggcup's worth of Flash liquid. She gets to work. Halfway through scrubbing the sink, she realises she's starting to shake with hunger. Damn Neil! If he hadn't stuck his oar in at the supermarket, she might actually have been able to buy herself some proper food. Still, there's Samuel's leftovers. They will have to go to Llanfairpwll first thing in the morning and stock up at the Co-op. She does not want to make more trips to the supermarket than are absolutely necessary. Luckily there's a fairly large freezer compartment in the kitchen. She rummages in the changing bag, making a mental inventory of their supplies. Five mini-boxes of raisins, half a Tommee Tippee cup of diluted orange juice, three muesli bars, most of a packet of pasta, a jar and a half of tomato sauce and two pots of yoghurt. And, of course, what's left of the family bag of apples. It is easy for Maggie to ration herself to the remains of Samuel's pasta and an apple. During her time at Jesus College she had survived on less. And she knows that a couple of mugs of hot water will trick her stomach into feeling almost full. Standing at the sink, she gobbles the pasta. Then she decides to rest in one of the armchairs whilst she eats the apple. But within seconds she is back on her feet, opening the front door.

The smell of the sea, the reassurance of its regular sounds, is so overwhelming that she has to sit down on the wall. If he wakes, she will hear Samuel from here. It's a warm evening and the strait is absolutely still. The lights of Dinorwig are coming on. She looks at the blue shadows of Snowdonia and allows herself a flicker of a smile. They are here. They have made it.

There is only the sound of the sea to disturb them. And yet Maggie cannot sleep. She's holding herself on the edge of the bed, anxious not to disturb Samuel, who is sprawled on the centre of the mattress. She cannot even close her eyes, because when she does her mental list of things she must remember, things she must do tomorrow and things she has done today, grows larger. And she has to check – to keep checking – that he is not about to tumble from the bed.

At 3 a.m., having just fallen asleep, Maggie is woken by a cry.

'Mum-mee!' Samuel moans. 'Mum-mee!'

His voice is like a thump to her chest, restarting her slowing heart. She reaches over, strokes his head, mumbles, 'It's all right, Gee-Gee's—'

'Mummy!'

She puts on the bedside lamp and he scrambles upright. 'We're at Gee-Gee's house, remember?' She is instantly annoyed with herself for not insisting upon 'home', as she had when they'd first arrived. The hour and the look of fear on Samuel's face have forced this half-truth from her mouth. 'Go back to sleep,' she says.

But there is no chance of that. His mood has already swung from distress to interest. He sits back, his big head swivelling as he takes in the details of this new room. He points to Dustin Hoffman above the bed. 'What that?'

Maggie runs a hand over her face. Her heart is still racing from the sudden waking. She tries to pull him to her. If she can hold him, perhaps he will be lulled back to sleep. She has done this before, of course, soothing the boy when he hasn't napped long enough by running a finger across his temple, singing or cradling him in her arms until his eyes droop. But that was in his seaside-themed bedroom, with his winking moon night-light and very efficient blackout blind, his blue-striped sleeping bag from John Lewis and all his stuffed toys to hand. Now Samuel evades her grasp. 'Up,' he says. 'UP.' And he wriggles to the edge of the bed.

It is useless to resist the force of his curiosity. She must rise from the bed and allow him to explore. At three in the morning it is important to avoid a tantrum.

'OK. Let's look around,' she says, resigning herself to a few more hours without sleep.

'Look round,' agrees Samuel.

She shows him the room, opening Joe's drawers and allowing the boy to grab her brother's clothes and toss them to the floor. There isn't much: a couple of bobbled grey jumpers, several out-of-shape black T-shirts, a pair of thick cords and some greasy jeans, thrown in the bottom of the wardrobe. 'What this?' Samuel asks, claiming each item with a chubby fist. She explains, patiently, sometimes embroidering the truth when she's fed up with simply stating the facts ('That's a grey bobbled jumper made of rabbit hair. Joe wore it when he was picking up his prize for being the sulkiest teenager alive' or 'That's a pair of blue jeans. Joe wore them in the Levi's advert he shot in 1989'). Despite her tired limbs and the prickling feeling around her eyes, Maggie starts to enjoy herself. This is a good way, she thinks, for Samuel to make himself at home, a good way for him to become acquainted with Joe.

Under the bed they discover photography magazines, odd socks, old tissues, leadless pencils. But Samuel is more interested in the rack of CDs next to the bed. Maggie opens each case and allows him to examine the contents. She's pleased to see that her brother's taste has not changed: Bob Dylan, Johnny Cash, Sam Cooke singing gospel, Elvis at Sun Studios. Nothing post-1975. She puts 'Mystery Train' on the CD player and does train-noises for Samuel, who laughs.

When he is tired of pushing the stereo system's buttons, he takes hold of the side of a flimsy shelving unit and rocks it.

'Samuel!' says Maggie, reaching out to steady the thing, 'Samuel, no—'

His tongue pokes from the side of his mouth as he concentrates on getting the unit in both fists and pulling with all his might.

Maggie sees the shelves – warped, empty and made of the thinnest MDF – about to topple and swipes Samuel out of the way just as the whole thing falls with a dull thud on the bed.

Maggie looks into Samuel's shocked face. 'Are you OK?' she asks. 'Poor Samuel! What a noise . . . !'

But after a moment of stunned silence, he simply points to a large, flat package that's propped behind the wardrobe. 'That?' he demands, stumping over and managing to drag it some way into the room.

Reaching out to stop the package tipping and knocking Samuel over, Maggie sees something written on the brown paper. *For Maggie. With respect and admiration. Ralph Wichelo.*

Then she recognises the size and shape of the thing, and she stops and takes a breath.

'Present!' Samuel declares, and starts to grab at the paper with clumsy fists.

It must be the portrait. She has never seen the finished article. She has often wondered what it looked like, and what Ralph had done with it. Even when she'd managed to stop thinking about Ralph himself, she'd thought of the painting almost every day, brooding on what mysteries her uncle had revealed on his canvas.

'Open present!' Samuel says, having managed to remove a small square of paper from the package.

Dustballs fly as she joins him. Together they rip the paper away in large sheets. She props it against the wall and stands back before looking properly. The image is, of course, of Maggie at sixteen, lying naked on the sofa in the boathouse's front room.

She stares at the picture for a full minute, trying to take it all in. Samuel smacks it with the flat of his hand, making the canvas flex. When she grasps his wrist to stop him, he screams, alarmed by the sudden fierceness of her grip.

'Stop hitting. Gee-Gee wants to look.'

'Hit!' he shouts, squirming to bring his hand back. But she keeps hold of his wrist. 'Hit!' he repeats. 'Hit!'

'Stop,' she says, managing to keep her voice calm but firm. 'Just stop.'

She knows she should console him, but she cannot take her eyes from the picture. It is a beautiful thing: the colours seem to vibrate, the brushwork is vigorous and yet subtle. What she's shocked by is not her nakedness, but the look of absolute happiness on her face. Her cheeks are pink, her eyes bright, her mouth lifted in a shy smile. The openness of that look is something she no longer recognises. It is a look full of hope. She remembers those long afternoons with Ralph as he worked and refused to answer her questions. That will be me, she'd thought, back then. One day I will do that, too. I will work on canvas and I will not have to explain myself.

As it was, she didn't even manage to study A-level Art, switching at the last minute to Sociology.

Samuel is bucking around now, trying to loosen his arm, wailing. Letting him go, she shoves the picture under the bed before lifting the shelving unit back into place. Then she picks him up and holds him tightly, nuzzling his sweaty hair. After a few minutes he goes limp in her arms. She sits on the bed, leaning against the headboard so that Samuel can lay his head on her breast and sleep. Maggie, however, remains awake until dawn, thinking about the canvas and about her failure to live the life that the girl in the painting seemed to promise.

Eight p.m. in the Shaw house. A sharp knock at the door.

Nula leaps to answer it, hardly noticing as her foot nudges her glass of red, which tips and spills across the rug.

She yanks the door open, ready to laugh with relief, to tearfully berate Maggie; ready for things to go back to normal.

But it's not Maggie and Samuel. It's Greg, scowling at his phone. 'Sorry,' he says, pushing past her into the hallway. 'Forgot my keys. Have you been trying to call me?'

She closes the door. 'They're not back.'

Greg looks up.

'Maggie and Samuel. They're not here.'

Nula sees the briefest flash of panic in his eyes. Then Greg's calm exterior slides into place. He takes a breath and nods. 'OK. I'm sure it's nothing to worry about. Have you called her?'

'I can't get through.'

The colour drains from his face, but he doesn't flinch. 'Let's sit down, yeah?' He takes her arm and guides her into the sitting room as if she's an old woman barely capable of walking. And for the moment this is exactly what Nula wants. As they sit on the sofa, she clings to his arm. Greg has to shake himself free from her grip in order to place his phone on a cushion and loosen his tie, as if preparing himself for a challenging meeting.

He eyes the wine-stained rug, but manages not to mention it. 'You've tried calling her?'

'I just said so! They should have been home hours ago . . .'

'She didn't mention going anywhere? A change of plan? Some play-date or other . . . ?'

'No. Tuesdays are always the same. Toddler group in the morning, but then playing at home.'

'Of course.' He glances again at the rug. 'First things first. I'll call the hospital, just in case.'

And she watches him pace the room. He is careful not to step in the small puddle of wine as he speaks calmly and politely to various receptionists and gathers the information he needs. No one going by the name Samuel Shaw or Maggie Wichelo has been brought in so far.

Then Greg starts to leave messages for Maggie. Nula sits and listens to the distant ringing tone, the familiar, uncharacteristically jaunty message: 'Hi, you've reached Maggie. Leave a message if you have to!' At first Greg's messages are friendly but authoritative. 'Hi, Maggie. Greg. Call us, OK? Nula's a bit worried.' After ten minutes the messages become openly anxious. 'Hi, Maggie. Please call us. We don't know what to think. It's Greg.' After fifteen minutes they are exasperated. 'Maggie. Greg. What's going on? This is bang out of order.' The vein in Greg's forehead becomes pronounced, as it always does when he's overheated or stressed. It makes Nula think of some cartoon character, blood vessels popping, steam exploding from his ears; she's laughed at him for it many times: 'Blood's up, Greg,' she usually says, pressing a thumb to the soft pipe and grimacing. Looking at it now, she wants to smash it down, iron it out with her fist. Greg is calm in a crisis. He prides himself on it. She cannot allow him to be otherwise.

Finally Greg's messages become pleas, his voice wheedling.

'Whatever this is about, we can sort it, OK? Even if it's about me. OK? There's no problem, Maggie. No problem. Just call. OK?'

Nula sits, still in her work shoes, watching. She can smell her husband now. The stewed-meat smell from his armpits makes her nauseous. 'What did you mean,' she asks: '"Even if it's about me"?'

His phone is still attached to his ear. He holds up a hand for quiet.

'Don't shush me,' she says. 'Tell me what you meant.'

He frowns at the screen, shakes his head. 'I'm just trying to get her to call.' His thumb swipes at his phone. 'Is she on Facebook?'

Nula closes her eyes. 'Of course she's not, Greg.'

Greg shrugs. 'Have you checked? Don't suppose there are many Wichelos.'

'She's not on Facebook.'

'Everyone is, these days.'

'Not Maggie,' says Nula.

Whilst he tries again, Nula slips upstairs. Samuel's cot has been straightened, as always, his toys put away in the boxes stacked on one side of the room. There is no Leggy Monkey on his mattress, but that's not unusual: he often takes the toy with him. Then she opens a drawer and notices it isn't as full as it was this morning. She'd stacked a few ironed T-shirts and trousers in there last night, whilst he was asleep, and they have gone.

Nula runs down the stairs to find Greg on his hands and knees, spreading salt granules over the wine stain. He looks up, and she thinks he's about to tell her, as he always does, that his mother taught him this trick. But something in her face stops him from speaking.

'Some of his clothes have gone,' Nula says. 'I think you should call the police.'

The police arrive. No sirens, but the presence of their car in the street will be enough for the neighbours to presume another break-in. There's one every few months up here. No one will knock on Nula's door to ask, but the car will be registered and they'll all be double-locking tonight, making absolutely sure to set their burglar alarms in the morning.

Without lifting his phone from his ear, Greg answers the door and shows them into the sitting room. Nula takes in the two figures: an older man in baggy jeans, a younger woman in uniform, her jacket bulky and misshapen. The fluorescent strip which says 'Police' on her breast is grubby and makes Nula think of Samuel's blue waterproof jacket, which needs a wash. Has Maggie remembered to take it? It's summer, but you never know. She feels a sudden urge to check, and stands to do so, but the older man holds out a hand and says, 'No need to get up, Mrs Shaw. Detective Mike Walters. Let's get straight on to some questions, shall we? We want to get this sorted out as quickly as we can.'

Nula does not move. 'I have to check something . . .' she begins, then falters.

'Tea?' Greg offers, a hand on Nula's shoulder.

Detective Walters shakes his head. 'This is Constable Finch.'

Nula looks at the woman. Pale-blonde hair, a flat, open face. Too young, she thinks, to have children of her own.

'Can we sit down?' asks Detective Walters.

Nula sinks into her chair. Greg sits on the edge of the sofa with the police. 'Sorry,' he begins, still looking at his phone, 'I've got to keep this on in case . . .'

'Of course,' says Detective Walters.

'I'm sure she's going to call. All this is probably a panic over a flat battery!' As he places his phone on the arm of the sofa, Nula notices that her husband's hand is trembling.

Detective Walters nods, but does not smile. He dabs at his pointed nose with a tissue. 'We just have to ask you some questions—'

'They've only been gone a few hours. Bound to be a rational explanation,' Greg continues, almost to himself. 'A mix-up. Communication failure. That's all this is.'

'Can we start at the beginning? Your son and his nanny weren't here when you arrived home, is that correct, Mrs Shaw?'

'Yes.'

'And what time was that?'

'Around six-thirty.'

'And who saw Samuel last? Was it you, Mrs Shaw?'

'Yes.'

'And when was that?'

'This morning,' Nula says. 'His nanny, Maggie, arrived for work at eight-thirty. I handed Samuel over to her, and went back to bed.'

'You didn't go to work?' Walters has a pair of very fashionable spectacles, too large for his thin face.

'It had been a bad night.'

'We've had a lot of those,' said Greg.

'Bad as in . . . ?'

'Lots of waking. He's having nightmares – dreams – at the moment.'

Walters frowns at his notebook. 'And what happened then? After you went back to bed?'

'Nothing. That is, I got up—'

'When was this?'

'Ten. Ten-fifteen.'

'You weren't working today, Mrs Shaw?'

'It's Wichelo. I kept my name.'

'Oh. Like Maggie's?'

'Yes. We're cousins.'

Detective Walters looks at Greg. 'You didn't mention that on the phone.'

'It didn't seem important,' said Greg. 'Is it important?'

'I don't know.'

Nula has an urge to tell Detective Walters to get his grubby jeans and stupid glasses off her sofa and go out to look for her son. If only these people would leave, Maggie and Samuel might come back. What if Maggie arrives to find a police car at the house? Won't that make her panic? Won't that delay Samuel's safe return?

'So what happened after you got up, er, Ms Wichelo?'

'I went downstairs—'

'Were your son and his nanny still in the house?'

'No.'

'That didn't strike you as unusual.'

'No. Maggie always takes Samuel to toddler group on Tuesday mornings. So I got my things together and I left for work.'

'She didn't leave a note?'

Nula shakes her head.

'Anything gone missing?'

'Some clothes. Trousers, a couple of T-shirts . . . And she took his changing bag. But she always takes that.'

'Right.' Detective Walters scribbles something on his pad, then says, 'Constable Finch will take a look around, if that's OK. Perhaps you could show her the way, Mr Shaw?'

Greg flashes a glassy smile at no one in particular. Nula almost reaches for his hand, wanting him to stay with her, not to leave her alone. Instead she says, feebly, 'Don't be too long' as he leaves the room.

Detective Walters lowers his voice. 'Have you noticed anything unusual about Maggie, lately, Ms Wichelo? Anything at all?'

Nula almost smiles. 'Most things about Maggie are unusual.'

Walters raises his eyebrows.

'What I mean is, she can strike people as a bit odd. Bit of a loner, as my mother-in-law describes her.'

'Is that how you would describe her?'

'Lonely, maybe. She's a good nanny to Samuel. She's done wonders . . . We've always said it. She's very dedicated.'

'And that's never caused a problem?'

'Why should it?'

'No reason. Some mothers might feel threatened.'

Nula pauses. 'There's never been a problem between me and Maggie,' she says, her throat constricting.

In her study, Nula sits bathed in the blue glow of her laptop. Detective Walters has asked her for a recent picture of Maggie and Samuel. She opens a large file of photographs containing all the images Maggie has emailed her over the past year and a half. It is rare for her to look at these photographs. For a few weeks Maggie had sent a couple each day, and whilst Nula knew her intention was reassurance, after a while the frequency with which the photos arrived in her in-box became rather irritating. She didn't say anything to Maggie. She just stopped replying, and soon the emails became less frequent.

She clicks on 0079, and there is Samuel, grinning at the

top of a slide, a trail of snot running from his nose to his upper lip. Quickly, she opens another. 0086. She has no recollection of this one. It is of Maggie and Samuel at Whipsnade Zoo, where she took him for a treat. It must have been taken by a passing stranger. Nula imagines Maggie asking some man to take the picture, perhaps not exactly pretending to be Samuel's mother, but not saying the word 'nanny', either. Such an unappealing term. Who would want, these days, to define herself as a nanny? Nula has often wished there were some other way of describing Maggie's job, something that isn't a throwback to that long-dead era of governesses and housemaids, something with fewer connotations of servitude and middle-class assumption. But there is not. There is no word at all, in fact, which perfectly describes Maggie's relationship with Nula's son.

In the picture, the two of them are standing in front of the penguin pool. Everything in the photo looks slightly grey – the light is odd; perhaps it's late afternoon. Even Samuel looks grey and tired, dwarfed by his overlarge new coat. Maggie is crouching beside him, arms around his waist, saying something in his ear. She was often in this position. It had sometimes felt to Nula that she had to stoop to hear her own child, whereas Maggie was always already there, at his level, alert to the slightest nuance in his voice or expression. When she felt this way, Nula told herself that she was being neurotic; that it was Maggie's job, as a professional child carer, to be attuned to Samuel. It's different, she had told herself, when it is not your job, but your duty. As she zooms in on the picture, she flinches at that word, at the thought that this is how she has viewed motherhood. Perhaps that's what's been wrong, all along.

Tears come to her eyes. She makes Samuel's face bigger and

bigger on the screen so that she can see the smear of yoghurt at the corner of his mouth, the line of dried snot below his nose, the crust of sleepy dust in the corner of his bright eye. And she thinks: I should have been there to wipe those things away; and she cries some more, and she enlarges the photo again and again until her son becomes a blur of pixels.

An hour later, after the police have left with a copy of the picture, Lilly and Jeff arrive. When Nula answers the door, her mother-in-law's cheeks are as white as paper; she is without a necklace or lipstick. She grips Nula's hands, searches her face. The evening's warmth comes in behind her, intimate and disturbing with its lingering smells of barbecue and suncream.

'Greg called us,' says Lilly. 'He was in such a state . . .' Then she's in tears and Greg and Jeff are leading her into the kitchen, offering her brandy, a chair. Nula remains on the doorstep, breathing in the darkening night. She watches the couple across the street – Sarah and Finn Draycott – as they unload their sleepy children, Josh and Eve, from the back of the Mercedes estate. Finn balances bags from his fingers, car keys in his teeth, slams the boot shut with an elbow. Sarah steers the children into the house. The lights go on. As Sarah reaches up to the window to let down the blinds, her eyes meet Nula's and she raises a hand, briefly, and gives a small, sympathetic smile. Nula finds herself pretending not to have seen Sarah. She closes the door and leans against it. Could her neighbour know, already? Of course not. But something in that wave, that look, makes Nula's heart race. If Sarah knows, then the whole street will know that Samuel and Maggie have gone. The whole street will know that Nula has been careless enough to let her little boy disappear.

Not long after she'd had Samuel, Nula had met Sarah Draycott in the street. Her neighbour was running home after dropping Josh and Eve at school and was dressed in pink trainers and an expensively plain tracksuit. Her red hair was pulled back and her face was shining healthily with perspiration. She had greeted Nula warmly, with a moist kiss on both cheeks, and had leaned enthusiastically over Samuel's pram. For once he was sleeping soundly, and Nula tried not to worry about Sarah's proximity and heavy breath. It was, after all, fairly unlikely that a droplet of sweat would wake a baby.

'He's utterly beautiful,' Sarah exclaimed. 'You must be so proud.'

Nula suddenly felt like weeping, because it was true, but she'd never said so herself, and did not expect anyone else to say it.

'How's the feeding going?' What every other mother asked. A way of finding out whether you were breast or bottle.

'Good,' said Nula. 'Fine.' What she always said. A way of not giving this information.

'Getting *some* sleep?' Sarah grimaced, laughed.

'Not much.'

'Great, though, isn't it? I mean. Amazing,' said Sarah. 'I've never looked back.'

Nula wanted to agree. She knew, even then, that Sarah had chosen to be a stay-at-home mum, giving up her teaching career to look after her kids. But Nula also wanted to tell Sarah that she was finding the whole thing exhausting, boring, difficult; that, every day, she longed to be back at work. Most of all, she wanted not to cry in front of her neighbour. And so she smiled thinly and walked on, mumbling something about it being time for a feed.

*

Inside the house, Lilly, Greg and Jeff are all sitting around the kitchen table, drinking brandy and staring at Greg's phone. When Nula comes in, Lilly stands. 'They'll find him, love. They will find him,' she says, gripping Nula's hands once more. Nula senses that Lilly wants to hold her, and she pulls away. 'I need to look for something,' she says. 'Sorry.' And she goes upstairs, knowing none of them will follow her. None of them will want to face the monster that is a mother whose child has disappeared.

She slips into Samuel's bedroom, closes the door behind her and sinks to the floor. She should, she thinks, be crying now; the sight of her son's bedroom should be enough to have her wailing. Looking at the wooden cot, the stacked boxes of toys, the basket of stuffed animals, the framed poster of *Where the Wild Things Are*, the rug with its pastel-coloured boat on a fish-infested sea, the huge wooden fire-engine that Jeff made for Samuel on his second birthday, she realises that, when she thinks of Samuel, she doesn't think of him in this room. She thinks of him playing downstairs, building brick towers, racing trucks. She thinks of him playing with Maggie.

Despite Nula's confidence that she would be left alone, Lilly appears. Nula does not move or look up from her position on the floor. Her mother-in-law stands close to her, in silence, staring at Samuel's fire-engine. Nula had stowed it up here, rather than in the sitting room where most of his toys were. She'd known that, as it made no sounds and had no buttons to press or levers to pull, her son's interest in it would be limited. It was Greg who'd loved it. He'd immediately admired the craftsmanship that had gone into the vehicle, the smoothness of its finish, the old-fashioned brass bell and ladder.

'You know,' Lilly says, 'I was never sure about Maggie. She's such a *quiet* little thing.'

Nula closes her eyes. She is only surprised this conversation hasn't taken place earlier.

'She's a long way from her family, isn't she, down here?'

'Wales isn't so far away, Lilly,' says Nula. 'It's practically in the British Isles. And her dad's somewhere near here—'

'Bit of a loner, I've always thought,' Lilly continues. 'And doesn't she dress oddly? All that black.'

'What is it that you want to say?'

'Nothing. I don't mean anything . . .' Lilly gives a cough, and her voice becomes strangled. 'It's just . . . I blame myself – I should have offered to have Samuel for you, when you went back to work.'

Nula swallows. 'I didn't want you to have him,' she says, simply. 'We've been very happy with Maggie. She is – was – wonderful with Sammy.'

There is a long pause. As Lilly cries quietly, Nula clenches and unclenches her fists and feels herself on the brink of screaming.

Finally Lilly gives a sigh, sniffs and seems to compose herself. Nula presumes her mother-in-law will go now. Instead, Lilly strides across to Samuel's fire-engine, pats its shiny surface and says, 'Jeff made Greg a car when he was small. He spent months on it in his workshop. A replica of an Aston Martin. Greg barely looked at it. I felt so sorry for his father.' Her voice wavers again. 'It's hard for fathers, though, isn't it? With sons.'

If Lilly doesn't leave soon, Nula may have to slap her mother-in-law very hard.

'It's simple for us. We know they're ours and we just . . . get on with it. I always found it easy, with Greg. He was such a caring boy, and I knew all I had to do was love him. I didn't give it a second thought.'

Nula stares at her mother-in-law.

'She'll bring him back,' says Lilly, nodding. 'No woman in her right mind would steal another woman's son. Would she?'

Nula has no answer to this question other than a long, loud wail.

At eight-thirty the next morning, Maggie and Samuel are asleep. With one hand on the child's side, she dreams of nothing.

'Maggie.'

For a moment she's back in her Oxford flat, waking to an empty space and the ghost of her brother's presence.

'Maggie?'

She opens her eyes.

He's put on weight. There are creases around his dark eyes, flecks of grey in his stubble, like ash.

'Joe,' she says.

'Who's this, then?'

She looks at Samuel and can think of no response.

Their eyes meet and he says, 'Been a while, hasn't it, little one?'

When he's handed her a mug of very brown tea, made himself comfortable on the sofa, filled a cigarette paper with Amber Leaf, rolled it with skilful fingers and taken a few puffs, he says, 'So', as if he's about to begin asking her to explain, but when she looks at him he lapses into silence.

She has left Samuel sleeping in the bedroom. For so long she's wanted him to meet Joe, but now he is actually here it doesn't seem the right moment. And she'd forgotten her brother smoked. She will have to ask him to extinguish his cigarette when the boy's in the room. She thinks of Nula's habit of going outside for what she calls 'the occasional indulgence'. Her slightly lascivious wink as she utters the phrase. The way she sprays herself with Chanel afterwards.

'What have you been up to?' she tries, brightly.

He takes a long drag, blows smoke from the corner of his mouth. 'This and that.'

A lengthy, snorting snore comes from the bedroom. The smell of Samuel's dirty nappy has followed them. She knows better than to wake him to change it, though.

'Noisy, isn't he?' says Joe.

'Always,' she says. 'Especially when he's sleeping.'

He sips his tea. 'Maggie—'

'Yes?'

'What the hell's going on, then?' He strokes his earlobe in a way which makes her realise that he has come to look and sound like their father. The tics and movements Joe once parodied have become natural to him.

'I've come to see you,' she says. 'Can't I come to see my own brother?'

'OK,' he says. 'All right.'

'Look,' she begins. And the line that comes into her head is: *I've brought you this boy. Now we can be a family again.* But the words seem too ridiculous to utter, and Joe is not looking at her, and she's confused by his voice. He has acquired a bit of a Welsh accent. And so she says, 'I can't tell you everything. Not yet. But can we stay here for a while?'

He takes a gulp from his mug, then sets it on the floor. 'Sounds a bit mysterious.'

'We just need somewhere to stay for a bit.'

He looks out of the window. 'Thing is . . . I'm not here much, lately. I just popped back to get some stuff. Half-day today. I'm over at Nic's, mostly.'

'I thought we could spend some time together.'

He nods and smokes his cigarette in silence.

Samuel lets out another long snore.

'Mum told you about Nic?' he asks.

She looks at the floor.

'If you're up here, you could go see Mum, couldn't you? You could pop up to the house?'

She puts a hand over her mouth, and it's enough to make him change tack.

'Yeah. Well. Up to you. But I know she wants to talk—'

'She writes,' says Maggie. 'And I read her letters. So I knew.'

'Right.'

'Is she nice? Nic?'

Joe seems to think about this. 'Nice enough.'

Maggie nods in what she hopes is an understanding way.

'Does Mum know about . . . the boy?' Joe asks.

'Not yet.'

'Mummy!' Samuel shouts.

Maggie's eyes meet her brother's.

'You know,' he says, grinding out his cigarette in a saucer, 'I always knew you'd come back. Didn't think it would take this long, though. And I didn't think you'd be bringing your *kid*.'

All she can manage is a very quiet 'Yeah'.

'Let's meet him, then,' Joe says, standing.

On the threshold of the bedroom, he catches her arm. 'Do you see Dad?'

'Not much,' she says, wishing she could say *Not at all*. It would hurt her brother less if their father had failed her, too.

Since leaving Anglesey, he's lived alone in a small flat near his mother just outside Oxford. Every other Saturday he meets his daughter for cod, chips and peas and a glass of Soave. Lately he's suggested they meet somewhere else, where the customers aren't all over sixty-five. After years of looking after his own mother, he's had enough of old people. You could have looked after *us*, Maggie thought, instead of running away. But she'd smiled and said it was a good idea.

The sight of Joe makes Samuel stop shouting for his mother.

'Who are you then?' Joe says.

Samuel looks uncertainly at Maggie, then holds out his arms.

'Sammy,' says Maggie, picking him up, 'meet your Uncle Joe.' It seems pointless to pretend. She means to tell Joe everything, when the time is right, so why not say the boy's real name?

Joe lets out a laugh. '*Uncle Joe,*' he says. 'That's me, I suppose.' He offers a hand and the boy grips his finger and squeezes, hard.

'Nice to meet you, little man,' says Joe.

'Lidd man,' repeats Samuel.

'I'd better change him,' Maggie says, reaching for the nappies and wipes.

She nods towards a thin brown towel hanging on the back of a chair. 'Put that on the bed for me?'

Joe does as he's asked, but turns away at the sight of Samuel's shit-filled nappy, holding his nose. Samuel laughs, and copies the gesture.

When she's cleaned the boy up, she kisses his cheeks and presents him again to Joe, holding him on her hip for her brother to admire.

'Who do you look like?' asks Joe, narrowing his eyes. 'Mummy or Daddy?'

'Joe—' warns Maggie.

'Daddy!' shouts Samuel, looking at Maggie. 'Where Daddy?'

'In Oxford,' she says.

'See Daddy?'

She's aware of Joe watching her, wanting to know. She had told herself that, whatever happened, she would not lie to Samuel. She might not tell him exactly what was going on, but she would answer his questions as directly as she could. But now Joe is listening, and Samuel catches hold of her cheek and angles her face towards his in an effort to squeeze an answer from her. 'See Daddy?' he asks again.

'Soon,' she says. 'Soon, my love.'

Joe goes to the Co-op and fetches some food. After they've eaten a late breakfast, Maggie lets her brother take Samuel onto the beach. From the boathouse door, she watches Joe help the boy along the stones. They stay close to the house, both of them looking back at her frequently, as if they can't quite believe she's still there. Joe points out the brown jewel of a dead jellyfish to Samuel, who pokes at it with a stick. Maggie starts to shout some warning at them, then stops herself. She tells herself that she must trust Joe. Her brother may be the only one she can trust. He picks up an empty crab shell and offers it to Samuel, who examines it carefully, bringing it close to his face and sniffing it. Joe laughs, then holds Samuel's hand in the air and waves it and the crab at her.

She waves back, thinking Joe would make a good father. Samuel has taken a shine to him, and already Joe talks to him in the clear, straightforward way that Maggie likes. She hates it when adults use supercilious tones with children, something Greg often does with his son. 'Oh, it's a BLUE train, is it? I could've sworn it was turquoise . . .' *Wink, wink.* Often she's wanted to point out to Greg that his tone requires another adult as an audience, and it can only distance, rather than involve, his child.

Watching her brother grab Samuel's arm to prevent him stumbling on the stones, she remembers the time Joe caught her hand on the groyne. Had he really held on then, or had she imagined it? When she'd had his approval, did she also have his love? She remembers how cool and large and unfamiliar his fingers had felt. She had hardly dared to hold on, although she'd wanted to clasp his hand and never let go.

And, much later, Nula's fingers were tight on the back of Joe's neck. Maggie had seen them lying together near Plas Coch. She had cycled all the way there one evening, after Nula had mentioned Joe's interest in the place. He'd looked small then, compared to their cousin, his legs skinny, his shoulders barely visible beneath the shield of her arms, his blue T-shirt pulled up to show his pale torso. Maggie's first crazy thought had been that it was a game; Nula was pretending to gobble Joe up and soon they would roll away from one another, laughing. But as she'd watched them together, it dawned on Maggie that Nula was Joe's now, and Joe was Nula's.

'Joe!' she calls. 'Sammy!'

They look at her.

'Come back in now.'

The wind has turned suddenly fierce. It seems to blow Joe and Samuel back to the boathouse. Joe carries Samuel on his shoulders, and the boy drums the top of Joe's head in delight. 'UP!' he shouts, 'UP!' Stepping from the door to greet them, Maggie laughs, has to hook the hair from her mouth, and is almost knocked sideways by the strength of the gust and by her joy in seeing Samuel carried by her brother.

At the threshold Samuel grasps Joe's ears and pulls, not wanting to dismount. As Maggie holds the door open, Joe is helpless. The door is too low for Samuel to remain on his shoulders, but Samuel, refusing to come down, clutches at Joe's nose and almost falls. Joe cannot move forward or back, for fear of dropping the boy, but he is yelping in pain now at Samuel's elated pinches.

'Sammy!' Maggie scolds. 'No!'

Samuel starts at the sharpness in her voice, and begins to cry.

Released from pain, Joe manages to dislodge the boy from his shoulders and holds him out to Maggie, but Samuel shakes his head. Does Joe smirk as he cradles Samuel to his chest? Maggie isn't sure. To hide the shock of Samuel's rejection, she busies herself with boiling the kettle, preparing hot drinks.

Joe places Samuel on the rug and gives him an old copy of *Practical Photography* to rip up.

'Don't you want to keep that?' Maggie asks.

Her brother collapses on the sofa. 'I don't go in for that stuff any more.'

'But you're still at the camera shop?'

'And that's exactly why I don't go in for it.' He stares at his lap and flicks an imaginary piece of fluff from his jeans.

She brings them tea. 'Got any toys you could bring over?'

'You didn't bring any?' asks Joe.

Samuel destroys an article on maintaining Fuji stock, and throws the shreds over his head.

'We had to leave in a bit of a hurry,' she says, placing her mug on a high shelf and sitting beside Samuel on the floor. 'It was a bit . . . tricky.'

'There's a Pound Shop in Bangor. We could get him some stuff there.'

Yes, she thinks. We could. We really could. She imagines the scene: she and Joe holding Samuel's hands as they do one-two-three-and-swing down the aisles of the Pound Shop. Samuel's excitement at being let free in a place filled entirely with plastic tat. It would be a delight, and a torture. But, of course, it cannot be.

She rips a page from the magazine, then rolls it into a tight ball and throws it at Joe, hitting him on the chest. Without hesitating, he picks it up and throws it back at her. It bounces off her forehead.

'Goal,' he says.

Samuel demands, 'MINE!'

Maggie hands him the paper ball. He tries a throw, but the ball travels no further than his own feet.

'So,' says Joe, looking at his watch. 'Didn't you want to talk . . . ?'

'Yes,' she says, giving the ball to Samuel again. 'But . . .' She glances at the boy. 'Maybe when he's in bed.'

'Come on, Maggie. I've got to get to work soon. It would be nice to know *something* about what you've been up to, all these years.'

She had meant to tell him sooner. She'd meant to explain, straight away. Back in Oxford it had all seemed possible, but now, with her brother sitting above her, blowing on his tea just as their father always does, she cannot think of any way to begin.

Samuel has started eating the ball of paper. Holding him

tightly around the waist, Maggie claws the stuff from his mouth, flicking tendrils of soggy print from her fingers.

'Can you stay?' she asks Joe. 'Just for tonight?'

'I'm not sure . . .'

'The sofa's not too bad . . .' Maggie says. 'We could catch up. Properly.'

Samuel coughs out the last of the paper and throws his arms around Joe's legs.

Joe puts a hand on the boy's head. 'All right,' he says.

All afternoon Maggie waits for her brother's return from work. Joe is coming back, she tells herself; everything will be all right because Joe is coming back. She considers another play on the beach but, seeing a few dog walkers on the shore, thinks better of it. Instead she lets Samuel mess about with the ripped-up magazines. They toss them at each other and all around the boathouse. They lob them at the walls, stuff them down the back of the sofa and into the cracks between the floorboards, then they soak them in the sink. Samuel becomes so excited by this storm of paper that he can't stop moving. He jumps and rolls on the rug, bounces on the bed, climbs on the back of the sofa, all the while singing a tuneless song. His face is crimson and his skin gleams with sweat. Maggie lets him do as he likes. As he chucks soggy paper over her head and tries to shove it down her top, shrieking with laughter, she starts to laugh, too. And then she cannot stop laughing, because she's done it – she is actually here, with Samuel, and Joe is coming back. She collapses on the floor, holding her sides, and an ecstatic Samuel throws himself on top of her. When she senses his hysteria might turn into tears, she picks him up and runs to the bed with him, where they hide together under the covers. She shines a torch into the darkness and tells him stories. He loves these tales, the ones she makes up about the crocodile and the moose who catch a bus into town without realising the bus is made of chocolate. Halfway there the bus melts and they have to lick up the remains. Maggie mimes the licking, running her tongue along Samuel's hands, prompting him to do the same to her.

Later, after she has tidied up and given Samuel his tea, Maggie sits him on the draining board to flannel him down. He shivers a bit at first, unused to this type of bathing and to the roughness of the old fabric, but his face lights up when she allows him to pour water from his sippy cup over himself and the sink. Then she tucks him in bed, surrounds him with pillows, sings and rubs his back until he is asleep. It doesn't take long – it has been another exhausting day. She tells herself that soon he will be used to these new surroundings, these new routines.

As she waits for Joe to return with the fish and chips that he's promised, Maggie considers looking at the painting again. But she doesn't want to disturb Samuel. So she paces the sitting room, wondering what to do. She looks at the armchair and tells herself *I am tired and hungry and I should sit down*, but, like Samuel this afternoon, she cannot stop moving. She must get on with something straight away, otherwise she will have to think about what she's done. Until now, she has thought only of getting Samuel out of the Shaws' house, out of Oxford, onto the island, into the boathouse. This afternoon she'd been glad that they had made it. They'd got this far, they were together. They were happy. They were laughing. That had seemed to be enough. She had told herself it was enough.

But now Maggie must work out what to do next.

She grabs the balding scouring sponge and wipes the kitchen

table. Joe should be back by now. It should take him only half an hour to get here from Bangor, even in his old Ford van. She goes to the window, looks at the cobalt strait. The tide has come in, its irresistible movement flooding the beach. The water is very close to the boathouse. She can hear it reaching for the wall outside, touching the stones with little kisses and slaps.

Maggie tries to focus instead on Samuel's breathing. We are together, she thinks. We are together. We laughed all afternoon. It is enough. She presses the sponge to the window, trying to wipe away the smears, but can only make them worse.

Kiss, slap, goes the water. Slap, kiss.

What has she done?

She could look at the painting.

But she must not think of that. She must not think of anything.

Move. She must move. She sinks to her knees and begins wiping the floorboards with the sponge. She can make the place fit for Samuel, and for Joe. If she can clean it properly, perhaps she will know what to do next. Fetching a plastic bowl from beneath the sink, she fills it with hot water, then chucks in the last of the Flash. It is a relief to kneel on the floor and delve her hands into the soapy liquid. Inhaling the chemical scent, she scrubs at an uneven board beneath the window. The sponge begins to come apart, leaving stringy balls of green nylon in the water, but she does not stop. She will take the curtains down next, wash them in the sink. They'll dry outside in no time. Then the cupboards will need a going-over. Perhaps she should call Joe's mobile and get him to bring some cleaning supplies, too.

As she's squeezing out the water, she remembers Nula telling her the story of Samuel's birth. *The week before, I couldn't stop hoovering. I even polished the bloody letter box!*

Maggie drops the sponge into the bowl and watches the grimy water shift and resettle. Outside, the strait slaps the wall again.

The front door opens, making her jump. Joe goes to the table in silence. The place fills with the smell of vinegar and hot fat as he throws a carrier bag and his keys on the table. He doesn't acknowledge her in any way. Maggie immediately recognises his mood. Imagining the worst – the police, or Nula, outside – she flies to the window. But the evening is quiet; all she can see is the grey glitter of the strait as the sun goes down.

She waits for Joe to speak.

He focuses not on her, but on the plastic bag as he spits out the words. 'I've just had Mum on the phone. She said the police had been round.'

Maggie puts a hand on the windowsill to steady herself for what's coming.

'They were asking about a little boy who's gone missing. Apparently he's Nula's son. And, apparently, you're his nanny, and you've also gone missing.'

Maggie listens for Samuel's breath. For the breath of the sea.

Still he does not look at her. His lips have shrunk, his chin is drawn inwards. Each cheek is dotted by a small red spot of rage. He raises his voice. 'Since when have you been working for Nula? Were you going to mention that, Maggie? At any point? To any of us?'

'Please don't wake Samuel . . .'

'The fucking *police*, Maggie!'

Maggie screws her wet fingers together. 'It's not as if you ever asked me anything, is it? After I left, when did you call me? Come and see me? You didn't. You were all glad I'd gone.'

Joe looks at her, baffled. 'We're not talking about that. We're talking about the police. Here. Now.'

Hands trembling, Maggie picks up the bowl and empties the dirty water down the sink. 'I would have told you. I would have told you everything, if you'd asked, if you'd *ever* asked—'

Joe stands over her. With obvious effort, he lowers his voice. 'I'm asking you now. Let's start with the boy, shall we? Is that boy in there Nula's son?'

Maggie says nothing. She wrings out the sponge, places what's left of it on the draining board.

Joe spins her round to face him. '*Tell me.*'

Maggie cannot look at his face. 'Did you tell Mum I'm here?' she asks.

He lets out a sound that could be a laugh.

'Joe? Did you tell her?'

He doesn't say anything for a minute. Instead he paces the room, occasionally emitting a strange sound, or kicking a table leg.

Maggie sits at the table and watches him. It will pass, she thinks. This rage will pass. And if he had told her mother, she would be here right now. Wouldn't she?

'Is his name even Samuel?'

She nods. 'I meant to change it, but I couldn't.'

Joe leans across the table and yells so loudly she jumps. 'You're not even any good at this, are you? I've got no idea what you're up to, but you've fucked it all up! They'll be here soon, you know that, don't you?'

With a shaking hand, Maggie reaches inside the plastic bag and manages to put a chip in her mouth. It is tepid now, and hard, but she chews, swallows, then takes another. 'We should eat,' she says, very quietly. 'We should eat and we should think.'

Joe covers his eyes with his hands.

'Joe,' she says, 'we need to keep our strength up.' She pushes the bag of chips over to him. 'Please eat.'

It is what their mother would say. *Keep your strength up.* As if strength was an innate part of you, and all you had to do was fuel your body and out it would pour, the power that had been there all along.

'Joe, I had to take him,' Maggie says. 'He needs me. And I thought this would be the best place. Here, with you—'

'Oh Jesus!' says Joe. And he sounds like a frightened child.

Maggie takes this as a good sign. A sign that perhaps she can explain and he will understand. She swallows another lump of cold potato and begins. 'Nula doesn't want him, Joe. She doesn't deserve him. It's just like before. She didn't want—'

'OK,' says Joe, reaching for his coat. 'Let's go.'

'What?'

'I know a place. We have to go. Right now.'

'Samuel's asleep—'

'Now!' He grabs her arm, pulls her to her feet. Then they're face-to-face, Maggie rubbing her arm and trying not to cry with pain, Joe filled with dramatic, angry plans, and she is there again, in the rooms of their early childhood, him the teacher and her his pupil. And it is a relief of sorts to be yanked to her feet and told what to do by her elder brother; it's a relief to believe that his will is stronger, that he is better equipped, that he is the one on top of the desk, pointing his ruler and barking instructions.

'Get the boy,' he says. 'And get in the van.'

Joe said there wasn't time for the car seat, so Maggie clasps Samuel on her lap. The boy sits upright, enthralled by being in his first-ever van, digging his elbows into Maggie's chest as he tries to reach up and see more. He would love, Maggie knows, to sit on Joe's lap, to grasp the wheel and steer his own course along this deserted road. Maggie managed to put a cardigan over his pyjamas and throw a few bits of food, some nappies and clothes into the changing bag before her brother accelerated away from the boathouse. He told her to leave her car where it was; he would deal with it later. The important thing was to get somewhere else. He did not use the word *hide*.

They speed down the lane towards the main road. At every bump, Samuel giggles. It's getting darker now and the headlamps flash up at the dense trees, reminding Maggie of the stageset for *Babes in the Wood*, which she and Joe had seen together in Oxford when they were children: those dark painted trees hanging overhead like black flames, threatening all hell within their branches. She expects ghostly animals to leap before them. None do. Nothing, it seems, will interrupt the path of Joe's van.

Once on the A-road Samuel's eyelids waver in the half-light until he relaxes completely in Maggie's arms, his head searching for the soft place between her breast and shoulder. Finding it, he slumps against her. 'Sleep,' she whispers into his hair.

Joe squints into the grey shapes of the road ahead. Maggie has no idea where they are; Joe knows the island much better than she does. They have been driving for fifteen minutes before she asks where they are going.

Joe does not respond.

She doesn't feel she can ask anything else.

After a series of narrow lanes they reach a patch of woodland, where Joe parks the van by a gate. 'Carry him,' he grunts. 'The road doesn't go any further.'

As soon as he opens the door for her, she smells and hears

the sea. A piny saltiness fills her lungs and makes her want to cry because this is not a holiday, as the scent suggests. Hoisting the moist, sleeping boy onto her hip, she follows her brother as he leads them into the pines. Joe walks fast, and it's difficult to keep up; Samuel asleep is a dead weight and she has to stop frequently and hoist him up again, being careful not to wake him. Branches creak and swish overhead. Ferns and grasses brush her hands. Even in the twilight the undergrowth is loud with the incessant drone of insects. Her arms and back are aching, but she daren't ask Joe to carry Samuel. The trees become thicker, the ground more uneven. She stumbles on a tree root and has to stop again and transfer Samuel to her other hip. Joe strides on without looking back, Samuel's changing bag slapping his leg. He says, 'Not much further' and she manages to keep going until the trees clear a little, and suddenly they are right at the island's edge, the silver sea glaring back at them.

'Round here,' says Joe, and they crunch along the sand to another patch of pine trees. Joe holds back some branches and shines a torch, and there it is: a tiny caravan.

Inside, it is surprisingly cosy, even if it does smell of wet wool and ancient air freshener. Joe snaps on a battery lamp, revealing the extent of the place: one room with a bed/sofa, a hob and sink; but someone has taken pains to prettify it, hanging frilled curtains decorated with a strawberry print and placing a few matching cushions on the bed. Maggie manages to keep Samuel asleep as she lays him on the mattress. Joe flings across a blanket from the corner cupboard, then pulls the curtains closed. Maggie lies next to Samuel, who has begun to stir, and strokes his back. Joe stays close to the door, ready to leave. He tries to speak, but she shushes him, pointing at the boy. Once she is sure Samuel is deeply asleep, she sits up and whispers, 'Whose is this?'

'Nic's.' He rubs his face.

'Does she know we're here?'

'What do you think?' A look at his watch. 'Christ. It's late.'

Maggie glances round. 'Where will you sleep?'

'In my own bed. I'll come back tomorrow. And by then you'll have a plan.'

'Joe, I had to take him—'

'I don't want to hear it.'

She grabs his hand and peers at his tired face. 'Nula's getting rid of me, because she can't stand that I'm closer to Sammy, better with him . . . And his dad is such a creep, always trying it on . . .' Maggie can hear the hollowness of her explanations. Her words seem to drop to the floor, already meaningless. But she can't stop talking. 'And they're . . . they're unfit parents, Joe. I had to take him.'

He stares at her, bewildered. After a moment he says, 'You'll have a plan about how you can get that boy back to his mother with the minimum of trouble for you, and zero trouble for me, OK?'

'He needs me.'

'If you don't have a plan, you'll be on your own. I'll call the police. Do you understand?'

There's a pause. Maggie has registered the exasperation in her brother's voice and, because it is easier than arguing, she nods.

'Good.' He closes the door behind him.

She leaves the battery lamp on, not wanting Samuel to wake to another unfamiliar, dark place. It buzzes and flickers, gives off a cold, greenish light. But it is better than nothing. Samuel sleeps, his small face a pale circle that she runs her finger around, thinking of how soft, how unformed, he is; how good he has been; how he hasn't once, yet, asked for his mother – not in any very serious way – and this must mean that she was right to bring him here.

Tomorrow she can talk to Joe again, and he might change his mind, especially if he spends another day with the two of them.

The caravan rocks slightly in the wind. The curtains give a shiver. Still in her summer coat, she lies on the mattress and tries to breathe in time with the boy. In, out. In, out. In, out. But his breathing is faster than hers, more urgent, despite the thumping of her heart, the racing of her thoughts. And she gives up and wraps herself around him, a frame to his centre; and, after a long time, she sleeps.

It is six-thirty in the morning and for the last hour Nula has been standing at the bay window in her sitting room, watching the street. Since Samuel disappeared two days ago, she has been wondering if this is what she has secretly wished for. It is, must be, her fault that he has gone, because there were times, many times during the first nine months of his life, when she wished someone would take him from her, just – she reassures herself – for a few moments, just so she could sit and think of nothing for minutes at a time, or read a book, or walk out of the house alone, without knowing where she was going, and could meet another adult without children, perhaps a man, a man who would look into her eyes and listen to the words coming out of her mouth.

After her return to work, she'd felt better. And what does that mean? She is, she reminds herself, a woman who wanted to be away from her child. She is a woman who needed someone else to care for her son because she was unable, unwilling, to do so herself. What does that make her?

There are many women, after all, who have killed their own children. Up to half the women in Broadmoor have killed their own children. She had read that somewhere once, and now cannot stop thinking about it. Who were they, these women? Why didn't anyone talk about them? Did they wake up one warm June morning, the street almost silent apart from the rumble of an approaching rubbish truck, and find their children gone? Was there a moment of uncertainty? Did they, like her, not quite know if they had brought this about themselves?

Another magpie flies past. So many of them on this street. Greg salutes each and every one. She's told him: don't give them respect. It just encourages them. Makes them feel welcome when they are not.

She watches Sarah Draycott wrench back her thick flowered curtains, wearing only her pink bra (why do you still notice such things, she chides herself, when your son is gone?), and she shrinks from the window, fearful that Sarah will see her there and judge her behaviour inappropriate. Should mothers who have lost sons stand and look out of windows? Shouldn't they be wailing in the street? Or conducting their own hunt for the child? Probably Sarah has already judged her for having employed a nanny in the first place. Perhaps such an act was all the encouragement Maggie needed to take Samuel. Was there something in her own behaviour or expression that said: for God's sake, take him off my hands? Can't you see I'm desperate? Take him from me. Release me.

Why else would this happen to her?

Later that morning, Detective Walters comes to the house to ask Nula the same questions again.

She is alone and doesn't offer Walters a drink of any kind. Greg has gone out, saying they needed bread and it was pointless, wasn't it, this hanging about. Nula hardly heard his excuses, and felt no urge to stop him leaving.

Once Walters has parked himself on her sofa, he touches the rim of his glasses and says, 'When I spoke with your husband yesterday, he said that you might believe he had an affair with your son's nanny.'

Nula blinks. It is the first time anyone has spoken this thought aloud.

'He claims that this is not the case, but he says,' Walters takes his notepad from his pocket, flicks through some pages and begins to read, '*Nula probably thinks I was having a thing with Maggie. But I wasn't. I'm not.*'

'Well,' says Nula. 'There you are.'

Walters gives a small cough and settles back into the cushions, as if for the duration. 'Why would your husband say such a thing, Ms Wichelo?'

'Perhaps because he wanted you to convey that information to me.'

'So is it your opinion that your husband was having an affair with Maggie?'

Nula sighs. 'Maybe. Yes. I don't know . . .' She grabs a handful of her own hair. 'It's not something I can really think about right now . . . You must see that.'

'We're finding it tough to progress, Ms Wichelo, without more information about your son's nanny, and what her motivations for taking your son might be.'

'If she's taken him,' says Nula.

Walters makes a little steeple with his fingers and peers at her over its arch. 'The two of them were last seen at the toddler group almost forty-eight hours ago. Although we can't rule anything out at this stage, this fact strongly suggests to me that your son's nanny is our prime suspect. I appreciate that this is a difficult thing for you to face, but if she was having an affair with your husband, well, that might explain some things. Mightn't it?'

'Shouldn't you be talking to Greg about this?'

'I'm talking to you, Ms Wichelo.'

'Call me Nula, for God's sake.'

Walters takes off his glasses and pinches the top of his nose.

Nula wonders how much he needs these glasses. He takes them on and off so frequently that they seem more a prop than a necessity.

'OK. Nula. Perhaps we should think about where she might have gone. We know that her mother lives on Anglesey, and we've just found some CCTV footage of the car she hired in a Bangor supermarket car park . . .'

'So she's up there . . . ?' says Nula, sitting up straight. 'If she's up there, why aren't you there, looking for them?'

'We have a team in the area. They've yet to sight the car again, but they have visited Maggie's mother,' Walters states, keeping his eyes on his notepad. 'She says she hasn't seen her daughter for years. There was a . . . rift of some kind. She says she's tried to contact Maggie by letter and phone, but Maggie mostly ignores her efforts and rarely speaks to her.' He looks up. 'Does that sound plausible to you?'

'Possibly. Is Maggie on Anglesey?'

'We don't know yet, Ms Wichelo. The footage is from more than twenty-four hours ago. She could well have left the area by now.' He pauses. 'Any idea about why there was a rift between Maggie and her mother?'

Nula is still trying to process the information about Bangor. 'I'm not sure how any of this is relevant to finding my son . . .'

'We have to explore our best leads. And, at the moment, this is our best lead.' A flicker of irritation passes across his face. 'I'm sure you understand that.'

Nula says nothing.

'Obviously we're keeping an eye on Mrs Wichelo's place, and we'll inform you if there's progress. But, in the meantime, can you think of any reason why Maggie and her mother might not be on speaking terms?'

'I . . . I only know her parents split up when she was about sixteen. Her father lives somewhere near Oxford – but you know that already.'

'Any idea about the cause of the split?'

'None whatsoever.' Which was the truth. Nula's mother had told her about Aunt Fiona and Uncle Alan's divorce. Nula hadn't been very surprised. She'd barely seen them in the same room that summer.

'Can you think of anywhere else she might take him? Any places that were special to her?'

She thinks immediately of Plas Coch, but dismisses it as *her* special place, no one else's. Maggie was not involved in all that. She was too busy learning about art with Ralph to notice. And her father was, as usual, too busy with art to notice anybody else at all, least of all Joe.

She very nearly smiles at the thought of him, even now, even here in front of Detective Walters, even with her boy missing and her husband buying bread as a way of delaying leaving her, she almost smiles. His eyes. She can see them, those big brown doggy eyes that followed her everywhere that summer. His beautiful hair, heavy with curls. His clever hands.

'You'll let us know if you hear anything, of course . . .' Walters says, rising.

'Of course.'

As he's leaving he turns to her and adds, 'We're doing all we can. But we do need your help.' For the first time, Nula can hear a little desperation in his voice.

When Lilly phones, Nula is bundling Samuel's dirty washing into the machine. Keeping busy, Greg says, is important. Daily tasks. Nula has been sitting all morning, first talking to Detective Walters, then watching her phone, and has only just managed to remember this thing she should do. Not wanting to look at her son's clothes too closely, to smell them or to touch them, she bunches a whole load together in a towel and chucks them in the machine.

'I've thought of something,' says Lilly, before saying hello. 'I don't know. I think it might be useful.'

Nula pours laundry liquid into a ball, cradling the phone beneath her chin. This isn't the first time Lilly has called today, but it is the first time Nula has picked up on seeing her mother-in-law's name flash on the screen. 'What?'

'Maggie talked a bit about her brother to me. Joe, I think he's called.'

'And?'

'It's probably nothing. It's just – she told me she missed him. She didn't say things like that, personal things, normally, did she? And I wondered . . .'

'When was this?'

'It was one morning in the park . . .'

'Sorry,' says Nula. 'You'll have to explain. When were you in the park with Maggie?'

Lilly's voice hardens. 'I used to meet her there sometimes. I wanted to see Samuel, and she didn't mind.'

'She never mentioned it.'

A pause. Then: 'It was only a couple of times.'

Nula takes a breath. Doesn't matter. Get to the meat of it. 'So she missed her brother. How does that help us?'

'She said she'd like to take Sammy up there, one day. She said something about needing to make things right, with her brother. I didn't think anything of it, at the time . . .'

Nula drops the Ariel ball onto the floor tiles.

'Do you think I should tell the police?' asks Lilly.

'No need,' says Nula, and hangs up.

She can see him, suddenly. She can see Joe with Samuel. The two of them watched by Maggie. How can she not have thought of it before?

Leaving Samuel's sleeve reaching down to the floor from the wet drum, Ariel leaking all over the floor, Nula grabs her bag from the kitchen table and opens the front door. As she reverses out of the drive, Greg appears, a loaf cradled to his chest. It takes him a moment to realise what's happening, and by the time he holds out a hand to stop her, she's in the road, accelerating towards the T-junction.

For all these years Nula has avoided a return, even in her mind. She'd thought it was enough that she had obliterated the physical evidence of those days. The clinic in Summertown, with its pastel prints of striped deckchairs and fishing boats, should have been the last of it. The absolute last.

But she has to return. And now that she's on the M40, steering wheel gripped in both hands, it feels inevitable that this is how it should be. Inevitable that she has to go back again, that the last of it hasn't even started yet.

As she drives, she stretches her neck and seems to be able to see every detail of the road with immense clarity. The sweep of grimy rain thrown at her by a passing lorry doesn't slow her progress. She clicks the wipers to double speed, checks the clock on the dashboard: 12.20. If she doesn't stop, if she can keep just above the speed limits, she could be there by half-four. She could be there for Samuel's teatime. With a sudden stab in the stomach, she realises she has brought absolutely nothing to offer him. Perhaps she should stop on the way, pick up a special treat: some Pom-Bears, a packet of Buttons. She's never allowed him such things, but now she can hardly remember why. She eyes the fuel gauge: almost a full tank. No need to stop, then, until she is on the island.

She is only just past Birmingham when she realises it's no good. A pain is spreading from her groin into her back. She has no choice but to pull in at the service station to relieve herself. At the last minute she indicates and veers into the left-hand lane, causing a woman in a Saab to flash her headlights furiously. As she drives into the huge car park she almost mounts the kerb and has to tell herself, out loud, to slow down. 'He'll still be there,' she says. 'Maggie won't harm him,' she says. 'God knows what she's up to, but she won't harm him.' She slots the Nissan into a space as close to the service station as possible. Flinging her door wide, she jumps down. The swing of her skirt knocks her bag onto the concrete below. Phone, compact, hairbrush, tampons, lipstick, all slide across the ground. Her compact is immediately crushed under a T-bar shoe. Nula glances up and a woman in her sixties begins to apologise.

Ignoring her, Nula grabs the rest of her stuff and runs towards the automatic doors, leaving the shattered compact, and the woman, behind.

'Rude!' she hears the woman say. But she keeps going.

The warm stench of toilet cleaner and other women's knickers comes up to greet her as she enters the Ladies. She lunges into the nearest cubicle, yanks down her pants and almost cries with relief as the steady stream of piss flows into the pan. For a blissful moment it's enough to have reached the toilet and opened her aching bladder. Soon, though, she's wiping herself hastily, cursing the stringy excuse for toilet roll, readjusting her skirt. She risks the disapproval of several other women by not washing her hands.

Outside the toilet, a fearsome-looking plastic donkey is

rocking a three-year-child old back and forth. A man with his sleeves rolled tightly to his biceps watches the girl, a bored smile stuck to his face. Close to the exit, Nula turns her back on the racks of newspapers. There was a photograph in this morning's paper. One of her and Greg with Samuel at Waddesdon Manor. 'SEARCH FOR MISSING 2 YR OLD & NANNY' ran the headline. Greg squinting at the camera, Nula looking at Samuel, instructing him to smile. They must have got it from her Facebook page. 'HAPPIER DAYS' the caption read. It had slipped through her letter box at seven this morning, and she'd stared at it for a few moments, unable to fully recognise herself, before leaving it where it had landed, splayed on the doormat.

She hesitates beside a bucket of soft toys, her eye caught by a pale-blue monkey with legs almost as long as Leggy Monkey's. Picking it up, she sees it is sporting a violently red plastic hat and has a look of gormless surprise on its face. It seems quite necessary to take it. Leggy Monkey will have to be replaced; it will have been soiled by this whole experience. There is a long queue over at the till, and she has already been delayed by her own clumsiness. So she slips the blue monkey into her bag. His head peeks over the top, but she doesn't stop to try to hide him; she simply lets the doors slide open for her, walks purposefully out onto the tarmac and points her key fob towards the waiting Nissan.

At seven in the morning Maggie wakes to the sight of a huge eye. Wet breath warms her forehead.

'Gee-Gee wake?' Samuel asks, and she remembers where she is, and why. 'Home?' he asks, looking around him, bottom lip trembling. 'Gee-Gee home?'

She clears her throat. 'No, no. Somewhere else now.'

His face crumples. 'Home!' he demands. 'Go home!'

She sits up and tries to put an arm around him, but he moves away.

'This is our . . . holiday home, Samuel,' she tries. 'It's a caravan. Like camping? It's an adventure. A caravan adventure for Gee-Gee and Sammy.'

Samuel studies her, still dangerously close to tears. 'Want Joe.'

'He'll be here. Later. Joe will come back.' She swings her legs from the bed. 'Let's get you some milk, shall we?'

It is best, she's learned, to give him no time for tears. To press on to the next thing, regardless. But as she pours what's left of the milk into his bottle, sniffing it first – just about all right – Samuel falls from the bed. It's not far, and there is a mat on the floor, but there's a dull thud, and then a fatal pause before he starts to shriek.

In her haste to comfort him, Maggie knocks over the milk; it swamps the small counter. Knowing there is no more, she tries to sweep some of it back into the bottle with her hand. By now Samuel's roars of pain and fury are filling the caravan and she has to leave the mess and attempt to lift him. He pushes her away and roars some more.

She crouches next to him. 'Poor Sammy,' she says, 'where does it hurt?'

'Mummy!' he cries. 'Want Mummy!'

'Gee-Gee's here.'

'Mummy!'

'It's OK . . .'

'Mummy!'

'Show me where it hurts.'

'Mummy!'

'That was quite a bump.'

'Mummy!'

'Let Gee-Gee see.'

'Mummy! Mummy!'

His face looks set to burst with pain and rage. He throws back his head and screams, hardly able to take enough breath. When she tries to reach for him again, he bats her arms away. All she can do is sit back on her haunches and watch as he howls and howls and howls. After a few minutes, she covers her head with her arms. The milk drips from the counter onto her hands and hair, but she cannot move; she can only try to be still and protect herself from Samuel's utter fury. His screams cover her, they make her shrink until all she can feel is wave after wave of pure noise.

Into this, Joe walks.

Maggie does not hear him come in. She can't hear anything save for the screams. She has heard Samuel scream many times before, but never at this pitch, for this long. Then she's aware of someone reaching over her head, and for a second she hardly cares who is doing the reaching, as long as the noise will stop. Whoever this is, the noise will stop. And it does.

Slowly, she peels her arms away from her head. The howling relents, becoming interspersed with low whimpers and hiccups as Joe clutches Samuel to his chest and tells him that it's OK, it's all right, Joe's here and Mummy will be here, and everything will be all right.

When Samuel is quieter, Joe says, 'Call her. Now.'

The sweet, sickly smell of milk is on her hair and hands.

'Maggie,' says Joe. 'If you don't, I will.'

'Give Samuel to me,' Maggie says, standing and brushing the sticky hair from her face.

'You've got to phone her first.'

She fishes her phone from her pocket and shows the screen to him. No signal. 'Give him to me.'

Samuel is making long, drawn-out moans, like a cat announcing, quietly but insistently, its hunger. He looks at Maggie with big, terrified eyes. When she holds her arms out to him, he reaches for her.

After she has rocked him, cradled him to her chest, stroked his sweaty hair from his eyes and given him some of the milk that Joe has brought, the three of them sit together in silence on the bed. It is a bright morning; Maggie can hear the sea combing the shore, the terns chattering and her brother sighing. He keeps on sighing and taking a breath, as if he is about to say something. But each time he gives up.

Samuel grips Joe's sleeve and says 'Cr'van 'venture!' And Joe smiles, a little bit.

Maggie says, 'You loved Nula, didn't you?'

Her brother gives a mirthless laugh. 'Maggie. That was all a long time ago . . .'

'But you really loved her. I know you did.'

'It doesn't matter, now.'

'It matters to me. I lost both of you. And then there was nothing left. Just me and Mum in that cold house.'

Joe flips the lid of his Amber Leaf tin and begins to roll a cigarette. 'You went to Oxford, though, didn't you?'

'Fat lot of good it did me. I was a useless student.' Maggie lifts Samuel into the air and kisses him on the cheek, making him laugh. 'Sometimes,' she says, 'I look at him and I see you.'

Joe slides his eyes towards his sister.

'I think: he could have been Joe's.'

Samuel giggles again.

'Even if he was,' says Joe, 'he still wouldn't be yours.'

A silence passes. Joe lights his cigarette and takes a puff.

'What were you thinking, Maggie? What on earth were you thinking?'

She says the only thing she knows to be the truth: 'I didn't know what else to do.'

Joe rubs his chin, swallows. 'Have you made a plan?'

'I – I just need more time.'

'You don't have time. The police will be here soon enough. Even if I don't call them, they'll work it out . . . I'm trying to help you.'

'I know. Thank you. I'm going to call her.'

'When?'

'In a few minutes. I just have to change his nappy, then I'll walk him somewhere I can get a signal, and I'll call her.'

'Promise?'

She nods. 'Can you put that out? It's not good for Samuel to be around cigarette smoke.'

Joe peers at his cigarette, but ignores her. 'I have to get to work. I'll leave early and drop into the boathouse to pick up the rest of your stuff. I'll be back about five, OK? You'll have called her by then, won't you? You'll tell her to come here? You'll sort it out?'

'I'll tell her,' she says.

'If you don't, Maggie—'

'I'll sort it out.'

'Good.' He touches her on the shoulder. 'It's the right thing to do.'

When Joe has gone, she opens all the windows to let out the smoke and allows Samuel to empty the kitchen cupboard of all the pots and pans. She looks at her phone. No signal and a 'Battery Low' warning. The charger is still at the boathouse. If she were to walk, right now, onto the beach with him she could probably get a signal. She could do what her brother wants her to do. She could, she thinks, tell Nula that Samuel has been having a nice holiday, and that he is safe. She could even say that Greg had authorised her to take Samuel on this little trip. Hadn't he told his wife about it? He was supposed to. How typical of him to forget.

And Maggie can see Nula arriving within hours, kneeling on the sand in her beautiful shift dress and silk cardigan and embracing her son. She can imagine Samuel's face on seeing his mother again; she can see the light that would switch on behind his eyes. And she can picture herself walking the other way. But where would she go? The caravan is not hers, nor is the boathouse. Oxford would not welcome her, and she has no desire to go back there and listen to her father's sighs and stories of his allotment. She thinks of her drawings of Samuel, and remembers how her damp flat has damaged them. She thinks, briefly, of her mother, of walking all the way to Fiona's door, calling out that word – *Mum!* – and asking her for . . . what? She can barely remember, now, whether she seeks forgiveness for herself or for her mother. Perhaps both. But it is not possible for Maggie to imagine any further than that doorway, with its broken bell and dark wooden door, which remains closed.

She looks at Samuel and he throws a pan lid down and smiles, suddenly: a wide, cheek-dimpling, room-illuminating smile. And she makes her plan.

Smiling back at him, she says, 'We're not giving up, are we? Maggie's not giving up.'

It is a calm day, a warm breeze coming off the sea. Maggie and Samuel are in the pines, hurrying towards the road. 'This is our caravan adventure!' Maggie says as she carries him through the thickest part of the wood, keeping the twigs from his face with one hand. In the changing bag she has a little money, a bottle of milk, some spare nappies and the bag of crisps that Joe brought last night. Samuel has never before eaten real crisps, and she congratulates herself on having this sacred, forbidden treat with which to bribe him. They may need such things, later. He looks up at the flickering branches and points excitedly to the blue sky. It doesn't seem nearly as far to the gate this time, and Samuel enjoys running some of the way on the soft ground, bouncing on the fallen needles, crunching pine cones beneath his feet. Maggie hides behind a tree, but is careful to jump out and say 'Boo' before he really misses her. Still, when he catches sight of her, he barrels over and she holds him as though he had in fact been lost.

Once on the road she looks up and down. No cars, and no bus stop. The larks are singing, up, up, up. The fields are bumpy and green on both sides, dotted with sheep. They walk close to a farm's wire fence. 'Look!' she says to Samuel, 'sheep!'

He looks at the animals and frowns. Then he holds his arms out to be carried. 'Just a bit further,' she says, switching on her phone and checking for a signal. Two bars. Ignoring all her missed calls and messages, she reaches into her pocket and finds Neil's card still there. Dials the number. No reply. She switches the phone off again.

When a Land Rover approaches, she hoists Samuel to her hip and sticks her thumb out. Surely a young woman with a toddler will not have to wait long for a lift. The driver slows down a little, taking in the sight of Maggie and Samuel, but she doesn't stop. It isn't until she's driven away that Maggie fully acknowledges the danger of their situation. Something in the woman's stare alerts her to the risk she is taking on this exposed road. At the next junction she turns into a smaller road with trees hanging over one side and carries Samuel beneath them, calculating that this will at least give them some cover. They have not been walking for long when a newish small car approaches. This time the vehicle comes to a stop a few yards down the road and the passenger door opens.

Samuel wriggles free of Maggie's arms and runs towards the tail lights. In the driver's seat is a woman in her mid-twenties with very short blonde hair and large earrings. 'All right, there?' she says.

'God, thanks so much!' Maggie begins. She's been rehearsing this speech in her head as they walked down the road. 'Our car broke down back there – we're a bit lost, not even sure where I left it! – so I need to get to a garage.' Glancing into the back of the car, she sees – thank God – a child seat with an abandoned carton of juice lying next to it.

'You poor things. Hop in. I'll take you to the next village. There's a garage there.'

'You're a life-saver,' says Maggie, opening the back door and shoving Samuel into the seat.

The woman looks round. 'And who are you, then?' she asks the boy.

'This is Stevie,' says Maggie.

'Stevie!' shouts Samuel in an outraged tone, which makes the woman laugh.

As they drive, Maggie is careful to keep looking out of the side window, so as not to encourage too much conversation. But the woman is eager to chat.

'You on holiday?'

'Kind of. Staying with family.'

'That's not always a holiday, is it? Whereabouts?'

Maggie hesitates. 'Beaumaris.'

'You've come a long way.'

'Yeah,' Maggie laughs. 'We went for a bit of a drive . . . He was up so early this morning, I didn't know what to do with him. And we got totally lost.' She knows it would be better to say as little as possible, but she adds, 'I've never been good with directions.'

She looks back at Samuel, but he is busy squashing the carton of juice, dripping what's left of its contents onto his trousers.

'How old is he, then?'

'Two.'

'Gorgeous! But we always think that, don't we? My Nia, she's a little sod – pardon my French – but she's absolutely bloody gorgeous.'

A silence passes. A sign says: GAERWEN 6.

'How far's the garage?' Maggie asks.

'Not far. I know the guy there. He'll give you a lift back to your car, no bother. You come on your own, then? Just the two of you?'

'Pardon?'

'Sorry. Shouldn't ask, really. It's just I'm on my own, you know? Nia's dad's with another family. But she's fine with me. I'm all she needs.' The woman glances at Maggie.

Samuel says, 'Sheep!' and points.

'I'm on my own, too,' says Maggie.

'That's a shame,' says the woman, indicating left.

'Not really,' says Maggie. 'I've got Stevie.'

'Yeah,' says the woman. 'That's a good way to look at it.'

Samuel shouts 'Stevie!' again. Then he starts to laugh.

'Bless,' says the woman.

Having told Maggie to say that Rhian sent her, the woman drives away from the garage, beeping the horn in farewell.

Maggie waits for a moment with Samuel on her hip, waving. When she is sure Rhian's car has disappeared round the corner, she walks back to the small village green, where she'd noticed a bus stop on the way in. The timetable says a bus to Llanfairpwll is due in fifteen minutes. She lets Samuel climb on the war memorial, being careful to replace the rain-battered, artificial poppy wreaths he dislodges. No one joins her, no one walks past. It is ten-thirty in the morning. There's a newsagent opposite, and a disused pub. She considers going into the shop to buy Samuel some juice, but thinks better of it. In a place like this the two of them will have been seen and noted.

The day is getting hotter and, with a stab of annoyance, she realises she has forgotten Samuel's suncream. Ridiculous to have come without it. Her first thought is that maybe she can persuade Joe to bring some with him when she sees him next. Then she remembers Joe's sighs earlier this morning, his hand heavy on her shoulder, and she has to blink back a sudden urge to cry, because she knows she is on her own now. She has not done what her brother asked. Joe will not be coming back.

Maggie sits on the bus stop's bench for a minute, gazing at the dark circles of abandoned gum on the paving slabs. A wave of panic makes her legs weak. But then Samuel is grasping her knees, asking to come into her lap. She hauls him up and kisses his hot cheek. She still has Samuel, and she must protect him. To steady herself, she breathes in his warm scent.

Fishing in the changing bag, she finds his bright-yellow sunhat. He hates wearing it, but with the help of the crisps, which have him hopping on the spot with excitement, she gets the thing on his head, where it sits like a squashed sunflower.

When the bus arrives it is almost empty. Samuel holds Maggie's hand tightly as they board: this is a new experience for him. She sits him on her lap and lets him slap at the dirty window and shout 'BUS!' for the ten minutes it takes to reach Llanfairpwll. Once there, they wait for their connection in the shelter by the old railway station, watching the coachloads of tourists disembark with cameras poised to take photographs, purses ready to open. Most of them appear pretty disappointed by what greets them: a massive Edinburgh Woollen Mill and a very long word on a sign. Maggie looks no one in the eye and tries to keep Samuel amused with the *BIG RED BATH!* book she finds in the bottom of the changing bag, covered in rice-cake crumbs.

When the next bus arrives, it's empty apart from two teenagers sitting on the back seat, heads locked together over a single Game Boy. It is humid on board and soon Samuel is asleep, his heavy head deadening Maggie's arm against the window as she watches the strait and the sky open up on either side of the bus, flooding it with reflected light. For a moment or so it feels good to be over the water again, to be on their way. Then she remembers where they are going, and a sick feeling rises through her body as she clasps the boy tighter.

She has to wake Samuel when they reach Bangor bus station. For a while she carries him, but halfway into town she tries to coax him into walking. He screams so loudly that she immediately picks him up again and manages a few more paces before giving up. 'You'll have to walk for a bit, Sammy,' she says. 'Gee-Gee's tired.' This explanation does no good. He rips the sunhat from his head and throws it to the ground, his face growing redder. Fearing he will shout for his mother again, Maggie lifts him once more and struggles slowly past the Pound Shop, Greggs and Sue Ryder – briefly she wonders if they might have a buggy going cheap – towards her goal.

In the sunshine it looks a different place, the large windows sparkling, the huge yellow letters glowing brightly. Leisurely pensioners wheel trolleys through the automatic doors, some in pairs, some alone, none looking anything but satisfied by the prospect of spending the next hour or so in the aisles. Maggie locates a trolley. Samuel's nappy is hugely wet; as she lifts him into the seat she feels the tight pouch of soaked cotton. She heads for the changing room. Nappy first. Then the café. Then Neil.

Inside the changing room, Maggie studies her own face for the first time in two days. Her skin, always pale, looks deathly under the strip-light, an arc of shadow scooped under each eye. There is a large patch of dryness on her cheek, lined like the skin of an ancient apple. She blinks and rubs roughly at her face to bring some blood up. Her hair is lank and the milk that dripped into it earlier is now beginning to smell like vomit. Samuel, reclined on the changing table with his trousers round his ankles, gazes up at her and grabs fistfuls of it, as he always does when she changes his nappy. 'Gee-Gee hair, Gee-Gee hair,' he says, dreamily, which is usually her cue to lean over and tickle him on the face and tummy with its ends. But as she leans forward he yanks it hard, almost pulling her off-balance. 'No,' she says, 'no pulling.' But he doesn't stop, and before she knows it, she's yelling, 'Samuel! No!'

Immediately he starts to cry, terrified by the strange noise Maggie has created in this small room. Taking steadying breaths to keep herself from shouting again, she watches as his eyes disappear behind a crumpled mask of fear, and finds that this time she does not have the strength to comfort him. Letting him cry on, she completes the nappy change and carries him out of the room, abandoning the trolley. He is so shocked by her silence that he grips her neck and his screams subside into whimpers.

Maggie finds the café, buys two cheese sandwiches and two cartons of apple juice and sits at a plastic table. Samuel continues to whimper on her lap, hiding his face in her T-shirt. It's not until she has finished her sandwich and drained her juice that she feels able to say, 'It's OK' and try to smile at him. She opens the second sandwich packet, tears off a piece of white bread the texture and consistency of foam and offers it to him with a shaking hand. He snatches it and eats, his eyes never leaving her mouth, as if trying to ensure that it won't open and make that terrible sound again.

As the boy watches her, Maggie becomes aware of someone else's eyes on her face. Looking up, she sees sandy hair and pink cheeks. But it's not Neil. It's a young woman, holding a tray. When the woman smiles uncertainly, Maggie looks away. 'Come on, Samuel,' she says, handing him another piece of sandwich. 'Eat up. We'll need to go in a minute.'

But the woman has approached their table. On her tray are a bowl of bright-red soup and a large paper cup of Coke. 'Don't I know you?' she says, squinting slightly.

'Don't think so,' Maggie mumbles, wiping Samuel's face and hands roughly with a napkin, pushing back her chair. Samuel shouts in protest and snatches the rest of the cheese sandwich from her hand.

'You don't go to Cheeky Monkeys, do you?'

'We've just moved here, actually,' says Maggie, hoisting Samuel onto her hip. 'We're in a bit of a hurry.' She pushes past the woman. Samuel waves over her shoulder and, through a mouthful of bread and cheese, shouts, 'BYE-BYE!'

'Wait,' the woman calls.

Maggie can see the exit. A few strides and they will be there, a few more and they will be out on the street. What was she thinking, coming here again? Places like this are not possible now.

The woman is determined. 'Wait!' she shouts.

But then, so little is possible now.

Maggie picks up her pace, but Samuel starts shouting 'WAIT!' too, and then there's a heavy hand on her arm. She stops, closes her eyes. *Not yet, not yet, not yet*, she thinks. There must be somewhere else we can go together. Somewhere else we can be together. Don't take him from me yet.

'You forgot this,' says the woman, holding out the changing bag.

Maggie stares at it, at the woman's beautifully manicured hand on its strap, and a sob pushes its way up her chest.

'Are you sure we've never met, love?' The woman's voice is soft now, kind.

Maggie can only shake her head.

'Not easy, is it?' The woman says. 'They can be little buggers, can't they?'

With Samuel still shouting, 'WAIT, WAIT!' and spitting bits of sandwich in her hair, Maggie says, 'Thank you. Thank you very much.' She accepts the bag and makes for the automatic doors.

Nula reaches over to stroke the ear of the stolen blue monkey. When did all cuddly toys become so soft? She remembers her own teddies being rather rough, their fur brittle compared to this silken fabric. Passing through the cramped, grey towns of North Wales as quickly as she can, she allows her thoughts to settle on Samuel. She feels certain, now, that she will soon be with him. Having this stolen monkey with her seems to confirm it. At the thought of him, a whimper escapes her mouth. She bites back the tears, glad to have to slow to a stop at some traffic lights and watch a mother drag a screaming toddler across the road in front of her car, shouting at her child to 'Come *on*, hurry *up*,' both of their faces pink explosions of fury.

Taking a breath and driving on, she remembers Samuel after one such outburst. She had carried him, screaming and kicking, from the car to the house. He had been almost asleep when they'd arrived home and was livid at having been disturbed by his mother. Inside, everything she'd tried had failed: her special soothing voice, a chocolate-biscuit bribe, a promise of television. In the end, she had left him to convulse with fury on the floor of the sitting room until he was too tired to continue. When he was done, he had waddled to where she was sitting on the sofa and rested his hot head on her knee, leaning against her, utterly exhausted. 'Mummy,' he'd said.

She'd wanted to cry, then, not just because the noise had stopped, but because of the sudden, pure need in his voice. It was a need that seemed too large for her to meet.

Afterwards she had shared a hot chocolate with him, feeding him mouthfuls of milky froth from her spoon. When they were almost done, he had taken the spoon from her and held it against her mouth until she'd opened her lips and pretended to swallow. Then he'd shrieked with delight, and they had done it again and again. When she took him up to bed that night, he was almost asleep before she reached his room. In her arms he felt totally limp, almost too heavy for her to manage. But she had made it to the armchair and sat with him in her lap, allowing him to give up completely, allowing herself to watch as he fell helplessly towards sleep.

V

'There's not much more we can do here, Maggie.'

She'd been coming to the boathouse every afternoon for the last month, and now the school holidays were almost over. Removing her clothes and stretching out naked in the warm, damp air had become routine, and instead of watching Ralph's every move as he picked his way around her – sometimes crouching to squint at some nook of her body, sometimes peering so closely at her flesh she could feel his breath – Maggie had taken to closing her eyes and listening, as she had on those first few visits here, to the sounds of the boathouse. But now she heard not just the various twitches and grinds of Ralph's paintbrush, but also the sea lifting and rearranging the stones outside and, occasionally, the white peacock in the vicarage garden down the lane. *Listen to me*, it seemed to say. Listen to my stuttering mew and imagine my staggering, pointless beauty. Stop listening to him. Listen to me.

'Couple more sessions and we might be done.' He was frowning at the canvas.

She sat up. It was the most he'd said in days.

'Don't move.'

She lay back down. He hadn't once offered to show her what he was doing, or talk her through his process. Not that she had really expected him to do either of these things.

But she had thought she might get something in return for coming here and stripping off every day.

'Break in five, OK?'

Halfway through the afternoon they always had this break. Usually Ralph stayed in the boathouse, smoking, whilst Maggie sat on the wall outside, looking out at the strait, wearing the oversized T-shirt she'd learned to bring with her, wondering how long she could keep him waiting. But today Ralph paced impatiently behind her as she gazed at the mountains. On clear days they looked close enough to run up. When it was overcast they sank into the clouds and seemed as unreachable as distant planets.

'When you've finished,' she said, 'can I have a go?'

Ralph stopped walking. He finished his cigarette, then threw the end over the wall onto the stones beneath.

She expected him to stall her by pretending not to understand what she meant. But he seemed to know well enough. 'When I've finished,' he said, 'it'll be time for you to go back to school. And you've got years ahead of you in which to *have a go.*'

Maggie folded her arms across her chest.

'Right now it's time to get on,' he said. 'I want to finish this thing.'

She didn't move.

He let out a long sigh. 'Look,' he said, sitting next to her on the wall. 'The thing is this. You don't need me. You can just do it. On your own.'

When she turned to protest, he removed his glasses, caught her chin in his hand and looked at her so intently that for a moment she thought he might kiss her. But instead he said, 'Honestly. Trust me. Teaching is all bullshit. And I am a particularly bullshit kind of teacher.'

'We'd better get back inside then,' she said.

There was a pause. He was still examining her face, as if he hadn't seen it before now. 'It's going to be a good painting,' he said. 'And that's because of your *remarkable* way of lying on that sofa.'

Maggie's father had announced that a fuss was to be made about Fiona's forty-fifth birthday. He was going to make dinner, and they would all eat together al fresco, around the new patio table and chairs he'd picked up at the garden centre in Pentraeth. It would be just family, of course, but that family was to include Nula and Uncle Ralph. Piqued by Ralph's refusal to teach her anything at all, Maggie had told him she would not be coming that afternoon as she had to help her father get ready for the evening. Ralph had said he'd almost finished the painting anyway, and could probably get on well enough without her.

Now, though, she sat in her bedroom looking at the book on Paula Rego that she had taken out of the library. When the house wasn't filled with the high whine of the Hoover, Maggie could hear her father singing 'You Ain't Seen Nothin' Yet', nah-nah-ing when he didn't know the words. He had sent Fiona to the Tre-Ysgawen spa for the day and was, as he had promised, giving the place the once-over. 'He looks like Freddie-fucking-Mercury,' had been Joe's comment to Maggie on seeing his father in an apron. Maggie had offered to help, but Alan had refused assistance of any kind.

She turned a page. She had meant to ask Ralph his opinion on Rego, and many other artists. She'd meant to ask him how he had become an artist. How he knew what to paint. What he thought to be the point of painting at all. But it was difficult

251

to speak properly when you were naked. And it was difficult to speak at all when the other person was so absorbed in what they were doing.

Her father appeared in the doorway. 'Do me a favour?' he asked.

Maggie nodded.

'I've forgotten to buy paper napkins and I can't really leave the cake . . . Can you pop to the Spar for me?'

It was all the excuse she needed to jump to her feet and head for the door.

She did not go to the Spar. Instead she headed down the lane, to the boathouse, taking the Rego with her. Today, she would not take her clothes off. She would ask him what he thought of the work of Paula Rego. As she walked, she imagined the scene: they might sit together on the wall, overlooking the strait. They might exchange knowing but appreciative comments about the view. She might share his cigarette and tell him how she found Rego's use of light and dark so astonishing. She might tell him how she found the work deeply, beautifully worrying. And he might tell her that he was almost ready to show her how she looked on his canvas.

The sunlight crawled across her shoulders as she walked. She'd quickly changed into her sundress before leaving the house. A strap hung down one shoulder, but she didn't bother righting it. As she neared the house she could hear the shouts from tourist boats on the strait. The white peacock was nowhere to be seen or heard. The tide was high and the beach had all but disappeared under the water.

His door was closed. She stopped on the steps, surprised that he hadn't left it open, as he usually did, even though he was not expecting her. After a slight hesitation, she knocked, loudly. There was a scraping inside – the unmistakable sound of his boots on the floorboards. Then a long silence.

'Ralph?' she called.

On the strait, someone screamed in mock-terror. One of the boats from the Plas Coch hotel. Maggie knocked again. No one came. She looked across the strait, at a loss for what to think or do. He was in there. She had heard him. Setting the Rego book down (she'd inserted scraps of paper between the pages to mark the paintings she particularly liked), she grasped the door handle and tried to turn it. It didn't move. She took it in both hands and tried again. Still it would not budge. As she waggled the thing, growing increasingly irritated, it dawned on Maggie that someone or something was resisting her on the other side of the door. Someone or something was holding the handle firmly in place.

'Ralph?' she said again. 'It's me. It's Maggie.'

No reply.

'I heard you in there,' she said.

Nothing.

And then it came to her. He was in there with Nula. He was with his daughter and Nula was holding the handle. She had claimed Joe, and now she would take this from her, too.

Maggie let go of the handle and walked to the side of the house. The reflected glare of the strait made it difficult to see through the window. As she shaded her eyes, the shapes in the room gradually came into focus. From here it was impossible to make out who or what was behind the front door, but she could see, on the sofa where she herself usually lay naked, what looked like her mother's handbag. And, in the middle of the floor, her mother's green sandals, the straps still buckled, as though they'd been kicked off in a hurry. For one single second Maggie stared at these items, puzzled by what they could possibly mean. Where was Nula, then? Why were the three of them in there?

Then she understood. Nula was not in the boathouse, but her mother was. She hooked up the strap that was hanging off her shoulder and, leaving her book where it was, ran from the house and all the way up the lane.

At home, her father had moved on to cleaning the toilet. He was on his knees, wearing a pair of rubber gloves the colour of cooked liver, scrubbing beneath the rim. Maggie stood behind him, watching Alan's freshly dyed head bob up and down.

He turned to her, smiled briefly, then went back to the toilet. 'Nice dress,' he said. 'Wearing it to the party?' He attacked the pan with new vigour.

'Maybe we should cancel. They don't sell napkins at the Spar. And it looks like rain.'

Alan gave a laugh. 'Bit late for that. The pie's ready for the oven. Cake's made. Presents wrapped. No napkins, you said?'

'No. Dad—'

'I suppose it's not that important. We can use kitchen towel, can't we?'

Maggie sat on the edge of the bath and said nothing.

'Kick-off in an hour. Don't get that floor dirty.'

She covered her mouth with a hand.

'Sorry,' said Alan. 'It's just I want it all to be right. For your mum.' He looked at her. 'What is it, love?'

'Nothing.'

'You know,' he said, tossing his rubber gloves in the sink, 'moving here has been good for this family. Being in a landscape. It's nourishing for the soul. Makes you feel part of something.'

Maggie examined his face. It was true, for him at least: his skin was tanned, his shoulders bulkier, from working outside. Without his ties and work-stripes he looked younger. He seemed always to be in shorts, these days, and polo shirts with things like 'SURF' and 'WAVE' and 'POWER' printed on them. Life here suited him.

And, thought Maggie, maybe it was true for Joe, too: hadn't he found freedom on his motorbike, and found Nula, too?

Perhaps, she thought, it was even true for her mother, who, it now seemed, had good reason to seem distant, distracted.

All of which left Maggie utterly alone.

At seven o'clock Alan summoned his children and Nula to the patio table, upon which was an open bottle of champagne and six plastic flute glasses. He'd tied pink balloons to every available surface (the guttering along the old dairy, the hook above the back door, the whirligig washing line) and had moved the stereo system into the kitchen, so they could all hear *Total 70s Party!* coming from the window. Despite Maggie's hopes, the evening sky was clear and it was still warm. The chickens burbled and the oven hummed. Alan clapped his hands together as his wife appeared through the back door. She was wearing a tight, lurid green top with wide black trousers and a pair of heeled mules. Maggie noticed, for the first time that summer, that her mother had lost weight. Fiona smiled at them all through her lipstick, her eyes skimming quickly over Maggie's face.

'Happy birthday, darling,' said Alan. Joe clapped a bit. Nula and Maggie did not.

Alan poured the champagne. 'Ralph's coming, too,' he said, raising his glass.

Fiona took her drink and nodded, very quickly.

'Nibbles!' Alan declared, handing round a large bowl of crisps.

'How does it feel to be forty-five, Aunty Fiona?' asked Nula. She was wearing a short black dress and the same black pumps she'd arrived in. Her tanned bare legs shone as she stood very close to Joe.

'Life's begun,' said Fiona, with a small smile.

Alan put an arm around his wife. 'I'll drink to that,' he said.

By seven forty-five there was still no sign of Ralph, and Alan said he had better serve the starter or the pie would be ruined. The sky was turning a dirty yellow and the air was beginning to cool; Fiona had thrown a black cardigan over her shoulders. Beneath the table Joe's hand was on Nula's naked knee, but no one except Maggie seemed to notice. Not even Nula, who was sipping her champagne. As Alan handed round the halved avocados dressed with a dollop of Hellmann's, Maggie berated herself. What had she expected? That Ralph might actually desire her in some way? Or, more ludicrous, that he'd respect her enough to take her ambitions seriously? Or even enough not to fuck her mother? Since the evening had begun, Maggie had been waiting for her mother to look her in the eye. It hadn't happened yet.

As she watched Fiona chew her slightly under-ripe avocado, Maggie began to wonder if she had been wrong about what she'd seen at the boathouse. If something had been going on, wouldn't her mother be so mortified that she would not be able to appear at all? Wouldn't she have feigned illness, fainted or vomited with shame? But there she sat, her plum mouth closing on forkfuls of avocado. Perhaps she hadn't been in Ralph's bed. Perhaps she had been there to talk to him. It was possible, wasn't it? Possible that her mother knew about the painting sessions. Possible that she was concerned enough for her daughter to go and talk to Ralph herself.

But when Ralph arrived, without apologising for being late, and Fiona's voice tipped into song as she said his name – twice – and thanked him for coming, Maggie's stomach lurched. Perhaps her first assumptions had been right, after all.

'Don't get up,' Ralph said, sitting beside Nula. 'Avocado! My favourite.'

Maggie looked at her plate.

'Happy birthday,' he said, handing something wrapped in newspaper over the table.

'What is it?' asked Alan.

'Let her open it and see,' said Ralph, shaking it in Fiona's direction.

Fiona blushed and looked confused. A hand flew to her throat and she laughed. 'You shouldn't have,' she said.

'You don't know what it is yet,' said Ralph.

'Go on,' urged Nula, 'open it.'

Fiona tore the paper away from the gift. Seeing what was inside, she gasped. 'Oh Ralph . . .' she began, then stopped and held his gaze.

'It's to say thank you,' said Ralph, 'for your hospitality.'

In silence, Fiona held it up for them all to see. Maggie recognised the small canvas straight away as one of Ralph's studies of the strait. This one was calmer than the rest: swirls of blue and yellow beneath a greyish sky. Maggie didn't think it the best of the ones she had seen.

Nula looked at Joe. Joe looked at Nula. Alan looked at his wife, then his brother. Ralph looked at Maggie.

'It's wonderful,' said Fiona. 'It's too much.'

Ralph held up a hand. 'It's yours.'

Nula said, 'But you never give your work away.'

'Nonsense,' said Ralph, smiling round the table.

Fiona was studying the painting, turning it this way and that, letting out little sighs.

Alan looked over her shoulder. 'Compact, isn't it?' he said.

'But powerful,' said Fiona.

Ralph smirked and tucked in. 'Great avocado,' he said. 'Just right.'

'Have you finished the actual painting, yet?' asked Maggie, fixing her uncle with a stare.

There was a pause.

'Maggie,' said Fiona, '*this* is the actual painting.'

'No,' said Nula, pushing away her uneaten avocado. 'It's a study. A sort of practice run. But you're still very lucky,' she continued. 'R.V. Wichelo doesn't come cheap.'

Ralph put his fork down and clasped his hands together. 'There are no practice runs in art,' he said. 'Every work is an important part of the process.'

Nula snorted.

'Well,' said Alan, stroking his earlobe. 'Whatever it is, it's a great gift. Thank you.'

'It's nothing,' said Ralph. 'Really.'

Maggie's mother was staring at the canvas still, as if trying to work out what it represented.

'I'll get the rest of the food,' said Maggie, rising and hurrying indoors.

The kitchen was unbearably hot from the oven and the steaming veg on the stove. Maggie leaned her head on the sweaty wall and took a few breaths. She could hear her father asking Ralph how his work was going, and Ralph answering his questions with dismissive one-word sentences. She found herself thinking of the day her father had allowed her to eat whatever she wanted and she'd vomited it all up, and how she had felt so sorry for him afterwards, and she was suddenly struck by the fact that her mother was not the only one who had betrayed him. Hadn't she kept the nude modelling secret? When she'd received her GSCE results a week ago she had refused her father's offer of a celebratory lunch out, impatient to get to the boathouse instead. What would he say if he knew that she, Maggie, grade-A student, spoiled daughter, had been posing naked for his brother?

A plastic chair made a cringing noise over the patio and Maggie straightened herself up. Alan appeared in the kitchen, his forehead slick with perspiration. 'How's that pie doing, Maggie-May?'

As he removed it from the oven, a great whoosh of heat hitting them both, Maggie wanted to cry. Chicken-and-mushroom pie with home-grown veg. This was winter food. Hopelessly so. Even her father should know that you don't serve pie and gravy on a plastic patio table. She foresaw that her mother's disappointment would swiftly be followed by triumph, for her father had got it wrong, again. And yet it was beautiful, the lid golden and puffed, topped with her mother's initials, FW, fashioned in pastry.

'I'll take it,' she said, grabbing a pair of serving gloves.

He looked at her, clearly reluctant to hand over his creation.

'Give it to me,' she insisted.

'I'll just put a mat on the table,' he said, handing over the heavy dish and dodging in front of her.

She followed him outside.

'Dinner is served!' Alan announced.

Nula, Ralph, Joe and Fiona all turned to watch Maggie open her hands and let the dish fall to the floor. There was a thud, rather than the satisfying crash she'd imagined, as the earthenware cracked and its contents splurged out of its bottom, the perfect pastry collapsing with a pathetic slump on the patio tiles.

Nula swerves the car around another sharp bend. She has been stuck behind a tractor for the last ten miles and it's past four o'clock now. Rocks veer up on either side of the Nissan, with sheep balancing on their edges. She overtakes another slow car, swearing loudly. These tourists, these mountains, these stone bridges, these lumps of sheep, these chattering streams – all of them are merely in her way. She must simply get through, leave them behind. Now that the island is close, her impatience is barely containable. It surges up her legs, through her stomach and along her arms to her fingertips, making them twitch. She'd calculated that avoiding the motorway would save her time at this hour, but now she wishes she had chosen the other route. Signs warn of falling rocks, sheep in the road, hairpin bends, but she keeps up a steady fifty-five miles per hour. She wishes for Joe's motorbike, rather than this huge hunk of metal, imagining it singing around corners, accelerating towards Anglesey with lightning swiftness. It is a fantasy, though: in reality, Joe's motorbike had been under-powered, even if it had felt indescribably thrilling to travel through this mountain range behind him. It had taken her a while to have enough courage to look at what was flashing past rather than merely bury her face into Joe's jacket, but once she had she'd been shocked by the dangerous glamour of it all. From her father's car the landscape had looked like a pretty film unspooling; from Joe's bike she could feel the fierce freshness of the wind, see the sharp glint of slate, smell the rain coming up the valley. She'd pressed her belly into Joe's back and hoped for the best.

The beginning of something had so quickly turned into an end, but still she warms briefly at the thought of the two of them riding off to their place by the bank of the strait, where they were sheltered by the overhanging trees. For a few weeks, Joe was all she thought about. She thought about his shy smile and his capable hands and the hair curling up like a lip at the back of his neck, but she also thought about him pushing her down and keeping on and on and on, and not letting her go until she made those noises that she is embarrassed, even now, to think of.

She hadn't for one moment thought that the experience would end with a pregnancy.

On the day of her aunt's birthday party she had decided to break the news to Joe. He was in a serious and impatient mood, a mood she usually liked as it meant he had only one thing in mind. As they hurried along the shore, across the grass to their usual place, he tugged her hand so hard that several times she had to tell him to stop, to wait, to take it easy. Sometimes he looked back and smiled, or caught her face between his hands and kissed it, but he said nothing. It was a hot day and the strait was calm in the yellow light of the late afternoon. When they had found the place beneath the branches, he held her tightly, placing his hands inside her top and running a finger along the strap of her bra. Pulling away from him, she sat on the ground and folded her knees up to her chest. Joe knelt beside her and studied her face. He was just about to try to kiss her again when she said, 'I'm pregnant.'

She couldn't look at him for a full minute. Instead she focused on the hazy tops of the mountains. One was supposed to resemble an elephant, Joe said, but she could never see it.

He touched her arm. 'What do you want to do?'

She had expected shouts of horror, or perhaps even a demand of proof, rather than this softly uttered question to which she had no answer.

'You're sure?'

'I was a week late – I'm never late – so I did a test . . .'

'You need time to think,' he said.

'I suppose so.'

'It's a shock.'

'Yes.'

There was a long silence. Joe kept his hand on her arm, and Nula kept her eyes on the mountains.

'I'm sorry,' he said.

'Why?'

'It's my fault, isn't it?'

'Not really,' she said, lying back and closing her eyes.

After a while, Joe lay beside her. 'Actually,' he said, 'I'm not sorry.'

She reached for his hand. 'I'm not, either.'

'Really?'

She opened her eyes and looked at him. He was smiling. There was no way to take it back now. 'Really.'

After that Joe was full of plans, to which Nula listened whilst watching the light shift through the leaves overhead. He was supposed to be starting a photography course at the Tech in a week or so, but he could get work instead, he was sure. He knew the guys in the processing shop in Bangor pretty well now and they'd mentioned there might be something there. And she didn't have to go back to Oxford, did she?

263

Maybe she could finish her A-levels here? Whatever happened, he would look after her. They could live in the boathouse, he suggested; his parents wouldn't charge them much rent.

At this, Nula sat up. 'Joe,' she said, 'have you forgotten? We're cousins.'

She said it incredulously, as if only an insane person would forget such a thing, but the truth was that she herself had stopped thinking about this fact weeks ago. They'd known each other so little before the summer that it was easy for her to dismiss their blood ties as largely insignificant; it wasn't, after all, as if they were actually committing incest. Not in the way people normally used that term.

'It's not illegal,' said Joe. 'Is it?'

Nula looked at him.

'Anyway,' he continued, confidently, 'we could live somewhere else.'

'But you love it here.'

'I was thinking of the other side of the island. Amlwch or somewhere. No one will mind there.'

The expression on his face was so serious that she had to laugh. Then he dissolved, too. The two of them laughed until they cried, and afterwards they lay together in the red dirt until their entwined hands began to prickle with cold.

Leaving her father's pie splattered on the patio, Maggie ran from her family and kept on running, out of the village, down the lane, past the chapel with the box of bones, right down to the beach beside the boathouse. It was almost nine o'clock and the light was fading fast. The sky swirled pink and grey above her head. She picked her way through lumps of dried seaweed, their spiked tendrils prickling her toes, and sat near the water. She grabbed handfuls of stones and threw them at nothing. One of them looked like a brain and she stared at it for a while, running her thumb over its pits. Then she hurled that one down too. She did not turn to look at the boathouse. She wasn't sure if she had hoped for Ralph or her mother to follow her. She knew she was disappointed that *no one* had. The terns and oystercatchers stalked the shallows as she cried. Plunging her fingers into a mess of wet seaweed, she squeezed at the tough bulbs until small gulps of warm liquid yielded to her fists. Where was her mother? Why wouldn't she follow, if she knew what Maggie thought she knew? Maggie again recalled the pair of shoes and the handbag she'd seen that afternoon. It did not have to mean what she thought it meant. But even if it didn't, why wasn't her mother here with her now? She remembered falling from the back of Fiona's bike when she was little: the shock of sharp gravel in the side of her face, the warm blood seeping over her lips, her mother's open mouth as she shouted, 'Help me' to a passing stranger; the yeasty smell of her lap in the back of the car on the return from hospital, stitched and bruised, but still buzzing from the attention of it all, from seeing her mother weep with relief (was it?) when her father turned up and said, 'She's fine, Maggie's fine, of course it's not your fault.'

Joe came. He crunched across the stones and sat next to her and put his arm around her as though that was what they always did, at times like this. As though no one else but he could possibly have come and comforted her at this moment. He asked no questions. He said nothing at all for a few minutes, but let her cry on his shoulder. It was wonderful to feel the solid frame of her brother next to her. She cried with relief, because he had come; and with anger, because her mother had not come.

'Well,' he eventually said, 'you certainly broke up that little party. Thank Christ.'

Maggie couldn't laugh.

He sniffed and put his hands in his pockets, but still he sat there, close to her. Together they watched the sky turn from pink to purple to deep blue, and the mountains all but disappear beneath the night.

She was just formulating a sentence that would begin her story about Ralph, about Fiona, about herself, when Joe said, 'Nula's pregnant. It's mine. I think we might keep it.'

When she looked at him, his whole face was smiling, lit by the unmistakable glow of happiness, and hope.

Joe talked and talked as they walked back up the lane towards the house. He outlined how he and Nula would live in another part of the island, how he would get a job in Bangor, or maybe

Caernarfon; how, when the baby was a little older, they might think of moving to Cardiff and investigate childcare options so that Nula could pursue a career in the media. He wouldn't expect her to be a stay-at-home mum. He would want to do his fair share. And she, Maggie, would be an aunty. Could she believe it? Could she even *imagine* it?

Maggie said, 'You're eighteen. And Nula's seventeen.'

'Yeah,' he said, almost as though this was an asset.

'What does Uncle Ralph say?' Maggie tried.

'Pretty sure she hasn't told him yet,' said Joe. 'But it doesn't matter what he says, does it? It's up to us.' Even he sounded a little unsure about this, however, and they were almost home before either of them spoke again.

'Joe,' said Maggie, catching his arm and squinting at him through the darkness.

'I know,' he said, still walking. 'It's mad. But it's what I want.' He paused, grinned. 'I think the baby should have a Welsh name, don't you?'

Maggie dropped her brother's arm and blinked at him.

'You haven't congratulated me,' he said.

'Congratulations,' she said. She was glad the shadows of the trees hid her face.

Whichever way she turned, Maggie couldn't sleep. It was humid and, having dropped her dinner on the patio, she was hungry. Nula was sleeping soundly in the camp bed. Maggie rose and opened the door, so the landing light shone into the room. She studied her cousin's face. Was it, she wondered, fuller, more adult, in pregnancy? There were the same thick eyebrows, the same glossy skin. The same way of sleeping as if dead. And yet, Maggie knew, at any moment Nula could be up and walking, looking in the fridge. Her own stomach gurgled. She would have to beat her cousin to it.

Downstairs she took a hunk of cheese and a cold sausage and stuffed them between two slices of bread. Standing at the counter in her nightie, she ate the whole thing quickly, then downed half a carton of orange juice. She grabbed a chocolate bar from the cupboard and let herself out of the house, first slipping Joe's leather jacket over her shoulders and pushing her feet into her mother's flip-flops.

She walked down the lane, eating as she went. The moon was high; the stars clustered and shone. The lane was knobbly beneath her plastic soles. She just had to make sure, she told herself, that her fears were not true.

The door to the boathouse was closed and all the lights were out. Maggie hammered on the wood with both fists. After a few minutes of as much noise as she could make, Ralph came to the door in his tatty towelling dressing gown and work boots.

'Christ!' he said. 'What the hell's happened?'

She pushed past him and planted herself in the centre of the room. 'Is my mum here?'

'What?'

She scanned the place for clues of Fiona's presence. No handbag. No shoes. Not a hint of Poison perfume. Just the soily smell of Ralph's sweat.

'What's the matter with you? What's going on?'

'You tell me.'

Ralph rubbed at his face. 'What time is it?'

'Are you having an affair with my mum?'

From beneath his hands, Ralph let out a small groan.

'She was here, earlier, wasn't she?'

'I don't know what you're talking about.'

'I came here. I tried to open the door. But I couldn't. And I don't know if you were holding it closed . . .' Now she was saying it, it sounded ridiculous. 'I looked in the window and I saw her shoes and her bag.'

Ralph nodded, slowly. 'Sit down, Maggie,' he said. 'Please.'

'I don't want to sit down.'

'Well, I can't explain unless you do. Let's have a drink, too, shall we?' He bent to the cupboard under the sink, produced a bottle of Scotch and half-filled two cups with the stuff.

'Sit,' he said, holding out the cup.

Maggie stared at the drink and pulled her brother's jacket tighter.

'I don't like it, either, but I always have it in the studio. In case things get rough.' He took a swig, grimaced. 'Right. Right. Let me get this straight. You think that because you saw your mother's shoes in here, that I'm – that we're – having a torrid affair. Is that it?'

'Yes.'

Ralph gave a short laugh. 'Well, I'm glad my reputation still holds.'

'That isn't funny.'

'Sorry. Let me explain.' There was a pause. Maggie took a sip of her whisky and hated herself for having to cough afterwards.

'You see, it's really quite simple,' Ralph continued, ignoring her spluttering. 'Your mother came to see me, true. When she got here, she said her sandals were killing her. So she took them off. It was pretty hot, wasn't it? Not like Wales at all.'

Maggie swallowed, took another sip, managed not to cough.

'Then we went for a walk. We must have been out when you came.'

'How did she go for a walk without her shoes?'

'She wore mine,' said Ralph. 'I've got surprisingly small feet.'

He fixed her with a stare.

'Why did she come here in the first place?'

Ralph took a drink. 'She didn't want me to tell anyone that.'

Maggie waited.

'She specifically asked me not to say anything about that.'

'Then how can I believe you?'

'Promise you won't say anything?'

She nodded.

'Your mother thinks Joe has a crush on Nula, and she came to talk about it with me. She thinks I should warn Nula, so that your brother's not, you know—'

'What?'

'Humiliated, I suppose. Nula's very . . . particular.' He grinned. 'Fiona doesn't think the feeling is mutual. She's just looking out for her son. That's all this is, Maggie.'

Maggie didn't find it hard to believe that her mother had failed to notice so much about Joe and Nula's relationship, and she wanted the rest to be true. But she said, 'Why should I believe you?'

'For the simple reason that I'm telling you the truth,' said Ralph. 'You don't seriously think your mother would – do you?'

Maggie took another drink. The stuff had improved. 'It wouldn't be the first time.'

Ralph leant forward. 'Really?'

She looked into her cup. There was a long pause. 'I'm sorry I woke you,' she said. 'I should get back . . .'

But Ralph was obviously still thinking about Fiona's affair. 'Poor old Alan,' he said, trying to hide his smile behind his cup. Maggie, however, saw it all too clearly. Looking down, she saw, too, that her mother's flip-flops were tiny; they only just fitted her own feet, and were much smaller than Ralph's. She remembered the footsteps she'd heard behind the door. She stood, suddenly. 'I've got to go,' she said.

He caught her by the wrist. 'I do believe that you have talent, Margaret Wichelo. You know that, don't you?'

Maggie pulled away from him. 'How can you know that? You haven't even looked at my work.'

'But I can tell, you see. I knew as soon as you came here . . .'
She headed for the door.

'I was hoping you'd come back, so I could teach you something, properly teach you—'

She opened the door and looked out into the night. Before leaving, she turned to face him and she said, 'Nula's pregnant. It's Joe's.'

Maggie runs through the supermarket car park and back to the street. Samuel starts to laugh at this game of being bumped on Maggie's hip. He is still spitting out bits of sandwich and shouting 'WAIT!' when she spies a bus stop on the main road and struggles towards it. She has no idea where to go. But maybe if she can keep travelling she can come up with a plan. They just have to keep moving.

Samuel's weight is almost impossible to bear now.

Not yet. Not yet. Not yet.

Distracted by the traffic, Samuel quietens and doesn't moan when she puts him down and leans, sweating, against the plastic shelter.

She checks in the changing bag and there is enough money for a couple of bus trips, but no more. Two nappies. Half a packet of wipes. The empty crisp packet. Her phone has run out of battery. She still has the bottle of milk, and she feels a tiny prick of pride at not having had to resort to that, yet.

She kneels before Samuel and grips him to her, kisses his cheek. 'Gee-Gee's so proud of you,' she says into his hair. 'You're such a good boy. We've come a long way, haven't we?' He tightens his hold around her neck, shouts 'WAIT!' again, and laughs.

The bus to Llanfairpwll is the first to arrive. Boarding it, she is careful not to look anyone in the eye. A middle-aged man rises and offers her his seat. 'Let Mam sit down, eh?' he says to Samuel.

Maggie collapses into the seat, heaves the boy onto her lap.

As they are leaving Bangor, Samuel reaches up and slaps her face with both hands, gently at first, but then harder. When she tells him to stop he laughs. 'That hurts,' she says. 'Samuel. Please don't.'

'Hurt,' says Samuel, hitting her again. 'Hurt.'

'No,' she says.

'Hurt!'

'No. Maggie doesn't want to hurt.'

'Hurt!' he shouts again.

Other passengers are beginning to throw annoyed looks in her direction. Maggie holds Samuel tightly, trying to pin his arms to his sides, but he wriggles free and hits her again, hard. She stares at him for a moment, her cheek smarting, and he doesn't look away. His eyes are bright with daring. For a second she wants to hit him back.

As the moment passes, she sees that all her plans, such as they were, are in ruins. Her brother has denied her the support she'd wanted. She has no money left. They have nowhere to hide. But, more importantly, she'd wanted to hit Samuel. It is this that shocks her into the realisation that this thing must end.

She sits for a moment, looking into Samuel's clear, defiant eyes, hardly knowing what she feels. Everything is falling away. And so she begins to sing, very quietly.

'Oh, the grand old Duke of York, tiddly pom . . .'

Samuel brings his hands back again, then pauses, listening.

'He had ten thousand men, tiddly pom . . .' Maggie sings.

He remembers his cue. 'POM!'

'He marched them up to the top of the hill . . .'

'POM!'

'And he marched them down again . . .'

'POM-POM-POM!'

She keeps singing, her eyes on Samuel's hands, which are suspended in the air, as if he's weighing up their chances. The song gets them to the Menai Bridge. Maggie notices the tall anti-suicide fencing on either side. The huge chains flash by the window, their giant iron loops crusted with grease. Seeing them, Samuel becomes silent and merely stares. Finally his hands fall to his lap and he relaxes against her.

Maggie stares too. She stares at the graceful arcs of the bridge and tries to imagine another way this could end. But all she can think of is her own weariness. She closes her eyes and strokes the top of Samuel's head. For the first time in two days she longs for her own bed. For the past few hours her head has pulsed with pain, and now her arms, legs and eyes ache with a new intensity. She longs for someone to comfort her, and there is only one person she can go to for that.

When they reach Llanfairpwll, she almost laughs. There's the train station, with its promise of escape. But she cannot travel any further. She is too tired, and so is Samuel, whose head has slumped against her shoulder. Her only option is to go back. And so she carries Samuel along the aisle of the bus. Passing the middle-aged man who gave her his seat, she nods and says, with as much enthusiasm as she can muster, 'Diolch yn fawr.'

'Croeso,' he replies.

They get off the bus and don't have to wait long for the next one, which will drop them a few yards from the farmhouse.

The bus doors swing open. It's almost empty and the driver barely looks at Maggie as she struggles to find the right change and keep her grip on the boy. Samuel, now a seasoned bus traveller, breaks away, runs to the back and tries to climb up on the seat. She helps him onto her lap and the bus shudders its way along the tree-lined roads, past Plas Newydd and into the village; and there it is, the farmhouse, directly on the road with the fields behind. When she lived there it had always seemed to Maggie that because it was on the road in this way, there was absolutely no chance of making the place into a proper farm. Real farms were at the ends of lanes, surrounded by fields. They nestled in hills or perched on mountainsides. They did not sit hunched on roadsides, like shops or pubs. From the moment they'd stepped from the car that day and her mother had squinted up at the dirty windows, Maggie had known it wouldn't be right.

'This is it, Sammy,' she says. 'We're getting off now.'

She can already see the front curtains twitching, the shadow of her mother's head at the window.

The door has been repainted a deep blue. There's a new bell, too, but the curtains are the same: long, cream, plain, the texture of Shredded Wheat. Maggie stands on the step, Samuel in her arms. For a split second she considers leaving him on the doorstep and running. She could flag down a car, persuade the driver to take her somewhere. A boat, perhaps, across to Dublin, then somewhere further away. But she catches the scent of Samuel's hair and she cannot move.

The door opens. 'Come in, before someone sees the pair of you.'

First casting a look into the street, her mother closes the door firmly behind them. They stand together in the hallway, Samuel hiding behind Maggie's knees. Her mother is wearing a pair of gold-rimmed spectacles, but otherwise hasn't changed:

the same hair the colour of treacle sponge, the same small frame and pale skin. It is the smell of the place, though, that makes Maggie want to crumple onto the carpet and weep. Poison perfume, Nescafé, dust, Flash.

'You're both safe. Thank God!' Fiona covers her mouth with a hand and takes a breath. 'Come in then,' she says. 'Come in and eat something.'

Maggie is unable to move or speak.

Fiona kneels before Samuel. 'And what's your name?' she says.

'Sammy,' says Samuel. He looks up at Maggie. 'And Stevie!'

'Well,' says Fiona, stroking his hair. 'Would you like some crisps, Sammy and Stevie?'

Samuel nods and Fiona takes his hand. Then she looks at Maggie and her face is so full of concern that Maggie feels relieved and shamed at once, and has to look away.

Fiona leads the boy to the kitchen, leaving Maggie leaning on the knobbled wallpaper in the hallway, trying to catch her breath. For a while she listens to her mother asking Samuel what flavour he'd like, whether he wants to sit on her lap, and would he prefer juice or milk? It is the first time he's been out of her sight in two days and she feels her legs weaken with the awful release of no longer being solely responsible for him.

When she manages to walk into the kitchen, Samuel is sitting happily at the table in Fiona's arms, stuffing himself with Quavers.

'Sit down,' says Fiona. 'You must be hungry.' It is as if she has been waiting for them. There are ham sandwiches on the table, a block of Cheddar, an open packet of Digestives. Maggie stares at the food.

'Well,' says Fiona. 'You are a very handsome young man, Sammy and Stevie.'

Samuel doesn't look up from his crisps.

'It's very nice to meet you. Do you think Maggie is tired? I think she must be very tired, don't you?'

Samuel nods, his fist closing on another handful.

'Shall we let her have a sleep?' says Fiona.

'No sleep!' Samuel protests.

'Tell you what,' says Fiona, standing and offering the boy a hand, 'come and watch telly for a bit whilst Maggie has a little nap, OK?'

Samuel looks at Maggie for a second. She nods, and he follows Fiona into the sitting room.

In her bedroom, beneath her duvet decorated with blue dolphins, Maggie collapses. She sleeps fitfully, dreaming of Nula. Her long limbs, clothed in cerise pyjamas, are coming down the stairs towards the kitchen, where Maggie waits, holding the fridge door open. The electric glow lights her cousin's shining face as she reaches for whatever she can find: a thick slice of roughly cut ham, a corner of sweating cheese; pot after pot of yoghurt. She reaches again and again and again, until there is nothing left.

When Nula had first come to the island, the suspension chains of the Menai Bridge had appeared like giant bunting, criss-crossing the sky in welcome. Now she takes the quicker route, across the Britannia Bridge, accelerating through the square mouths of its giant stone arches. It is past six o'clock and her lips are dry, her fingers twitching, still, on the steering wheel. Her phone buzzes again and she ignores it again. If Maggie has gone to see Joe, they will be in the boathouse. It's where he had wanted them to live, ludicrously, before she left; and it's where he had ended up living, by himself, when just about everyone else had gone.

Once she has crossed the water, something in her shifts: she'd been so sure, on her journey here, that her instincts were right, sure that this would be the place she would find her son, but now it strikes her that perhaps Maggie is already gone, perhaps she is already across a much deeper, wider stretch of water. If she had enough foresight to hire a car rather than use her own, what else might she have planned? She could be abroad, dragging Samuel through some port under a false passport. Russia, perhaps. Or she could be on one of those coaches to Poland. They don't even have border checks, Nula thinks.

She drives on to the roundabout, too fast, almost colliding with another 4x4 on the Llanfairpwll exit. She accelerates past the statue of the Marquis of Anglesey, Plas Newydd and Plas Coch, where she cannot help but glance down that shady lane. But she does not stop. Instead she turns into the lane towards Llanidan, her heart rising. She will try the boathouse first. Then the farmhouse.

Halfway along, the lane becomes too narrow for the Nissan, so she abandons her car by the church and runs towards the strait, the stolen blue monkey in her hand, ready. And it is all she can do not to call his name out as the trees whisper overhead and the birds sing their song. The light glows gently and the sheep look on, unconcerned. Once at the boathouse, she thumps on the door and she is shouting now, shouting his name over and over again, 'Samuel! Sammy! Sammy! It's Mummy!'

She knows almost at once that the place is empty: there's no car parked nearby, no lights on inside, but still she shouts because it feels such a long time since she has had legitimate cause to holler her son's name. She peers through the side window and the place looks the same as when her father had used it as a studio: the shabby sofa, the bare boards, the rag rug and the tiny kitchen. She tries the door again, forcing it with her shoulder, but she doesn't have the strength to break an entry. Then she is back at the window, checking for a sign that Maggie and Samuel have been there. At first she can find nothing – no Leggy Monkey, no changing bag or tiny sandals with Velcro straps, but then she sees a plastic bag by the bin and, sticking out of the top, an empty pot of children's yoghurt. Nula slaps a palm on the window, unable to shout any more. Slap. Slap. Slap. She swallows. He is not here, but he is close. There is hope. She sinks to the ground to wait for their return, cradling the monkey in her arms.

Joe's enthusiasm was stifling. The day after the party, he couldn't stop talking about the future: what they would do, how they would cope. He touched Nula carefully, gently kissing her stomach (which showed absolutely no outward sign of what was within), looking into her eyes in a searching, rather than a blatantly lustful, kind of way. At first she was relieved; it would have been so much worse if he had blamed her or insisted she got rid of it. But it wasn't long before she found Joe's change in attitude intensely irritating. Instead of sneaking down to the shore near Plas Coch for sex he suggested a trip to Bangor to look for work, or maybe to Amlwch for places to rent. He told her again that she didn't have to go back, that he would look after her and the baby. She couldn't stand that he kept saying that, so casually. *The baby*. As if it were already a reality.

So Nula went to visit her father.

When she got to the boathouse, the door was open. As she stepped inside she couldn't quite understand what was before her. The only evidence of Ralph having used the place as a studio were a few streaks of red paint on the floor. There was no canvas that she could see, the furniture was all in the right place, and there was no sign of the steel toolbox in which he kept his materials. He'd packed everything away, even though they were not due to leave until the weekend.

Then her father appeared in the doorway to the bedroom, wearing his shorts, a black short-sleeved shirt and a battered pair of plimsolls.

'Where's all your stuff?' she asked.

He looked at her for such a long time that, in the end, she had to drop her eyes. 'You came,' he said, and he walked slowly towards her and took her in his arms. It had been years since he'd embraced her in this way, and at first she stiffened. But after a few moments she found herself gripping his waist, tears pricking her eyes. He kissed the top of her head. 'I knew you'd come, eventually,' he said. 'You don't have to say anything, my darling. I know all about it.'

She tried to pull away from him, wiping her nose with the back of her hand. 'What are you talking about?' she asked, feebly.

'I think you know, Nula.' He paused. 'You've done a test?

'I . . .' She was still trying to catch up with how much he knew, what he was up to.

'Let's sit down,' he said, leading her to the sofa. 'I'm not interested in blaming anyone. I just want to help, all right?'

She stared at him, unable to comprehend his calmness. Eventually she asked, 'Who told you?'

'It doesn't matter. What matters is what you want to do about it.'

Nula swallowed and said nothing.

'You must have some thoughts.'

'Are you going to tell Mum?'

He reached for her hand. 'Listen to me. This is very important. Don't be like your mother. Don't throw your life away.'

Nula let out a disbelieving laugh.

Ralph lifted his chin. 'She'd never put it that way, I know, but that's what happened. She was twenty when she got pregnant with your sister. She had to drop out of art college and marry me, when she could have had a career as an artist.'

Her sister had always insisted on this. Nula had thought her parents met when her mother was Ralph's model, but Hester told her she was wrong. 'Mummy was an artist, too,' she liked to say. 'She had her creativity suppressed by Daddy.' Nula had always wanted to prove her sister wrong. As their father's favourite, she did not want her sister's version of events to be true.

Now she opened her mouth to speak, but her father raised a hand. 'I know what you think. But that having-it-all stuff, that's all bullshit. It's difficult for women. It's not the same now, I know. But it's not so very different, either.'

'Joe wants to keep it.'

Ralph raised his eyebrows. 'I've always liked him.'

'I don't *feel* pregnant,' said Nula. 'Do you think that's a sign?'

'Could be.'

There was a pause. Then Ralph said: 'It's a small procedure, you know. You can be in and out very quickly. They can do it with medication, these days, especially if we get there early. It's up to you. But I can sort everything out. If that's what you want.'

How did he know these things? Nula didn't want to ask that question, even to herself.

'I was packing up now anyway,' he continued. 'We could get it all – worked out – at home, couldn't we?'

'What about Mum?'

'She doesn't have to know. It'll only take a morning. And then everything will be back to normal.' He opened his arms to her again, and she found herself resting against his chest, closing her eyes, breathing in his familiar scent. 'My girl,' he said. 'You deserve more than this.'

He seemed to have all the answers, and they all seemed to make sense.

She began to pack a suitcase, unable to make a decision about whether or not to face Joe.

As she was folding her clothes, she imagined Joe coming in, standing close behind her, his hands working their way from her spine to her stomach, his chin resting on her shoulder. If he had appeared in this way, Nula might have stuffed the suitcase back under the bed and embraced him. But he did not.

Once she had finished packing, she went to look for him. She caught a bus, got off at the Plas Coch turning and walked all the way to the house-like tree and down to the shore. He wasn't there. Back at the farmhouse she tried to write something to him, but her pen hadn't made a mark before her father was knocking at the front door. She took the ring Joe had given her and placed it on the table in his bedroom, then changed her mind and put it in her pocket. It stayed there all the way back to Oxford, and it was there when she lay on the bed at the clinic in Summertown, waiting to be examined by the nurse who would prescribe the drugs that would make her vomit for three hours, bleed for six, and enable her to get on with the rest of her life.

The day after the party, Maggie's mother hung Ralph's study of the strait on the sitting-room wall. Every day Maggie tried not to look at it, and not to notice Fiona looking at it.

Nula and Ralph left without saying goodbye. Maggie soon gathered, from Joe's long silences and her mother's occasional comments, that Nula wasn't coming back at any point soon, and was not going to keep the baby. Not long afterwards Joe dropped out of the Tech, got a job and moved out of the family home and into the boathouse.

The first time Maggie went there to see him, he stared at the paint-chipped wall as she tried to inform him that their father was leaving because their mother had confessed to sleeping with Ralph. She arrived brimming with righteous anger, and wanted him to brim with it, too. Why, she wanted to know, couldn't she just leave with their father? Why did she have to stay here and endure the torture of their shameless, miserable mother? Her mother had told Maggie she couldn't move because that would mean settling in to another school. It was better, she'd said, to stay on the island and continue her education without disruption. Her father had said nothing on the subject.

'Wouldn't you have done what she's done?' asked Joe, still looking at the wall.

'What do you mean?'

'I mean, wouldn't you have wanted to bring an end to things
. . . with Dad? He dragged her up here in the first place. She
didn't want to come. She's been putting up with his moods
for years.'

'He's not the one in the wrong,' said Maggie.

Joe shook his head. 'It's not that simple, little one.'

'Since when did you take news like this so calmly?'

'Since when did you become a nude model?' Joe flashed
back.

Maggie stared at him.

'Nula mentioned it. In her letter.'

'How did she—?'

'You knew about Mum. Nula knew about you. People who
look for it find out this kind of shit. How could you do it,
Maggie?'

It wasn't me who fucked him, Maggie wanted to say. But
instead she gazed at the floor.

'Listen,' Joe said. 'I don't really care what they do, now. Or
what you do. I'm out of there. I'm just saving up, you know.
To get my own place. Maybe back in Oxford.'

'Oxford?' said Maggie. 'Why?'

There was a pause, during which Maggie tried hard to catch
up with her brother's current state of mind.

'Did Nula tell you anything?' he asked. 'Anything at all?'

She shook her head. 'Has she been in touch?'

'A letter,' said Joe. 'She says her dad helped her – you know.
I don't get that. She always seemed to hate him. And, it turns
out, with good reason.'

Maggie looked out of the window at the glittering strait.
She hadn't allowed herself, up to this point, to dwell fully on
what the information she had given to Ralph might mean for
her brother and Nula. Now it was clear to her: she had caused

this. Nula had terminated her brother's child, and it was her fault. She had ruined Joe's life.

'You just never know, do you?' Joe continued. 'You never know what people are really up to. Even the people you love.'

Each day when Maggie returned from school, she would find her mother on the sofa in her dressing gown, hemmed in by scraps of wet tissue, watching *Countdown* and weeping. Her eyes were bloodshot and her nose shone pink. She didn't seem to notice that her daughter was in the room. Maggie would sit helplessly beside her for a few hours, holding her hand and saying nothing, inhaling the over-sweet smell of her damp skin. During the second month of crying, Maggie held her mother's hand and looked at the television. When she was hungry, she took money from her mother's purse to buy ready meals and frozen pizzas from the Spar. At the till, she remembered how she and Joe had once felt intimidated by Glen, who was still there, leaning on the counter, chatting. But facing Glen now seemed pleasant compared to facing her mother. Sometimes Fiona would eat a triangle of pizza, but mostly she drank coffee. She shrank inside her dressing gown, leaving it sagging around her brittle body. Maggie could see every bone in her mother's feet.

By the end of the third month of crying, Maggie started going upstairs to her bedroom without even looking in on her mother. She asked Fiona for her Switch card and used it for trips to Safeway in Bangor. Walking the aisles, she deliberated over which brand of tinned soup or frozen lasagne to buy, wanting to delay her return to the farmhouse – and her mother's bones – for as long as possible.

After four months, Fiona seemed to recover a little. She got dressed. She began taking meals to Joe in the boathouse and bringing back his washing. Ralph's painting remained on the wall, but she no longer stared at it for hours on end. Then she regained her old cleaning job, pointing out that they couldn't live on Alan's payments alone. She enrolled in evening classes in Welsh poetry, saying she wanted to share Maggie's love of literature. She started using perfume again. Maggie hated this recovery even more than she'd hated the crying. She had understood Fiona's depression; it was what she'd expected. And wasn't it what her mother deserved, after treating her father so badly?

One day Maggie came home from school to find her mother sitting at the kitchen table, poring over her course work. 'You seem better,' Maggie said.

Fiona smiled and said, 'We're going to be fine, aren't we? Just the two of us. It's going to be OK.'

Maggie stared at her. She had that same look she'd had on their night out in Browns, before they moved to the island. The look of a complete stranger.

'It won't be long before I'm at university,' Maggie said.

'But that's almost two years away . . .'

'Twenty months. And then it'll just be you.'

Fiona said nothing more.

Joe never came to the house. Occasionally Maggie visited him, but she couldn't stand the smell of weed and bacon fat for longer than half an hour, and her brother didn't seem to want to do anything but smoke whilst she was there. He'd lost weight and let his motorbike rust behind the boathouse. He no longer talked about moving to Oxford or getting his own place. They did not discuss that summer, or what had happened to their parents. Once, when her brother was in the toilet, Maggie idly opened the door to his bedroom and took a peek. Covering the wall next to his bed were photographs of Nula. Some of them were out of focus, some just a smear of a hand or a knee. There were several close-ups of her sleeping face, and many, many photographs of her mouth, caught in what looked to Maggie to be a laugh, but could just as easily have been a scream.

On the shelf by his bed was the holey stone she'd given him, before their cousin had arrived on the island. Maggie put it in her pocket and slipped out of the door. She didn't go to the boathouse again.

Her mother took her to Bangor station. Fiona had offered, over and over, to drive Maggie all the way to Oxford, to stay and see her settled. But Maggie insisted on taking the train. It was a warm day in early October, and they stood together on the platform, basking in the glowing light, inhaling diesel and cigarette fumes. Her mother, still holding on to Maggie's suitcase, asked, again, what time the train was due. 'Five more minutes,' said Maggie, scowling up at the screen. She could not stand for this train to be even one minute late.

Since her father and Joe had left, Maggie had thrown herself into her schoolwork in order to achieve this moment, the moment she could say goodbye to her mother at Bangor station. Whilst reading her primary texts and crafting carefully argued, dispassionate essays about things she loved, she had imagined the scene many times: she would choose a seat on the opposite side of the carriage, so she could not see her mother as the train left the station. She would not look back. She would not wave. The seaside towns would slide by:

Llandudno, Colwyn Bay, Rhyl. The cheap caravans and chip shops and amusement arcades, and the beautiful sea. She would ignore them all and instead think about her future as a student of English Literature at Jesus College, Oxford.

'I'll miss you,' her mother said.

Maggie nodded.

'I know it's been tough for you, and I'm glad you've done so well, despite everything.'

Because of everything, Maggie thought.

'You'll call when you get there?'

'Yes.' Two more minutes left.

Fiona cleared her throat and seemed to sway a little. 'Maggie . . .'

'What?' The screen was changing, and the 10.25 to Birmingham New Street was now first on the list.

'I'm sorry, but I'm going to have to sit down.' Fiona was backing away from her daughter, stumbling through the small crowd that had gathered on the platform.

Maggie dragged her suitcase to the metal bench where Fiona was sitting, staring at the tracks, her eyes blank with pain. She reached for Maggie's hand, and Maggie let her mother's hot fingers rest upon her own for a few moments.

A voice announced the arrival of the 10.25.

'Mum,' said Maggie, trying not to sound annoyed, 'I've got to go. That's my train.'

Fiona managed to nod, but she clasped Maggie's hand with a fierce grip.

'Bye, then,' said Maggie, wrenching her hand free and turning to meet the gush of hot, stale air from the incoming train.

She did not sit on the other side of the carriage, as she had planned. Instead she stood by the doors, her suitcase resting against her leg. A bleach-and-piss stench from the nearby toilet made her gasp sharply. She scanned the platform for her mother's face. Fiona was still on the bench, her head sunk into her hands, her shoulders heaving. A man in a baseball cap was standing slightly to one side, eyeing her. Maggie touched the dirty window as the train pulled away and watched her mother grow smaller and smaller. Then she wiped her silty fingers on her trouser leg and went about finding somewhere to sit for the long journey ahead.

Her room at Jesus was large, wood-panelled and draughty. The small windows looked out onto the street and a wobbly standard lamp gave out a weak light. An ancient sink on iron legs was positioned in one corner. During her first couple of days at the college, Maggie took refuge in this room, trying to concentrate on her set texts and eating her way slowly through the sandwiches and fruit she'd brought with her. The unscheduled hours stretched ahead. She felt reluctant to leave until she had an actual tutorial to attend, and limited her expeditions to the nearest bathroom. Sometimes she couldn't face even this and instead hoisted down her jeans and knickers, climbed onto the sink and peed into it, hoping that no one in the college across the street could see into her window.

Most things about Maggie's first term at Jesus were baffling: the course, the rules and rhythms of the college, the other students. Because she had also been to a comprehensive school, a girl named Susie attached herself to Maggie. Sometimes Maggie accompanied Susie to second-hand bookshops or drank tea made with long-life milk in her room. When Susie asked Maggie about her family and friends back home, Maggie would shrug and say it was all so tedious, there was really nothing to tell. Nothing ever happened on Anglesey. Not to her, anyway. Susie would nod as if she understood, and then cheerfully proceed to bore Maggie with endless tales about her Christian boyfriend, who'd gone to Keele.

It wasn't long before Maggie made excuses not to meet Susie.

Once a week her mother called. Maggie assured her she was fine, and, no, she didn't need anything, and, yes, she was making new friends.

In a way, Maggie didn't mind being detached; she had become used to it. But she did mind not being good at her course. Suddenly the subject of English Literature became utterly bewildering to her. Instead of offering close readings of Heaney poems, as she'd done so expertly at school, she was expected to prepare a response to the whole of *Beowulf*, and to deliver this in a one-to-one tutorial with her tutor, Dr Edwin Jones. Dr Jones had a pink face, wore an Austrian hunting jacket, rubbed his knees a lot as he talked, and chuckled at his own incomprehensible jokes. He smiled at Maggie and seemed not to notice that she shook as she read her essays aloud. His chintzy college room was lined with tasteful watercolours, which made Maggie long for the mess and murk of Ralph's studies of the strait.

Sometimes, when she was wandering along the Cowley Road, Maggie considered passing Ralph's house. Her fury with him had subsided a little, replaced by fury with her mother. But every time she found herself thinking about lying naked on that sofa, Ralph's gaze bringing her to life, she vowed never to walk along the Cowley Road again.

One cold weekend during the second term, Maggie allowed her mother to visit. Fiona had arranged to stay overnight with an old friend in Oxford and they were to meet the next day for an early lunch in a French restaurant in Jericho. As Maggie walked there, the damp chill coming up from the pavements and through the soles of her thin shoes, she wondered if her mother had lied. Had she, in fact, spent the night with Ralph? Was she, at this very moment, fumbling for her bra in some hotel room while Ralph watched her from the bed? Pushing this thought from her mind, Maggie took the long route to the restaurant. The last thing she wanted was to be early. On her way she popped into the Oxfam bookshop and bought a couple of Edna O'Brien paperbacks in protest against her indigestible reading lists.

Fiona had booked for twelve and Maggie arrived at twenty minutes past to find her mother waiting in the street. She was wearing a light lipstick, which only increased her pallor, but when she saw Maggie she smiled with such warmth that Maggie let herself be embraced. For a moment she inhaled her mother's familiar perfume and felt her body relaxing; then she caught herself and pulled away.

They chose a table in the window. Fiona raked her fingers through her hair and took a good look at her daughter.

'You've lost weight,' she announced, firmly.

Maggie glanced at her baggy jeans. 'I just . . . forget to eat sometimes.'

'Well,' said her mother, 'we can feed you up now, can't we?' Impatiently, she flipped the short menu over. 'What are you going to have? There isn't much choice.'

Although Maggie had not meant to lose weight, she'd recently found herself enjoying the sensation when her newly protruding hip bones chafed against her stiff bed sheets. There was something pleasing about the angles that had appeared on her body, and something intoxicating about her ability to survive on less and less food. It made her think of Nula that summer, of how she never ate more than half of what was on her plate, and always seemed to get what she wanted.

Maggie ordered a grilled king-prawn salad and Fiona ordered steak frites. Fiona chattered nervously about the farmhouse; she was redecorating it, getting the heating sorted, the windows fixed; none of this was really so hard, after all. When you were on your own you just had to get on with it. She said she was enjoying the island more now; she'd made some friends in the village and had started helping out in the local school. Maggie nodded and sipped her water.

When her mother had stopped talking, Maggie asked, 'How's Joe?'

He hadn't been in touch since Christmas. Maggie had spent a week at home, but Joe had spent every day, apart from Christmas Day itself, working. On that day she'd watched other families arguing on the telly whilst her own avoided one another at all costs.

'Oh, you know Joe. He's in his own little world.' Fiona studied the backs of her hands. 'I try to help him, but . . .'

Maggie took this to mean there had been no improvements or developments in her brother's life.

She was careful not to catch her mother's eye as she enquired, 'Will you go and see Dad while you're here?'

Fiona unfolded her starched napkin with a deft flick and smoothed it across her lap. 'I don't think that would be a very good idea, do you?' she said.

A waiter wearing an oversized white apron and a slim black tie, who was the same age as Maggie and, she thought, probably also a student, presented their food with a heavily accented 'Bon Appetit'. Maggie wondered if his boss had told him to pretend to be French.

Fiona asked how the course was going. Maggie almost said

'fine'. But something tipped in her, some need to speak, and instead she found herself confessing, 'It's really bloody hard.'

'It's supposed to be challenging, though, isn't it?' said Fiona, focusing on spearing her chips. They were very thin and kept eluding her fork. 'And you did so well in your A-levels. I'm sure it'll be fine, love. I'm very proud of you, you know.'

Maggie pushed her plate away, suddenly revolted by the blackened legs and exploded eyes of her prawns. 'I'm not sure I should carry on with it.'

Fiona swallowed and wiped her mouth with her napkin. 'What do you mean? Do you want to change courses?'

Adopting the flat tone and blank look she'd so often seen her brother employ, Maggie said, 'I was thinking more of dropping out.'

There was a short silence. Fiona folded her napkin and nodded, slowly. 'OK. Well, let's not be too hasty . . .'

'I hate the course. I don't understand any of it. I want to leave.'

Fiona reached across the table and patted her daughter's hand. 'You know, if you want a break, you're always welcome to come back, Maggie. I'm sure we could talk to your tutors – maybe you could take a year out . . . you could come home, then, couldn't you?'

Maggie saw a hopeful expression pass across her mother's face. And she thought of what going home would mean. Joe sulking in the boathouse, still surrounded by photographs of Nula. Her mother tarting up the farmhouse, desperately trying to carve out a new life with tins of paint and Polyfilla. And all the while, Ralph's study of the strait glaring down at them from the sitting-room wall.

'God!' said Maggie. 'No. I wasn't thinking of that.'

Fiona blinked. 'Then what were you thinking?'

'Maybe staying here. Getting a job.'

Her mother gave a short laugh. 'What kind of job?'

Maggie gazed out of the window. It had started to rain heavily, icy drops making people stoop as they ran for cover.

'I've been thinking about working with children. Nannying or something. I've already done quite a bit of babysitting, for one of my tutors.'

This was true. She had seen the notice in the JCR, dialled the tutor's number and the following Friday she was putting Rosie, four, and George, seven, to bed in their comfortable Victorian semi off the Woodstock Road. George had been particularly sweet, begging her to read story after story. She couldn't remember the last time she had enjoyed reading so much; she'd relished speaking the words aloud. George had gasped and laughed at her emphatic telling.

Maggie's mother leaned back in her chair and sighed. 'So you're telling me that you're thinking of leaving Oxford University to become a *nanny*?'

Maggie shrugged. A young couple holding hands ran past the window, both soaked and shrieking. They looked deliriously happy.

'You've got a chance, Maggie. You can make something of yourself. Why would you waste that?'

When Maggie did not respond, Fiona's voice sharpened. 'Maggie? You must see how ridiculous you're being. Christ, if I'd had the chances you've had . . . well. Everything would have been very different.'

Maggie said, very evenly, 'It's not ridiculous. It's what I want to do.'

Fiona threw up her hands and made a small, choked noise of exasperation. Then she drew her chair closer to Maggie's and said, in a low voice, 'You know, when your father left, I thought that was it for this family. I'd ruined everything – I know it was all my fault – and that was it, and it served me right. But then you gave me hope . . .' Her voice wobbled and she put a hand to her throat. 'You worked so damn *hard*. You got a place at Oxford! Don't throw it all away now. Please don't do that.'

Maggie turned to look at her mother. 'You don't think I did it for you, do you?'

Fiona stared at her, her eyes wide with confusion.

'I didn't do it for you, Mum. I did it to get away from you.'

As she pushed back her chair, Maggie couldn't stop herself adding, 'While you're here, why don't you go and see Ralph?'

She stood and looked down at the grey roots of her mother's hair. She was about to get her coat when, very quietly, Fiona said, 'Ralph doesn't live here any more.'

Maggie hesitated.

'He left Eleanor,' Fiona continued, jutting out her chin, 'and he's in Scotland now. Some island or other. Apparently he's shacked up with one of his students.'

The fake French waiter passed by and asked, in English, if they'd like the bill. Her mother said yes, they would, they were leaving now.

Maggie had no choice but to sit down and wait for the bill to arrive. When it did, she winced as her mother grappled with her purse, shaking it violently and peering into its depths.

'I didn't know about Ralph,' Maggie said.

Emptying coins noisily onto the plate, Fiona said, 'It doesn't matter, does it.'

As they stood to leave, she grasped her daughter's forearm. 'You'll always be welcome at home, Maggie. That's all I can say. The rest is up to you.'

Maggie closed her eyes and waited until her mother had let her go.

The waiter appeared with their coats. Maggie snatched hers away, but Fiona let him hold hers out. Watching her mother blush and thank him as she struggled to place her arm in the sleeve, Maggie made up her mind to give up college as soon as possible.

It had been relatively easy. Her first job had been as a live-in nanny, which allowed her to leave Jesus immediately. No one seemed much to care that she didn't turn up for her tutorials and, after a while, the formal letters from the university, forwarded to Maggie by Fiona, stopped coming. Every morning Maggie awoke in her bright loft bedroom, pushed back the expensively smooth cotton sheets on her single bed and looked forward to a day spent in the park or at a toddler group with Theo, aged three. Theo was a boisterous, happy child who loved cranes and diggers, and if he was ever upset, all Maggie had to do to cheer him up was walk him past a building site. Theo's voice, when he called her, was loud and musical in a way she liked. 'Mag-gee! Mag-gee!' he would call, 'where Mag-gee?' And she would hear him, and go to his aid. Theo's mother said Maggie was a natural, and a wonderful addition to their family. Working for her gave Maggie an immense sense of usefulness and accomplishment.

At the weekends Maggie sometimes saw her father, but he was distracted by nursing his own mother, who had begun her slide into dementia. Whenever Maggie saw Alan, he looked and sounded exhausted – he'd stopped dyeing his hair, which was now thin and the colour of old dishcloths – and often had difficulty focusing on what she was talking about. He always, however, asked Maggie if she'd heard from her mother.

Sometimes she went to the cinema, or for a walk along the river. She began to draw again, taking her sketchbook to cafés and parks. She tried not to draw too many pictures of Theo, but couldn't help herself. He was so lovely, with his abundant curls and freckled nose and his unwieldy, expressive mouth. She was never quite satisfied with her drawings, but she told herself it didn't matter now. No one would ever see them, anyway.

Not wanting to complicate her life again, Maggie limited her contact with her mother to a weekly phone call. Sometimes she plucked up the courage to phone Joe, but he hardly ever picked up and never returned her calls. And, finally, she found it cleaner, simpler, to call home only once every few months, and rarely to answer her mother's letters.

But she dreamed of the island often. She was crab-fishing, slithering uncontrollably on the tangled bed of seaweed as a creature tugged at her line. Joe wouldn't look at her or help her reel in her catch, and her mother sat on the beach in silence, wearing her green sandals and gazing out at the mountains beyond the shore.

Nula hears the van before she sees it, its long splutter inter-rupting the early evening rhythm of birdsong and the murmurs of sheep. There is a scrabble of tyres and the wrench of a hand-brake, and then she's standing, running across the gravel and up the lane to where the vehicle has stopped. Joe steps from the van, alone. She freezes a few yards from him. 'Where is he?' she says.

He stares at her for a moment, speechless. But he is unable to hold her gaze for long. Instead he looks off, towards the strait. 'I told her,' he says. 'I told her to call you . . .'

'Where are they?'

'Hasn't she called?'

Nula shakes her head.

'Fuck!' says Joe.

A cold tremor rises from her belly to her back, travels down her arms and into the tips of her fingers. 'Just . . . just tell me. Tell me where my son is.'

'It's OK,' he says. 'He's safe. He's not far . . .'

She hides her face in her hands, dropping the blue monkey to the ground. 'For God's sake, where is he, Joe? Where is he? Where's my boy?'

'It's OK,' he says again. 'Look, I'll take you there.' He steps towards her, picks up the soft toy. 'Come on, Nula. Come with me.' He holds out a hand. She takes it.

*

They haven't made it further than the top of the lane before Joe's phone rings. Steering with one hand, he answers. 'Right,' he says. 'Bloody hell.' And then: 'It's OK. Nula's here. Yeah, she's with me. Good. I'll tell her. See you in a minute.'

He chucks the phone on the dashboard. 'They're at the farmhouse. With Mum.'

Nula's chest seems to collapse with relief.

'They're OK,' says Joe. 'Mum said Samuel's fine. He's had some tea and he's watching TV.'

She nods, dumbly.

As they turn into the village, he asks, 'If Maggie didn't call, how did you know to come here?'

She looks at him. 'I knew she'd come to you.'

He glances at her, a look of surprise on his face.

'Think about it, Joe. Who else would she go to?'

He sighs. 'I should have made more of an effort. I should've kept an eye on her . . .'

But Nula isn't listening, because now she can see Fiona waiting on the doorstep with Samuel. As the van pulls up, Fiona releases his shoulders and he bolts for the gate. Nula flings the van door wide and starts running, too. He is laughing as he runs, his face alight with recognition, and she reaches out and takes him back into her arms. It's as if she hasn't known quite what to do with her arms for the past couple of days. She remembers a similar feeling when she first returned to work, this nagging suspicion that she had forgotten something, as if she was carrying something else when she'd left the house, some weight that was now missing. She holds his little body so tightly and for so long that eventually he wriggles to be free. When she lets him draw back from her he clasps his hot hands on either side of her face and says, 'Mummy Mummy Mummy', and she says, 'Yes, my love, yes.' She presses his fingers to her mouth, trying not to let the tears become sobs.

She glances towards the door of the farmhouse. Fiona and Joe are watching from the step. Fiona smiles, waves a hand to indicate she should come inside. All Nula wants is to put her son in the back of the Nissan and drive home, to get him into his bedroom and in his blue-striped sleeping bag and hold his hand all night while he sleeps. But Joe is coming down the path, saying, 'Come in for a cup of tea? You'll need a rest', and she should call Greg and Detective Walters, and her mobile is nearly dead, and her back aches, and her bladder is full.

'Is Maggie in there?' Nula asks.

'She's asleep, apparently. Out cold. Just come in and get your breath.'

'One minute,' says Nula. 'No more. I can't face her. Not now.'

As they go into the house Fiona is full of praise for Samuel's good looks, his even temper, and Nula hasn't changed at all and how lovely it is to see her, despite the circumstances. Samuel walks around the place as if he has known it for years. He shows Nula the television and the sofa and asks for more Quavers. Nula can hardly hear what her aunt is saying; she cannot stop looking at her son. She had forgotten, in the short time that has passed, how big he is, how many words he has, how he is able to make his needs and feelings known without help from her. And were his eyes exactly that shade of green, before?

'Of course,' Fiona is saying, 'she's done a terrible thing, but . . .'

Nula scoops Samuel into her arms and hovers in the sitting-room doorway. As he keeps an eye on CBeebies, he touches her face with one hand.

'Mum!' warns Joe.

'But I can only think she wasn't in her right mind . . .'

Samuel's fingers seem longer, more dexterous, to Nula. She clasps his hand and kisses it again. Maggie is upstairs, she thinks. The girl who took my son is upstairs, sleeping, and I am downstairs, talking to her mother.

'No doubt some of it's my fault. I wasn't always there for her, but she cut me off almost completely, you see, after she went to Oxford. I lost her then, and I should've done more—'

'Let's not talk about this in front of Samuel,' says Nula. 'I just want to get him home.'

'I tried to contact her, so many times.'

She can see Fiona is close to tears, wringing her hands, her frown deepening as she takes shallow breaths. She looks old, too, her hair brittle, her chin collapsing into her neck.

'I have to call the—' Nula hesitates, glancing down at Samuel. His eyes are still glued to the screen. 'The p-o-l-i-c-e,' she spells out.

Fiona looks horrified.

'You must see I have no choice,' says Nula. 'I have to tell them I've found Samuel, at the very least.'

At his name, Samuel twists round. She smiles at him, kisses his forehead, and he snuggles back into her.

'Yes, yes, but—'

'And I need to let Greg know, too.' She places Samuel on the carpet. 'Watch your programme,' she says. 'Mummy will be back in two seconds.'

As Fiona shows Nula to the phone in the hallway, she grasps her elbow. 'Please,' she says, quietly. 'Please. Please help her. Don't let them deal with her too harshly. I couldn't bear it.'

Nula ignores her and starts to dial, keeping an eye on Samuel through the open sitting-room door.

302

Fiona squeezes Nula's flesh. 'You could tell them she's been under stress, that she's usually such a caring girl . . .'

'Please let go of my arm,' says Nula.

'You know, now, what it's like to lose a child.' Fiona's eyes are wild as she searches Nula's face.

Nula continues to dial.

'I just don't want to lose her again,' Fiona pleads.

'It's out of my hands,' says Nula, as Detective Walters picks up.

Joe offers them a lift back to the Nissan. Once in his van, she remembers the monkey she'd stolen for Samuel. But her son is still embracing Leggy Monkey, so she ignores the new toy, leaving it on Joe's back seat. The early evening light softens between the trees, and Samuel begins to doze off in her arms.

They arrive at the spot by the church where the Nissan is waiting. Joe turns to Nula and says, 'I know what she's done is unforgivable, but Maggie's been through a lot.'

Nula opens the van door. 'I'm the one who's been through a lot, OK?' Turning her back on him, she carries a dozing Samuel to the Nissan. As she snaps Samuel's straps together and tightens their grip on his shoulders, checking that the tension is just right, Joe stands beside the van, hands in his pockets. Nula shuts Samuel's door, walks past Joe and opens her own.

'It was good to meet him,' Joe says. 'And I'm not excusing Maggie, but—'

She stops, her hand on the door. 'Joe. Your sister took my son.'

He looks at the ground. 'I'm sorry,' he says. After a pause he adds, 'About everything. You know.'

She nods. How much longer until she can leave this place, get her son home?

'Drive carefully, yeah?'

'Thanks.' She has one foot in the car now.

'You know,' he says, gazing up at the trees, 'the baby was mine, too.'

A sound, somewhere between a surprised 'Oh' and an angry groan, escapes her lips.

She knows Joe is searching her face, expecting something. But Nula is unable to do anything but hang her head. She remembers the day he first brought her here, to the ruined church; how he'd shown her the box of bones and given her the ring; how he'd seemed to want some promise from her, when she'd only been interested in touching him.

Then she gathers herself. 'I'm leaving now, Joe, OK?' she says, planting herself in the driving seat.

'Sorry,' he mumbles. 'I shouldn't have brought that up.'

But she's already closing the door.

As she drives away, she looks in the rear-view mirror and sees him standing in the middle of the lane, waving his arms madly.

For a second she considers accelerating away, leaving him standing in a cloud of dust. Then she changes her mind and hits the brakes.

He's panting when he reaches the window. 'You forgot this,' he says, holding up the blue monkey.

She shakes her head. 'I didn't forget,' she says. 'I . . . got it for him, but I don't think he needs it, now.'

'Then I'll keep it,' he says. 'Maybe you'll come back for it, eh?'

And it's the same look in his eyes as when he gave her the ring, all those years ago. A beautiful, beseeching look.

Part of her wishes she could reach out and touch his face, trace the line of his chin with a finger and say yes. But instead she says, 'I'll never come back here.'

'Maybe I'll bring it to you, then.'

She shakes her head. 'Maybe,' she says.

Nula begins to shake. Samuel is safe and sleeping peacefully, she is already miles from the island, the police have informed her that they are on their way to arrest Maggie, Greg is expecting them back around midnight, and here she is, unable to stop shaking. Her jaw judders, her teeth begin to chatter. The hairs on her arms rise up. It is as if, she thinks, she has seen a ghost. First checking that Samuel is soundly asleep, she pulls onto the hard shoulder. It is a gloomy spot, overhung with trees and a craggy rock wall, littered with cigarette ends and plastic drink bottles. She calls her husband, gripping the phone in a shaking hand. 'I can't drive,' she says. 'I can't do it.'

Greg tells her to calm down, asks her where she is. Get to Chester, he instructs, find the best hotel, call him once she's checked in. He'll take a train, a bus – get there somehow – and the three of them will come back together in the morning.

Nula watches the odd bit of traffic streak by as her husband talks. He tells her that he loves her. He tells her that after this they'll be a proper family, won't they? They can put the whole thing behind them. Start afresh. He sounds so calm, so in control. As if he never doubted that Samuel would come back. As if he never doubted anything at all. As she listens to his voice, she closes her eyes and the shaking starts to subside. She is reminded of her father's voice that day in the boathouse when he'd told her what to do. She had been a good girl and had done everything he wanted.

And ever since, Nula has been stern with herself, telling herself that she must never think of it, because it was nothing. She must simply get on with each day as though nothing had happened. Nothing at all.

It's all she can do, for the moment, to listen to Greg's voice, to yield to its comforts. But as she replaces her phone in her bag and turns to look at Samuel – who is right here, and alive, and hers – she knows Greg's help will be a temporary shelter, and that she and her son will not stay within its confines for much longer.

It is past eight o'clock when Maggie wakes. She blinks, tries to remember where she is, what she's doing beneath all these dolphins. For a minute she considers the blue paint over the woodchip, the purple curtains, the pine wardrobe splattered with the remains of what were once stickers. All of it tilting towards the tiny window. Her mother has redecorated every other room in the house, but Maggie's bedroom has not been touched. Then she reaches over to search for Samuel's sleeping body in the bed and finds nothing but the edge of the duvet. His smell is gone. And his warmth. In a second she is on her feet, stubbing her toe on the chest of drawers in her hurry to reach the door.

'Sammy?' she calls.

On the stairs she hears the telly's blare, smells coffee. He must be asleep on the sofa, she thinks; even if her mother has called Nula, she can't have got here that quickly.

As soon as Maggie enters the sitting room she knows Samuel has gone. Fiona is sitting alone and upright in the armchair, mug in hand, corner lamp glowing on her lined face. Seeing Maggie come in, she reaches for the remote, turns down the volume on *Masterchef.*

'Where's Sammy?'

'Come and sit down, love.'

'Where is he?'

Fiona looks into her mug. 'What did you do?' she asks, very quietly.

'Where is he, Mum?'

'His mother's taken him home. He's where he should be.'

Maggie stares at the television. Someone is spinning sugar onto a disc of dark chocolate. The strands sparkle like gold thread. 'It's perfection,' a voice says.

'How did she——?'

'I didn't call her. She knew you'd bring him here.' Fiona puts down her mug. 'Of course she did. She'd worked it out.' She stands and holds her arms out to her daughter, and Maggie bolts for the door.

She is out of the house before Fiona can move. Along the front path, through the gate and across the road. There's the lane, and she takes it. The trees, full and green, block out the June evening and make Maggie disappear. The lane is as shadowy as it was on that first day she walked its length with Joe. She runs and runs along the stony path, past the chapel with the ancient bones. The racket of birdsong rises around her. All the birds are calling now. In one last blast they are singing out the day as Maggie races towards the strait.

She crashes out of the trees and onto the beach, and there's a bright smack of air and water and sky. Deliberately she does not look at the boathouse. She knows it is empty. Instead she keeps going, across the stones to the shingle, crushing the ghosts of crabs beneath her feet, slipping on humps of seaweed and skittering down to the water's edge where the seabirds flicker as they go about their evening business of toing and froing. She keeps going. Her father had told her about the treacherous strait, about the two tides that could easily catch you out, the sandbanks that shifted beneath the water so you never knew what was land and what was sea.

Maggie walks into the strait. It's a lovely shock as it soaks through her trainers and surrounds her feet. After a day spent carrying Samuel her legs are so tired that this rush of cool liquid is a welcome relief. She stumbles on the stones, has to push her way through the thick fronds of seaweed. Her jeans become heavy. She is up to her waist. She thinks of the note she meant to write to Joe. Because she's known all along that this was a possibility. If she couldn't keep Samuel and Joe in the boathouse, then the strait was always a possibility. Over the years she has thought, many times, of the words she would write to Joe to say sorry, and to say goodbye. She has never been able to come up with anything better than *Dear Joe, I tried to make things better because I know I made things worse and I'm sorry, because you are my brother.*

She walks on, the sand sinking beneath her feet. As the water meets her chin it sends a shiver up her body and her eyes seem to snap open for a moment and she sees mountains in the distance, so still and unknowable. And as the strait swirls around her she remembers how she had loved lying naked in the boathouse for Ralph. Her feet leave the bottom and she feels herself on that sofa once again. She closes her eyes, wanting her body to be all there is. Her limbs fight for a moment, there's coughing and kicking and arms splashing, but then they begin to give themselves up to the water, and she tells herself that all she has to do is let herself go under, and go under again, and go under again, and she will be fully present in this landscape. But she cannot do it. Instead she scrambles to find the bottom, and stands, and looks at the mountains, and is unable go forward or back.

Maggie.

A voice. Could he really be here, in this water, with her? It is so cold and she is so tired that she's no longer sure if she can feel her body or not, if she can form a thought or an image in her mind. She tries to focus on the voice, but there is just the cold. She has failed to be washed somewhere else by the current. The landscape will not yield to her.

Maggie.

She spits out another mouthful of seawater. Her feet find, then lose, a rock.

Maggie.

Her brother's voice. But there is another voice, too.

Maggie.

The voice of her mother, calling her back.

When they have hauled her out and onto the shore, wrapped her in towels and blankets, taken her into the boathouse and given her brandy, the police leave, saying she can have a moment. They'll wait outside with Joe for a few minutes whilst she recovers.

As they close the door, Maggie lets herself be held. 'What did you do, love?' Fiona asks again, gently. 'What on earth did you do?'

Maggie has no answer. The two of them hold each other for a long time, and Maggie can hear voices, crackles of static, coming from the policeman's walkie-talkie. She cannot stop shaking. Her teeth rattle in her head, her arms and legs judder. She closes her eyes and thinks about Samuel clasping her around the neck as they stood at the window of the Shaws' house and watched his mother disappear. The smell of the sea is on her hands and she inhales it deeply, feeling her mother's tears on her neck, like the tears Samuel had cried all those mornings – the tears that, she reminds herself, he allowed her to wipe away. She had been so happy when he surrendered to her embrace, but she thinks, now, that perhaps it was she who surrendered to him. And she sees herself stamping outside the back door in the rain, lost in the joy of getting wet with a thirteen-month-old boy, and she holds her mother tighter, and says that she's sorry.

There is a knock on the door, so loud it makes them jump apart and stare at one another, wide-eyed. 'It's time, Maggie,' a voice calls. 'Come on out now.'

Maggie says, very quietly, 'Help me, Mum. Please help me.' And Fiona says that she will do everything she can. Then she takes Maggie by the hand, and together they open the door and step outside.

Acknowledgements

I would like to thank the Society of Authors for their support in the form of an Authors' Foundation grant.

I would like to thank Katja Hofmann, for allowing me to write this book.

I would like to thank my parents for taking me to Anglesey, and showing me its wonders, so many times.

I would like to thank my cousin, Owena Roberts, for coming with me to the island and helping me to uncover our family's past secrets, even though they did not make it into this novel.

I would like to thank Poppy Hampson and David Riding for their continued support and friendship.

I would like to thank my dear fellow Owls: David Swann, for reading the whole thing and suggesting the title; Karen Stevens, for her astute readings and suggestions; and Edward Hogan, for reading everything, telling me what was wrong with it *and* how to put it right.

I would like to thank Ted, for bearing with me.

And I would like to thank Hugh Dunkerley, for his kindness, patience and love.